THE
ALARMISTS

THE ALARMISTS

DON HOESEL

BETHANY HOUSE PUBLISHERS
Minneapolis, Minnesota

Published by Bethany House Publishers
11400 Hampshire Avenue South
Bloomington, Minnesota 55438

Bethany House Publishers is a division of
Baker Publishing Group, Grand Rapids, Michigan.

Library of Congress Cataloging-in-Publication Data

Hoesel, Don.
    The alarmists / Don Hoesel.
        p.   cm.
    ISBN 978-0-7642-0562-0 (pbk.)
    1. Two thousand twelve, A.D.—Fiction. 2. Prophecies—Fiction. 3. Sociologists—Fiction. I. Title.
    PS3608.O4765A79   2011
    813'.6—dc22
                                                              2010041266

For my mother

Armed Forces Global Threat Assessment

November 27, 2012

- New Delhi, India: Indian Agricultural Minister announcing rice shortage due to massive crop losses.

- Dire Dawa, Ethiopia: Monitoring unusual seismic activity along Afar Depression. Possible pre-shocks.

- Bahawalpur, Pakistan: Pakistan moves 15,000 troops to Indian border.

- Niamey, Niger: Rumblings of military dissatisfaction with Aziz's government. May be centered on infantry companies in Tahoua.

- Novosibirsk, Russia: Continued drought forcing buckwheat prices up. Fighting in Novosibirsk as food stores dwindle.

November 30, 2012, 2:17 P.M.

From atop a rise—a mound of earth hardly a foot above the flat terrain that dominated the panorama—Colonel Richards looked in the direction of the sea that he knew lay off to the east, past the limits of his vision. From where he stood, it was difficult to imagine such a vast expanse of water in close proximity to this ravaged land—forsaken ground that filled the miles between the eastern sea and the mountains to the west. Stretches of solidified lava, fissures splitting the baked earth, and scraggly foliage designed to nurse the barest moisture seemed the only constants everywhere he cast his eyes.

As his team circled out with their instruments, Richards took a few moments to catch his breath, steadying his legs on the rock and letting the particle-filled wind whipping over the near barren ground burnish his unprotected face. He was familiar enough with the geology of the area to know the nature of the forces at work beneath his feet, the lava coursing through the rock, the three tectonic plates in unsteady federation. He marveled that despite its silent power, he could feel none of it through his boots.

He glanced at the Danakil gathered in a loose cluster some yards off. A few of the nomads squatted, sanafils skirting the mineral-rich ground. Others stood, the blistering sun at their backs, according the star a reverence conditioned by thousands of years of societal memory. Among the guides, there was not a single wasted motion.

The colonel drew a deep breath, filling his lungs with warm air, and turned to look back at the path they'd taken to reach this spot, his eyes finding the mountains that unfolded along the Red Sea down from Eritrea before straightening and heading due south into Ethiopia. Set against these larger masses was Erta Ale, which, while smaller than the mammoth range beyond, warranted a good deal more attention from Richards for the fact that it shared a geological connection with the activity that had shaped the land over which the colonel now walked, and the massive rift less than a click to the west of Richards.

That rift being the reason the colonel was there.

Twenty yards away a lanky man with a shock of brown hair sticking out from beneath his hat slung a pack from his shoulder and went to one knee. Unlike the guides, Richards's team paid the sun little mind. They were outfitted for the place, and for the short time they would be there, which meant they could carry out their assigned tasks with an efficiency that bypassed concern for things like sunburn or dehydration.

The man who had dropped to a knee pulled what looked like a long tent stake from the pack. Holding it close to his face, he touched a spot just below the rim and a small green light blinked on. A second reach into the pack produced a mallet and, placing the business end of the stake to the ground, he gave it several hard taps, driving it downward. A few steps away another man, darker skinned and more solidly built, wearing sunglasses against the glare, hovered with a device the size and shape of a personal game console. Once the first man had finished the work of pounding the stake into the ground, he gave a thumbs-up, at which the second man turned his attention to the device. The colonel stayed silent throughout, as the other members of the team continued their own work, and as the Danakil stood silent watch.

After a time, the man named Petros finished his analysis and looked back toward Colonel Richards. "Nothing abnormal, Colonel," he said with a shrug. "Just the regular seismic activity."

Richards answered with a nod. He turned to the rest of the team, who were busy performing their duties with an efficiency that suggested they were back in the lab rather than in one of the harshest environments on the face of the earth. Bradford and Addison were engaged in a mirror of the activity Petros and Snyder had just completed. Beyond them, Madigan and Rawlings ran an electromagnetic sensor over a patch of darker earth. Richards saw Madigan pause over one spot, but after a moment she shook her head and moved on. Soon Rawlings broke from her side and started back toward the colonel.

As the man's path took him past the Danakil, Richards saw him lift his sunglasses and give them a wink, though he might as well have been interacting with statues for all the response he generated.

"We're not getting anything, boss," Rawlings said. He closed the last few steps and took a spot on the rise next to Richards, turning so that he could see the activity from his superior's vantage point. "You want me to set up Spike?"

Richards rolled that thought around for as long as it took him to see Madigan complete another sweep and start back.

"Don't bother," he said. "It looks like this place is dead."

Rawlings nodded his agreement. "Maybe we'll pick up something closer to the rift."

"Maybe," Richards said, but his voice expressed doubt. More

than a decade spent investigating spots like this had given him a sixth sense for knowing when they would come up with a goose egg. And he had that feeling now.

"The data wasn't wrong," Madigan avowed, having intuited the colonel's thoughts. She had the electromagnetic scanner resting on her shoulder, the smooth base coated with a blanket of salt, gypsum, and sulfur.

"Of course not, Maddy," Richards said with a half smile. "No one's going to besmirch the data."

Maddy returned her boss's smile with a chagrined one of her own.

"Besides," the colonel added, "our presence here accounts for quite a few taxpayer dollars, so we'd better be nothing if not thorough."

"Are we going to give Spike a go then?" Madigan asked, and while she directed the question to the colonel, her eyes went to Rawlings.

Richards seemed to give the suggestion more thought than he had when Rawlings brought it up the first time, which brought a concerned look to Rawlings's face, but Richards was still convinced it would be wasted effort. If there was anything to find, it would be closer to the rift.

"Pack it up," he called and then watched as they did so.

As they finished up, Richards turned his attention to Rawlings.

"We'll need Spike once we reach the rift," he said, with something between apology and amusement.

Rawlings sighed. "Roger that, boss. Someone must be punishing me for something. This will be the third time we've rolled out Spike this week." He then repositioned his pack and started back the way they'd come.

After a last look around, the colonel was ready to follow suit until his eyes landed on Madigan. The only female member of Richards's unit wore a puzzled look, her eyes pointed north of their position. Richards tried to follow her line of vision but didn't see anything out of the ordinary.

"What's wrong, Maddy?" he asked as the rest of the team filed past, each covered to varying degrees with the ever-present dust of the place.

The captain glanced over at the colonel, then back at whatever had drawn her attention, and it was just as she opened her mouth that Richards saw it too.

"They're gone, sir," said Madigan.

Richards didn't respond. Perhaps five minutes had passed since he'd last registered the presence of the Danakil. Not long enough for them to have vanished like vapor—not over terrain as flat as this. He sent his eyes over the desert, searching for movement. Their sanafils, white when new, were now the color of the land, making them hard to see.

"There," Madigan said, pointing. "Northwest—maybe a mile."

It still took the colonel a few seconds to find them. They'd stepped off a ridge, much like the one on which the colonel stood, and headed straight toward an area thick with dragon trees and shrubs. Their path took them in the general direction of the rift, but Richards could see that their guides were no longer acting in that capacity. Richards and his team were in the process of being abandoned.

"What would have sent them running?" she asked.

The colonel pondered that as he watched the retreating nomads. They didn't really need the guides; the GPS systems and electronic maps they'd brought with them, backed by the technological might of the U.S. military, were enough to get them to within a foot of where they wanted to be. Still, there was something unsettling about seeing those in his employ fleeing across the desert. He turned to look in the direction of their SUVs.

"Good question," he said.

This time, he saw it before Madigan. At first he thought it could be a dust storm, but one of the benefits of having lived through several of those experiences was that one learned when a cloud of dust on the horizon was something else.

"Company," he said, and Madigan was moving to the trucks before he finished.

"Rawlings!" the colonel barked as he followed. Rawlings had just reached the first of the SUVs when he heard his name. He looked back at his commanding officer and then followed the line of the colonel's finger. Even over the fifty yards that separated them, Richards heard Rawlings curse.

Rawlings tossed off his pack and moved toward the back of the truck, and Richards could hear him directing the others, who, although not immediately clear on the nature of the danger, snapped into motion. Rawlings whipped open the door and began to pull out vests, tossing them to the others.

By the time Richards and Madigan reached the trucks, the other vehicles had closed much of the distance and the colonel stopped and watched for a few seconds. The Americans had no claim to this place; they couldn't control who crossed this land and who didn't. For all Richards knew, these strangers were locals, with more right to be here than his team had. Or they could be a research team—a legitimate one. This area saw a great many of those, all sanctioned by the Ethiopian government. There was no reason to believe this was anything other than one of those probabilities. Except that they were coming in much too fast, and as the lessened distance provided a clearer outline of the approaching vehicles, the colonel saw what looked like a makeshift gun turret.

"They're hauling, Colonel," Bradford observed. The soldier had donned a vest and held his AK-47 so that the barrel pointed at the ground.

Richards gave his team a quick once-over. Each pair of eyes was trained on the incoming vehicles. Richards counted three jeeps, all painted the color of the desert floor. Definitely not researchers.

"Bradford, Petros, back of Unit 2. Maddy, Rawlings, front side Unit 1. The rest of you with me."

Almost before the words had left his mouth they were moving, with two pairs heading in opposite directions. Richards took a few steps forward, and the remaining soldiers—and soldiers they were, despite their preference for science labs and high-tech gizmos—took flanking positions as the colonel waited for the visitors' intentions to become clear.

He didn't have to wait long.

Richards saw the uniform line of spewed dirt and rock tracking toward the SUVs before he heard the shots, and he reflexively pulled back behind the cover of the Toyotas. Before he could bring up the HK-416, he heard his team answering the assault in kind. He exchanged a look with Snyder, then took a deep breath and poked his head out from behind the truck.

The three enemy vehicles had stopped, forming a semicircle perhaps fifty yards away from the Americans. As he scanned the scene, Richards was relieved to find that the drivers had not elected to send their vehicles into the sides of the SUVs. Richards wouldn't have called it a tactical error, but having positioned his team around the trucks made them susceptible to an attack that utilized the sheer mass of the vehicles against them. But such an assault would have required something akin to the mind-set of a suicide bomber, and nothing in Richards's experience caused him to suspect such in Ethiopia.

He saw Madigan pop out from behind her cover, take a fraction of a second to acquire her target, and send a spray of 5.56mm bullets toward the back of one of the jeeps—toward a trio of men in dark clothing, their faces covered with scarves. All three, having spilled from the jeep to put the body of the vehicle between them and the Americans, ducked from the assault. But Richards's sharp eye caught the fact that while two pulled back on their own power, one slumped under the pull of gravity.

"One down!" the colonel yelled before stepping out and following Maddy's strafing with one of his own. He heard either Bradford's or Petros's rifle supplementing his rounds—saw large holes open up on the side of a jeep. During the barrage, one of his team lobbed a grenade across the distance between the opposing forces, dropping it behind their huddled forms. After the grenade detonated, leaving his ears ringing, he registered at least two casualties.

Bradford had eased out past the colonel, laying down a line of fire that pinned down their assailants. When the officer, his clip expended, pulled back, Maddy took up the cause. As Bradford reloaded, his back against the Toyota, he glanced at the colonel.

"They weren't ready for us, Colonel," he said. "They're way outgunned."

Richards nodded. Whoever these men were, they were equipped enough to handle just about anyone they might encounter in the harsh land between the small towns that dotted the desert—but not a unit with the training of the colonel's.

During a lull in the firefight, one of the enemy scrambled into the jeep mounted with the gun turret, shinnying over the back seat to pop up through the sunroof. The man—wide, dark eyes the only feature visible through his coverings—managed the task with far greater speed than Richards would have suspected, and he had the NSV turned on the American team before anyone could react. Advanced training or not, a 12.7mm heavy machine gun was a formidable weapon. Richards heard the rounds puncturing the skins of the Toyotas; he heard tires exploding. The gun turret suddenly changed the game; it was the kind of ordnance that could quickly take the advantage away from his well-trained team.

With the din of the machine gun filling the air, Petros pulled back from Unit 2, following the line of the SUV in a crouch. He stopped just after the cab, going to a knee below the curve of the windshield glass. After a beat, the sound of an HK erupted from the back of Unit 2, and as Richards poked his head around he saw the weapons fire draw the attention of the machine gunner.

Petros raised up, brought the rifle over the vehicle, set and pulled off a single shot, sending his target toppling back through the sunroof. In the moments that followed, all guns fell silent, leaving Colonel Richards hearing nothing save his own breathing and the groan of the desert wind.

Evidently, their attackers decided they'd had enough. A flurry of movement saw them launching themselves back into the jeeps, and in the brief period before they could send them speeding away from the Americans, Richards thought about having his team open up. Even if they didn't get them all, it would be enough to prevent an attack later on. What kept him from doing so was that, when it became apparent that their foes had disengaged, not a single member of Richards's unit fired a shot. And while a person in his position seldom took his cues from his subordinates, Richards had been with these men and women long enough to understand that the uniformity of their actions identified it as the right choice.

The colonel watched as the jeeps disappeared across the flatland, until the visual morphed into the dust clouds that had preceded their coming. As he did so, his team filtered back and Richards could see, without his eyes leaving their retreating assailants, that everyone was intact. Only when the dust clouds had vanished as well did he turn his full attention to those awaiting his orders.

"Injuries?" he asked.

There were none—a fact that freed Richards to pay more

attention to the three bodies splayed out on the desert floor. The colonel brought his weapon around and crossed the section of land through which deadly projectiles had flown only minutes ago. When he was close enough to confirm the three kills, he lowered his weapon and glanced at Madigan, who had followed a step behind.

"What do you think, Maddy?"

The captain cast a critical eye over the trio.

"Hard to tell," she said. "Could be the ONLF, maybe even al-Shabaab. You've got some cross-border clothing here. Macawis on these two, pants and shirt on this guy." She paused and gestured toward the third fallen man. "And this one looks like a local—an Afar."

Richards nodded. What he saw when he reviewed the deceased was a hodgepodge of, if not ideologies, at least ethnicities. If Maddy was right and this was the work of either the ONLF or al-Shabaab, he found himself leaning toward the latter: a terrorist group with a less stringent membership policy.

"Both of them are known to work in this area," Madigan added.

"Except that we haven't heard much from the ONLF since Ogaden in 2007," said Rawlings, who'd wandered over to poke one of the bodies with his weapon. "For all we know, this is Ginbot 7, or someone else entirely." He exchanged looks with both Maddy and Richards. "What I do know is that they didn't know who we are, Colonel. Didn't know how much firepower we have."

"Which means," Richards said, "they weren't coming after *us* so much as they were coming after any good-sized research team that might have a decent amount of valuable equipment."

Rawlings shrugged. "Your guess is as good as mine, boss."

Richards had to agree with him—it was only a guess. Adding to his irritation was the fact that the attack, while sparing his team any casualties, would serve to keep him from completing his project.

They wouldn't continue on to the rift now, not with blood spilled at their hands. And the odd satellite readings—the ones that hinted at something man-made happening within the natural forces fronted by the rift—would go unexplained. For now.

December 3, 2012, 2:33 P.M.

One of the benefits of holding a tenured university professorship was that by juggling classes and effectively using teaching assistants, the professor could free up enough time for some much needed weekday angling. Brenton Michaels hardly moved as he worked a brush pile, slow-rolling spinnerbait in search of one of the lake's larger fish—hopefully a bass, either the black or the white variety, which were occupied with chasing the shad through the shallows around boat docks and riprap, suspended in the medium depth water along the deeper drop-offs. He'd caught a nine-pound black bass in the same spot the year before: nowhere close to a record but large enough that he'd bragged about it. And the passing months had only allowed the fish in this reservoir to add weight and length. But that wasn't really the point. If at the end of the day he came off the lake without a nibble, it would still be worth it.

The lake remained placid as he floated the bait, and for the first time in two hours he glanced at the sonar. He'd angled every fishable section of these waters and could recite depths and brush pile and buoy locations by rote. He hadn't used instruments in years, at least not on this lake. But today he had a feeling that the fish weren't in their usual spots—that they'd gotten as used to his tricks as he had to theirs. The possibility tested his belief that the act of fishing was its own reward, and that made him consider firing up all his expensive gear for the first time in a long while. But the purist in him won out and he released a deep sigh and started to pull back on the line.

A moment later the muffled ring of his phone interrupted the silence. In a brief flirtation with spite he considered not answering it. But there were few who knew the number, and of those, none that he wanted to tick off. He rummaged around in a canvas bag that, in addition to the phone, held sun block, his shoes, and the largest Snickers bar money could buy.

After looking at the phone's display, he groaned before answering the call. "You do realize that interruptions like these can lead to the misshaping of malleable minds, don't you?" he asked.

The question resulted in the briefest of pauses on the other end before Abby, with her customary aplomb, said, "Your sophomore sociology class is up one flight of stairs and thirty-two steps down the hall. At the end of that minor odyssey is a midsized lecture hall, where at the moment Maureen Kellogg is lecturing a group of students who look a lot more interested than they usually do when you're actually up there doing your job. So I think it's safe to say that if you're involved with school in any way right now, it's a school of fish."

Brent smiled into the phone. Then he took in a deep draught of moist air, suspecting that his next question would pull him away from the pristine water.

"What's the emergency, Abby?"

"Emergency?" his admin asked. He could hear the sound of her rapid-fire typing in the background.

"If it keeps me from pulling in a ten-pounder, then it better be," he said.

Abby didn't answer right away, but when she did so it was with a brevity Brent had come to expect.

"Okay then," she said.

The next sound to hit Brent's ear was silence again, for she'd ended the call. When fifteen seconds later she answered his call back, he could imagine the smug smile on her face.

"Department of the Humanities. How may I direct your call?"

"Okay, what is it?" he asked.

"But it doesn't qualify as an emergency," she said. "Not enough to let the big one get away."

"Abby . . ."

"You got a call from the Pentagon. They want you for a consult."

The boat sat motionless on the calm water as he digested that. He'd rested the fishing rod across his knees, with the line following the curve of the boat beneath the surface where the neglected bait seemed content to do what it had done all afternoon, which was nothing.

"Oh," he said.

Calls to consult for one government agency or another, while not frequent, happened with enough regularity to render them unsurprising, and didn't even get him too excited. A request from the Pentagon, however, was a different matter. In the past fifteen years—after he'd achieved sufficient accolades to be recognized as one of the top experts in his field—he'd received two job offers from someone associated with the Pentagon. A shiver of excitement always accompanied signing his name to a nondisclosure agreement labeled *Top Secret*. He also knew that was why Abby had called, even knowing the message could have waited until he was off the lake.

When after several seconds it became apparent that his admin was content to allow the silence to continue as long as it would, the professor said, "Can you give me the broad strokes?"

He could imagine the look on Abby's face, pleased that she'd vexed him. She waited a little while longer before giving him the information.

"Colonel Jameson Richards," he repeated. "I don't think I've worked with him before."

"I got that impression too," Abby said. "He wants you in Washington tomorrow."

"Did he give you any idea what the project is?"

Abby chuckled. "Yeah, the Pentagon's all warm and fuzzy now. They *like* to talk about super secret stuff over the phone."

Brent smirked. "You know what this means?" he asked.

"You mean besides the fact that I'm going to have to scramble to find people to cover your classes again?"

"I love you, Abby."

"I love you too, doll."

Three hours later, Brent had his bag packed and was on his way to the airport.

3

December 4, 2012, 6:32 A.M.

Along a narrow alley that bisected a portion of the merkato, wooden stalls, wagons, and overflowing baskets of every size lined both walls, two deep in some places. In fact, so closely were these mobile retail outlets placed that the vendors who operated them were often forced to walk over, around, or under the goods of others in order to corral buyers for their own wares. The sense of industry in this stretch of real estate—an ebb and flow of entrepreneurial energy that spread out from the alley to consume an untold number of square blocks—was a free-form thing constrained by rules sufficient to keep it from giving way to chaos. And yet chaos was what it most closely resembled.

Set apart by a matter of feet from this flow of bodies and goods, two men sat at a small round table, customers of a tiny café that looked to have been dug out from a thick stone wall rather than built into the larger structure by conventional means.

Dabir had positioned himself at the table so he could look out on the alley, and the other man had pulled his chair around so he could do the same. It left them as something of a study in contrast, with Dabir's dark skin and regional clothing playing against the westerner's lighter skin and American dress. As the Eritrean sipped his drink he sent his eyes over the alley, looking for anyone who seemed more interested than should be the case. However, that was the beauty of a place like the merkato, he thought. They could have been discussing grain prices or arranging a transfer of nuclear material and not one of the thousands of people within the surrounding area would have known or cared. It was an anonymity granted by virtue of there being far too many people there to keep track of any two of them.

"We lost four men," the Eritrean said. He sipped at the tej again, his eyes on the people passing in front of the café.

"I'd heard three," the westerner said in perfect Amharic. He too nursed a glass of the honey wine.

At this, the Eritrean shifted his eyes from the alley to his table companion. "Three in the desert," he said. "Another died in the jeep as we drove." He studied the westerner closely, but could not see the man's eyes for the sunglasses. "I am curious, Mr. Standish. How do you have information about our losses?"

Standish's first response was a smile and a sip of the tej. Then he said, "You've worked for me for how many years, Dabir? And you're surprised I know something I'm not supposed to know?"

After a moment, Dabir answered with a slight nod. But when he spoke, his words held a hint of the defiance that made him such a good soldier.

"And yet your information has proved inaccurate," he said. "It is four—not three."

Dabir was gratified to see a hint of annoyance on the American's features, obvious despite the sunglasses he kept on even in the café's dim interior.

"You can be sure the widow fund will reflect that adjustment," Standish said.

"You are most generous, hälafi," Dabir said.

He returned his gaze to the alley, his field of vision occupied by a man selling fruit from several baskets and an Arab with head scarves that Dabir suspected would not move in this location.

"You did not tell us there would be American military in the area," he said after a while.

Again, Standish did not answer right away. Dabir saw his attention on the activity taking place beyond their table, following a man with a dozen or so plastic bins stacked on his head walk past the café—watching until the man disappeared from view. Only then did he speak.

"Your job is pretty simple, Dabir. Stick close to the border and harass anyone you can." He fixed his business partner with a look. "That requires a certain level of common sense on your part. If you see a group of people with better weapons than you have, leave them alone."

Despite the minor insult, Dabir would not be baited.

"They were dressed as researchers," he said. "We did not see weapons."

Standish finished his tej before responding. When Dabir moved to pour him more from the pitcher, the American waved him off.

"We both know this business isn't without its risks," he said.

"True. And yet the CIA cannot warn us when Americans will present themselves as targets?" Dabir asked. He was gambling. Standish had never made his affiliation clear. To Dabir, who had studied in Europe and whose understanding of global dynamics was more extensive than that of most of his countrymen, the probability that Mr. Standish was a CIA operative made sense. His money was certainly regular enough to be backed by the U.S. government.

The sunglasses served their purpose, though, as the Eritrean was unable to read anything in Standish's eyes.

"You'll need to recruit more men to replace the ones you've lost," Standish said, as if Dabir had simply misplaced the dead men. "You'll find enough in the account to facilitate that."

"Of that I have no doubt," Dabir replied. Whatever organization Mr. Standish was with—and Dabir had expended what resources he had available to try and answer that question, to no avail—they were always forthcoming with the money. As long as that held true, the mercenary would do as he was asked. "Again, you are most generous."

He stayed for several minutes after Standish had left, but he did not touch the tej again.

December 4, 2012, 7:21 A.M.

Brent walked out of his hotel room at 7:21 a.m. and by 7:29 was sitting in the back of a blue Ford Expedition headed for the Pentagon. The driver was a private, and beyond asking about Brent's flight and then loading his single bag into the truck, he hadn't said a word. He kept his hands at ten and two and his eyes on the road. From the hotel they made good time down the I-395, traveling the thirty-five miles in under an hour, which was good considering the traffic clogging the area regardless of the time of day.

It had been almost six years since his last trip to Arlington, and at least two since he'd been called to Washington. In fact, while it seemed silly to think it now, he'd begun to wonder if someone else was being called on to consult here in the Capitol. He'd been confident that was not the case, however. He kept up with the literature and so knew who was doing what in the field. The last few years had seen nothing groundbreaking—no hotshot bursting onto the scene to take any high-profile jobs being offered. To the best of his recollection, he was the last young hotshot to have upset the establishment. And while he was a good many things, *young* was no longer one of them.

The driver exited I-395 and took Brent the rest of the way on Washington Boulevard. As the professor watched out his window, the structure he could see from the freeway for the last few miles came into sharper focus. The driver maneuvered the Expedition around the mammoth building and through the security checkpoint that, once navigated, saw them arrive at the Mall entrance. The driver had the truck parked and had exited into the cool December air almost before Brent could reach for his briefcase.

"If you'll follow me, sir," the private said before pivoting on a heel and heading into the building, Brent's bag in his hand.

Inside, Brent and his escort were funneled to a security checkpoint, where the professor was forced to relinquish his briefcase, his belt, and the few coins in his pockets. The PFPA personnel who vetted him and his belongings did so with courteousness and businesslike efficiency. Soon he and the private were on the other side of the checkpoint, where they were met by a civilian who, despite the fact that she wore a mid-length skirt and a blouse, seemed no less professional than the soldier from whom she took the transfer of human cargo.

"Hello, Dr. Michaels," she said, extending her hand. "I'm Penelope Bridges, Colonel Richards's assistant. If you're up to it, the colonel would like to meet with you right away."

Brent took her hand and was surprised by her grip. "That's fine," he said. He bent down to retrieve his bag. "Lead on."

Ms. Bridges turned on her heel with much the same sharpness as Brent's driver and took off at a rapid pace. They were in the outer ring—the E ring—and Brent knew enough about the layout of the Pentagon to know that Colonel Richards likely occupied an office in E. Windows came with rank. What he didn't know was which floor the colonel might merit. His guide began to answer that question when she reached a ramp that, to Brent's surprise, led down to the Pentagon's two basement levels. The ramps were a throwback to a different era. As an attempt to preserve valuable steel for the construction of WWII-era battleships and weapons, the Pentagon had gone up without elevators. Instead, concrete ramps bridged the spans between floors. The one Brent and Ms. Bridges were taking led to the mezzanine level.

Exiting the ramp, Bridges led Brent along the E ring until they reached a corridor that turned toward the Pentagon's inner courtyard. A sign on the wall designated it as Corridor 3, which Bridges took toward the D ring, where she made a right. Brent dutifully followed his guide until they reached an office with bay number 29 affixed to the open door.

When they passed through the door, it took Brent a few moments to understand why it looked so strange. He'd been in standard Pentagon offices and the larger briefing rooms, even a few of the auditoriums, and the room he was in now was at least as large as the briefing bays. Yet the size had been accomplished by combining three or more offices into one large one. In the expanded space were a half-dozen desks, a few tables loaded with a variety of tools, electronics, and various items Brent couldn't identify, a large bookshelf, and other markers that spoke of the dual influences of scientific curiosity and military protocol. The place was a mess, but even the mess had strict rules.

As soon as Brent stepped into the room, at least four pairs of eyes shifted to him, yet only one man started in his direction.

"Dr. Michaels," Colonel Richards said. He crossed the room quickly and took the professor's hand in a stronger version of his assistant's solid grip. "Thank you for coming on such short notice."

"Not at all, Colonel," Brent said. "From what you told me over the phone, this one sounds pretty interesting."

It was as those words left his lips that something happening in the corner of the expanded office turned his head as if it were on a swivel. From the moment he'd entered the room he'd been hearing a noise, something like a low frequency hum. But such was the subtle nature of the sound that he hadn't realized he'd heard it until the last few seconds, although once it registered he realized he'd picked up on it right away.

At a large table in the corner, two military personnel—he could see uniforms under the lab coats, though he couldn't determine their ranks—were bent over a beaker that hung suspended over a Bunsen burner. Whatever was inside the beaker began to glow a strange green color. The two suddenly pulled back, looking undecided about whether they should remove the beaker from its place or pull the burner from beneath it. As the humming from the vicinity of the beaker increased, it became apparent that the time to countermand whatever was about to happen had passed. An instant later, the contents of the beaker spewed upward. It happened fast enough that Brent could only ascertain from the aftermath what had taken place—from the glob of green on the ceiling and the fine spray that coated everything within a few meters, including the two lab techs.

Taking his cues from those around him—all of whom had regarded the incident without alarm—Brent decided there was nothing to worry about. He watched as one of the lab techs removed his goggles, raised them up to study their slimed surface, and then wiped them on his coat. That done, he glanced toward the colonel.

"Well, now we know it doesn't like heat," he said matter-of-factly.

Colonel Richards appeared to digest that before answering.

"Lesson learned," the colonel said, then turned back to the visiting professor.

"It appears you have quite the operation here," Brent said.

Richards followed Brent's line of vision to the cleanup effort underway in the corner. "If you think this is something, Dr. Michaels, you should see the lab."

———

"So what kind of colonel are you?" Brent asked once he'd seated himself opposite his host's desk.

Richards raised an eyebrow, not a trace of humor on his face. "The regular kind," he said.

The dry delivery caused Brent to release a nervous chuckle. He gestured toward the closed door of the colonel's office, referencing the activity beyond. "There's nothing normal about what's going on in that room." He paused, shook his head. "Did I see someone out there levitating metal balls?"

"Strong magnets," the colonel replied.

"And the pile of junk that looks like a disassembled bomb?"

"Is a disassembled bomb."

"Who are you people?" Brent asked. "I mean, if it's not classified."

"Actually, it *is* classified," Richards said. "But not rigorously so for outside consultants."

The colonel's phone rang, and after a glance at the caller ID, he waved an apology to his guest and picked it up. "Richards," he said.

While Brent couldn't hear the other end of the call, he could hear the sound of the caller's voice. Whoever it was sounded excited—and loud.

After listening for several seconds, Richards cut into the caller's monologue. "Alright, follow secondary protocol until I get down there. Keep the room locked off. Understood?"

Brent didn't say anything after the colonel had hung up. From what he'd heard, he expected the man to bound up from his chair and go running from the room. Instead, the military man leaned back in his leather chair as calm as could be.

"We're army officers, Dr. Michaels," Richards said. "In addition to that, we're scientists. What you see going on out there is science, but with a twist."

"A twist," Brent said.

Richards nodded. "At your university, you have a science department, right?"

"Of course."

"And they're busy dealing with all the things that people are interested in—things that can either be marketed and sold or can put your school in a good journal somewhere, right?"

"Right . . ." Brent said, his responses coming slower now.

"Yes, well, we deal with the other stuff," the colonel said.

Brent attempted to parse that.

Richards, seeing the confused look on Brent's face, asked, "Are you familiar with Roswell?"

"You mean you investigate UFOs?"

"No, Professor," the colonel said flatly. "UFOs don't exist. You don't seriously think there are little green men at a military base in New Mexico, do you?"

"Well . . . I . . ."

"There aren't. But that doesn't mean we aren't investigating the possibility."

Brent let that sink in. When he felt he had a handle on what the colonel was saying, he said, "So your team investigates unexplained phenomena. You're ghost hunters. At least the army equivalent."

"My team investigates anything my superiors ask me to investigate," Richards said. After a pause he added, "And there are no such things as ghosts."

Brent pursed his lips and nodded, thinking this may have been the most interesting interview he'd ever experienced. "I'm confused," he finally said. "Why exactly do you need me?"

"Because we need a sociologist, Dr. Michaels." Richards leaned forward then, placing his elbows on the desk. "And from everything I've heard, you're the best."

Although it was flattering to hear something like that, what Brent was most interested in was what Colonel Richards hadn't said. Brent had been in the colonel's company for going on an hour and still he had no idea about the job he'd been called in to do. He was just about to bring this to Colonel Richards's attention when the colonel's desk phone rang again. Richards glanced down at the display and then back up at Brent.

"Now if you'll excuse me, Dr. Michaels, I have to go see about a fire."

———

"You realize I can't show you all of it."

"Classified?" Brent asked.

"Classified," Richards said.

From what he could gather through a combination of Colonel Richards's comments and his own impressions as he'd walked through a series of narrow corridors and past several nondescript rooms, the section of the subbasement the colonel's team occupied was a small portion of a much larger space. In fact, Michaels was now certain the perimeter of the subbasement—the Pentagon's basement's basement—expanded beyond the boundaries of the building above. Yet the professor had no idea how many *other* levels existed beneath this one.

What he did know was that the "all of it" the colonel couldn't show him must have been something, because what Brent had already been privy to was enough to keep him wondering for years. In one room—the first through which they'd passed after descending from the last of the official Pentagon floors—piles of disassembled hardware, computer parts, books and scattered papers, balls of wiring, copper coils, and electronic bits and interfaces he couldn't identify. And what looked like an Apollo-era space capsule occupying perhaps seven hundred square feet.

"What is this place?" Brent had asked.

"The Junk Room," Richards replied without breaking stride.

Now, having passed through a number of different but equally bizarre rooms, the professor realized that whoever Colonel Richards was, and whatever the purpose of his team, the job they had for him was also likely to be bizarre in nature.

The room they were in now stood apart from the others, primarily because of its cleanliness. The surgical table and the specimen jars filling the rows of metal shelving units spoke to the need for order and precision. As Brent followed Colonel Richards into the room, a woman dressed in scrubs was sliding a jar into place next to other jars just like it. They contained a dark, viscous substance. Brent couldn't begin to guess what it might be. But the truth was that he didn't need to understand everything he saw—didn't even need to know where he was in the building. He was there to entertain a job offer; whatever else happened around him was incidental.

That resolution remained with him for exactly two seconds, disappearing just as the colonel was about to step through the door opposite the one they'd entered. Before Colonel Richards could clear the doorway, a man met him going the other direction, holding a jar similar to the ones the woman behind them was arranging on the shelves. To avoid a collision, both men came to a sudden stop. That was when Brent got himself a good look at the pair of eyeballs sloshing around in the murky liquid, bumping up against the glass.

"Whoa. Sorry about that, Colonel," the man said. He looked past Richards to see Brent's eyes fixed on the jar in his hands. Glancing down at it, he said, "Almost lost the little beauty."

Richards stepped back to let the man pass, and Brent watched as he handed the jar to the woman, who then mounted a small stepladder to place it next to an identical jar on the room's highest shelf.

The professor turned to the colonel. "Okay, what was that?"

"What was what?" the colonel said.

"*That,*" Brent said, pointing to the jar on the shelf. "With the eyes?"

"Ah, that." After a pause, the colonel added, "How about we just agree you didn't see that, okay?"

Brent stared at Richards for a moment. "Classified?" he said.

"Classified."

"The eyeballs are classified. . . ."

The colonel nodded. "That's right, Professor. The eyeballs are classified." He stopped then and turned to face Brent. "But you didn't see any eyeballs, did you?"

The professor shook his head. "Nope."

Richards started off again, but Brent tossed a question after him.

"Are there any other body parts I should be on the lookout for?"

When less than twenty steps later their trip ended in a nondescript conference room, complete with a rectangular table, ten chairs, a laptop, and a ceiling-mounted projector, Brent almost felt cheated, his expectations growing with each new strange thing he'd witnessed on the way. Nonetheless, he took a seat in the chair the colonel indicated and waited for his host to join him at the table.

Once in the chair, positioned in front of the laptop, Colonel Richards tapped a single key and the projector sprang to life, casting the image of a large world map on the wall, color-coded to correspond with a legend displayed in the map's corner. What he noticed right off, though, was that the colors were confined to landmasses, and that they crossed both national and continental lines.

Brent shifted his attention to the legend, looking for anything that would help him decipher the nature of the map. He found that the only piece of information matching any particular color was a number. The numbers followed a straight count from one to ten; number one went with the color black and number ten with red. Each of the remaining numbers was given a color, and while Brent was no expert in this sort of thing, he suspected the black/one combo was the desired state of things, whereas the red/ten combo signified something extremely problematic—with varying degrees of undesirability in between.

"What am I looking at, Colonel?" he asked.

"Consider it our version of a Poincaré map," the colonel said.

Armed with that information, Brent looked at the projection again. Now that he understood more about the map's meaning, it seemed strange that the colonel and his team could plot Chaos Theory so neatly like this.

"I'm going to need a list of your initial conditions," Brent said. "And your topological mixing progression, if you have one. Plus the actual Poincaré data."

"Of course."

"Since all of your measures are land-based, can I assume you're using the Ricker model?"

The colonel nodded. "While we're not measuring population growth, we thought Ricker most closely matched what we're doing."

Brent studied the map once more. After a few moments, he said, "So what exactly are you doing, Colonel?"

Colonel Richards didn't answer right away, and when Brent pulled his eyes away from the map to glance at the man, he found Richards staring at the projection. Finally the colonel spoke.

"Tracking the breakdown of civilization, Dr. Michaels," he said.

From his spot in a small depression atop the escarpment, Canfield looked out over the oil field, a land as flat as any he'd ever seen. He could see them only because he knew they were there—the men in his employ crossing the quarter mile of brown grass separating the Hickson Petroleum field from Canfield's elevated position. Hickson Petroleum was but one of the many oil companies that leased space to drill in the Southwest's Spraberry Trend. Yet it was the one with the lightest security, which made it perfect for this operation.

Canfield stifled a yawn. He was in desperate need of sleep, but after the complications at Afar, he'd decided to give this one his personal oversight. He'd done a decent job explaining Ethiopia to his boss, though he doubted the man would accept two failings in a row—a belief strengthened by the tone of their last meeting.

"What happened at Afar, Alan?" Mr. Van Camp had asked him.

At the question Canfield had sunk back into his chair and drew in a deep breath. When he expelled it he shook his head.

"No one knew our government had anyone operating in the area," Canfield said. "Our liaison with the ONLF thought they were a research team."

He shook his head again.

"What have you heard out of Washington?"

Behind Canfield—who only a few days ago had shared a drink with a mercenary who knew him by the name of Standish—a series of monitors flashed a continuous stream of news feeds. Van Camp looked past Canfield, taking in the events captured by countless cameras, many of them owned by him.

"There's little coming out of the Beltway," Van Camp said.

"I imagine they'll keep it quiet until they know what they're dealing with."

It was the sort of statement that didn't require a response. Instead, Van Camp said, "Have you been able to find out anything about the military unit that surprised your mercenary?"

"Not as much as I'd like to know," Canfield answered honestly. "From what I've been able to gather, they're a small unit called the NIIU, led by a colonel named Jameson Richards."

"And the acronym stands for . . ."

"Non-Standard Incident Investigative Unit," Canfield said. He shrugged his shoulders. "My contacts weren't able to give me much about what that means except that most of their reports are protected by Level 5 security. And apparently they have a science facility in the Pentagon."

Van Camp seemed to ponder that, his eyes never leaving Canfield.

"I imagine all we can do at this point is try to determine why they were at Afar," he said. "Although in all likelihood it was an unfortunate coincidence."

Canfield had thought the same thing but was pleased that his boss had come to the same conclusion without much prompting. Diverting resources to study a small army unit would pull those resources away from where they were most needed; and they were already racing the clock to complete the work at Shackleton. He was grateful, then, when Van Camp switched topics.

"Four dead?" the man asked.

"According to Dabir, yes," Canfield said.

"And you're certain they were killed, not captured?"

"Dabir was certain." Canfield offered a grim smile. "He would have put a bullet in any of them himself had there been any doubt." He paused a moment before adding, "But in the heat of battle, who knows?"

"Who indeed?" Van Camp said.

It was that sort of question that caused a shiver to run up Canfield's spine, because it signified a potential lack of faith in Canfield's ability to accomplish the tasks assigned him. And causing Arthur Van Camp to doubt one's effectiveness was seldom a winning corporate advancement strategy. Hence his presence on a rock in Texas.

Canfield raised a pair of binoculars and watched his team of three men—dressed like the oil workers teeming over the rigs and drilling platforms—slip through a gate that an exchange of funds had assured would be temporarily unguarded. Once inside, the men set off in different directions, each with a mission to accomplish. As Canfield watched, he marveled at the lack of security. Apparently the thought of domestic terrorism had yet to take hold in the collective psyche of this region. He spotted the single guard walking the north line, but Canfield's men were by now well away from the gate.

With the binoculars, Canfield followed one of the men as he strolled over to one of the newest production trees. The man bent down as if to inspect the valve, yet Canfield knew he would be pulling the packs of C-4 from the riggers bag he carried, securing the explosives beneath the weld line. The process took less than twenty seconds, after which the man was heading toward the main gate. Thirty yards away, another man finished his identical task and started for the same exit.

Canfield watched him for a few moments longer before moving to locate the team leader, the one tackling the most difficult target—the drilling rig surrounded by almost a dozen men. The man had donned a pair of goggles and found a spot on the periphery of the activity. The rig was active, with the drill bit pulverizing the subsurface rock, the pieces then pulled to the surface by the cycling drilling fluid. In preparation for this operation, Canfield had studied the rig, noting the difficulty of accessing any vulnerable areas within joints secured under the topdrive. In order to blow the well, they had to find a way through the casing at ground level or locate a spot above the action.

Moments later, the C-4 attached to the production trees blew, with a noise sufficient to dwarf the sound of the drill and sending the ground rolling beneath the entirety of the field.

It took a few long seconds before the Hickson employees around the unfinished well moved, but once they started, and once they saw the flames and black smoke rising from the two obliterated production trees, they took off toward the conflagrations.

Canfield, though, kept his eyes on the team leader, a former army officer turned corporate mercenary. The man waited while the drill operator brought the unit to a lumbering stop and then hurried down the small ladder to follow his co-workers. A few seconds later, when the operative started to climb, Canfield lost sight of him. It seemed like forever before he spotted him again, descending and walking away from the rig.

Canfield's mistake was watching the drill rig a second too long. The flash, magnified through the binoculars, nearly blinded him. But what really shocked him was the power of the blast—sufficient to set the escarpment in motion a quarter mile from the site. His first thought was to wonder if any of his operatives had survived a blast considerably more powerful than he'd anticipated. But even with the possibility of casualties, he couldn't help but smile. He'd wanted this one to be memorable—to perhaps make up for the failure at Afar. In that he'd succeeded.

After watching a few moments longer, he made his way back to the truck parked on the other side of the rock, started the engine, and pointed the vehicle toward Hobbs, New Mexico.

Armed Forces Global Threat Assessment

December 4, 2012

- Caracas, Venezuela: Chavez sends troops to seize foreign-owned agriculture concerns in Mérida.

- Berlin, Germany: Bundestag approves measures to close borders, restrict immigration.

- Vienna, Austria: OPEC set to announce production cuts by two million barrels in December.

- Tehran, Iran: Ahmadinejad announces plans for second reactor at Bushehr.

6

December 5, 2012, 8:25 A.M.

They'd housed Brent Michaels in a temporary office, and true to his word, Colonel Richards had supplied the professor with all the data he could have wanted. Even better, he'd supplied Brent with someone to help him sift through the voluminous information.

Captain Amy Madigan, a petite blonde with piercing eyes and an easy smile, sat at Brent's left shoulder as he flipped through a stack of reports—all on U.S. Army letterhead, all signed and dated by Colonel Richards. In the few minutes during which he'd scanned the contents, Brent determined that the bulk of the reports detailed missions undertaken by the team over the last two years, mostly investigative jaunts to the world's far-flung places. What, exactly, they were investigating wasn't clear, but from what Brent could gather, few of the mission reports provided anything he would have called actionable data. In fact, most of them ended with a single phrase that the professor was starting to suspect was a motto for this team: *Information inconclusive.*

"So let me make sure I understand," Brent said. "The colonel wants me to investigate a perceived increase in worldwide sociological entropy and determine if there are any measurable factors behind it. Does that about sum it up?"

Amy Madigan tipped her chair back and seemed to give careful consideration to the professor's analysis.

"Well," she said, "if by 'sociological entropy' you mean why the world seems to be trucking toward crazy a little faster than normal, then yes, that's exactly what the colonel wants you to figure out."

That pulled a smile from Brent, though one tempered by the nature of his assignment.

"You do realize that trying to predict the future state of even a closed deterministic system is close to mathematically impossible," he said. "Even for a mathematician, which I'm not." He shook his head. "Trying to do so with the entire population of the planet is absurd."

As soon as he said it he realized how it sounded, but if Madigan was taken aback by a visiting professor insulting her work, as well as the work of her colleagues, she didn't show it.

"Of course it is," she agreed. "But remember, we're not asking you to project the model forward. We want you to track it in reverse—find the thing that set all this off."

"That's assuming there is one thing," Brent said. "Have you considered the probability that what you're investigating is just a series of random events, with nothing tying them together?"

"We have," Madigan said, "but we're pretty sure that's not the case."

"And what makes you so sure?" Brent asked, even as he mentally kicked himself for jeopardizing the promise of a substantial paycheck.

"Because that's what we do" was the captain's response.

Brent chuckled and pushed the stack of papers away. "I'm still not entirely sure *what* you do."

Madigan answered Brent's laugh with one of her own.

"That's okay," she said. "Half the time I don't know what we do either."

When Brent didn't answer, she let her chair fall back to the floor, resting an elbow on the desk. The shift in position revealed that she was wearing a chain, a small cross almost hidden beneath her uniform shirt.

"We have several labs down here," she said. "In one of them there's a car."

"What kind of car?"

"An Infiniti. A J30. 1995."

Brent frowned, unimpressed.

"The reason the car's here is because when it's parked on Seventh Avenue in Tacoma, right in front of the True Value, it won't start." At the professor's puzzled look she said, "You see, it will start anywhere else. In fact, if you push it a few feet up so that it's parked in front of the doughnut shop next to the hardware store, it fires right up."

Brent didn't say anything right away, for he was uncertain of the point.

"It's not just coincidence?" he finally asked.

"We've tested it. We've flown or driven that car all over the country, and every time we turn the key, it starts. But if we take it back to Tacoma and park it in front of the True Value, it's as dead as a doornail."

"Have you considered that it might be the spot as opposed to the car?"

"Of course we have. We've parked more than a hundred cars in the same spot and all of them started up just fine." She paused. "Well, except for the Mazda 626. It took us fifteen minutes to figure out it was out of gas."

"Maybe it's just Infinitis that are affected?"

"Uh-uh," Madigan said. "We've tried. Same model, same year. In fact, we even found one with the same mileage."

Brent nodded as if he understood what this was about.

"You see, Dr. Michaels, it's not the car and it's not the spot. But for some reason when you bring those two elements together, you have something unexpected." She reached across the desk and tapped the stack of papers. "We're the ones who bring the right things together, Professor. *That's* what we do."

Brent leaned back in his chair and considered that. In a way, Amy Madigan's explanation made sense. After all, when he looked at the mission reports, they resembled nothing so much as an accumulation of puzzle pieces to be assembled later.

"Tell me about Ethiopia," he said. "That was your last outing, right?"

Madigan nodded.

"What sent you out there in the first place?" Brent asked.

His experience working with military personnel had acclimated him to the normal reticence most of them had about revealing nonessential data. Madigan exhibited that now; he could see her batting the question around in her mind. Brent, however, seldom asked a nonessential question.

"A few of our satellites picked up some unusual readings along the Afar Rift," she said. "Like pre-quake seismic activity."

"I'm not as up on my geology as I'd like to be," he said, "but isn't that the spot where the ground ripped open? You know, all the shaking, the lava?"

"That's right."

"So aren't unusual readings kind of par for the course?"

She smiled and said, "Yes, but these readings seemed too regular to have been caused by natural forces."

"So that means . . ."

"That means they might have been man-made," she finished. At Brent's doubtful look, she added, "If you knew anything about the rift, you'd know that the forces that caused it operate miles beneath the surface. And while they might seem random, if you watch it long enough, if you gather boatloads of data over the course of years, you can come close to figuring out what it's going to do next."

"And these readings?" Brent asked after a moment.

"Too shallow to be connected to tectonic plate movement. And too regularly timed to be natural occurrences."

Brent had been honest in his initial admission: his expertise fell woefully short in the earth sciences. He had to take his cues, then, from Madigan, who exhibited no doubt regarding her conclusions.

"And now that you've been out there to investigate?" it occurred to him to ask.

"The readings have stopped," she answered.

Brent could follow her line of reasoning. Why would the phenomenon have ceased were it not something that could be controlled?

"Who would be responsible for something like that?" he asked.

Madigan leaned back in her chair, tipping it back again on two legs, and fixed the professor with a smile. "Dr. Michaels, that's why you're here."

———

Canfield allowed himself to indulge the slight limp caused by his egress from the hill that overlooked the obliterated oil field. He'd turned his ankle on the way back to the truck, stepping in a hole that he should have seen. He chalked it up to the weariness caused by business on three continents in four days—but he suspected Van Camp would simply see it as weakness.

While outside of the man's purview, he could let something like human frailty show itself. In front of his boss, though, he would have to walk a steady path to the man's desk, regardless of the pain.

His wife was another matter entirely. So rarely did he hurt himself that his wife's reaction had redefined "over the top." She wanted him off his feet so she could apply the ministrations a doting mate enjoyed affording. In fact, he thought Phyllis rather enjoyed his misfortune, as it fed her wont to fix things. That trait explained why he often returned home after one of his many trips to find that his house had become a refuge for some injured animal, or a motel for any one of their traveling neighbors' pets. It was a trait he didn't discourage; he knew the loneliness his job had imposed on her.

What he wouldn't do was to seek sympathy from his boss. Before he entered Van Camp's office, he braced himself against the pain and placed his full weight on his ankle. Van Camp trusted him to have a firm handle on each and every element of Project: Night House, and part of ensuring a continuation of that confidence was the unflappable persona Canfield exhibited. Like most men overseeing large corporations, Van Camp maintained a miserly grip on trust.

Van Camp, pen in hand, looked up as Canfield entered, and before he'd made it halfway across the room, Canfield knew he was about to be asked to undertake something distasteful. He could read as much on his boss's face: a manufactured reluctance accompanying a paternal smile—an expression that, in itself, was all theater.

Checking the sigh that threatened to emerge, Canfield took the seat across from the man who ran a global empire that few in the world could rival.

Van Camp set the pen on the papers spread out in front of him. "I apologize, Alan," he said. "I'd intended to give you a few days to rest from your recent spate of trips, but I fear I'm going to have to ask you to jump back into things immediately."

"I understand," Canfield said with a nod.

Rather than continue, Van Camp pushed back from the desk

and stepped over to the bar. He filled two highball glasses with bourbon and then returned, placing one of the drinks in front of Canfield. Despite the frequency of Canfield's presence in this office, Van Camp had never before shared a drink with him.

"Alan, I've been giving some thought to what we discussed when you returned from Africa," Van Camp said.

Canfield reached for the drink and sampled a bit of the expensive bourbon.

"I think it's time to end our operation in Ethiopia," Van Camp went on.

What kept Canfield from showing surprise was that he'd considered this a possibility. His boss was, like most successful businessmen, more cautious in his business approach than the general public suspected. Success did not come from embracing risk but from minimizing it. What he didn't know, however, was which project Van Camp wished to see ended.

They'd suspended—Canfield had thought temporarily—the work with the rift now that their machinations had attracted the attention of the American military. Coaxing an earthquake from an already unstable region wasn't all that difficult. Causing the earthquake to occur on a specific date and time, however, was much more complex. Such a thing required a great deal of planning and work, and so Canfield had assumed a temporary nature to the suspension—at least until Van Camp's considerable resources could make the necessary heads turn away. In Canfield's estimation, Project: Night House required success at Afar, considering the difficulty of ensuring the same level of success at Shackleton.

There was also the possibility that Van Camp meant the work of Dabir's team. In fact, he hoped for that—a desire that colored his response.

"While I don't necessarily disagree with you," Canfield said as the burn in his throat eased, "Dabir has proven himself to be a valuable asset. After Night House is finished, I thought perhaps we'd keep him on the payroll."

Van Camp took a drink and followed it with a slow head-shake. "What would he do for us that would mitigate the risk he presents?"

Canfield didn't answer. Instead, he took another sip of the bourbon and found his eyes moving to the only item on Van Camp's desk that could be called decorative.

He didn't know anything about Van Camp's personal history with the onyx carving—if it had been a gift, how long it had been in his possession, or if it held any sentimental value. His knowledge of the piece centered upon it having granted Project: Night House its name. The *Akbal*, the English translation of which had become the project moniker, was one of twenty symbols identifying Mayan calendar days. The carving showed what looked like a narrow mountain rising in the distance, with tree branches in the foreground. To Canfield it looked like a child's drawing, although he thought he understood the intent of the Maya. Commonly used symbols had to be easy to reproduce; anything intricate would have increased what, in today's terms, would have been called production time. That was a problem, and a solution, Canfield could appreciate. Something he could leverage in dealing with Dabir, who was a man he'd grown to, if not like, at least respect over the last few years. It made it easier that Dabir's team was but one of more than a dozen positioned at hot spots around the globe.

"I'll take care of it then," he said after a time.

The only acknowledgment from Van Camp was a repositioning of the man's eyes to the monitors that played out their scenes behind Canfield. For all Van Camp's aloofness, Canfield knew the man respected the intricacies of the various moving parts that would secure his success. Truth be told, he likely knew each of those parts—and their many variables—better than Canfield himself.

"What will you do about the team investigating Afar?" he asked, for the dual purposes of displaying the depth of his own detachment and because he honestly wanted to know.

Van Camp did not respond for several moments. In fact, such was the length of the man's silence that Canfield began to wonder if his boss had heard the question. He was about to repeat it when, with a refocusing of attention that pulled his eyes from the monitors, Van Camp caught him up.

"We watch them, Alan," Van Camp said. "We watch them and see if Afar was an accident, or luck. If it was luck, then we have nothing to worry about."

"And if it wasn't luck?" Canfield asked.

He'd worked for Arthur Van Camp for almost a decade—long enough to have been privy to most of the man's moods. It was a familiarity that made the ice that overtook the man's face so surprising.

"Then we may need to escalate things," Van Camp said.

With the finality intimated by such a statement, Canfield rose to leave. He didn't bother finishing the bourbon.

———

December 5, 2012, 4:50 P.M.

Dabir held on to the handgrip as the jeep bounced over the rocky terrain. The driver kept the sunlight behind them as well as he could, but the nature of the land forced the convoy of jeeps and the Toyotas driven by the Rashaida to tack in profile to the sun more than Dabir would have liked. Still, he knew the land would flatten out as they came out of the foothills and as they approached the border near Omhajer. If he'd timed it correctly, they would be upon the small farming community just as the sun went down. The farmers would never know death was coming until the first bullets were fired.

Dabir was ambivalent about what he was about to do, yet he had entertained and fought down that sentiment often enough over the last few years to not allow those doubts to affect him. When he'd first met Standish, the westerner had been candid about the results he expected for his money, although it had taken several months for Dabir to take his attacks beyond legitimate military and strategic targets. After the first massacre—the first time he brought his forces to bear against a group of people, a collection of nomadic families whose only crime was to make themselves available for such an action—Dabir had prayed for several hours, begging Allah's forgiveness. That remorse, however, had not stopped him from carrying out similar massacres against countless targets. Nor would it stop him tonight.

To supplement his ranks against his recent losses, he'd hired the Rashaida, who came with their own weapons and their own vehicles. There were six of them, in two Toyotas, which was the vehicle of choice for these industrious nomads, and Dabir would likely have them killed after the conclusion of this business. Mr. Standish was quite particular about witnesses.

Back in 2000, Eritrea and Ethiopia signed a sheet of paper that concluded a bitter war. Now, more than a decade later, Dabir thanked the tribal memory that carried the injustices of that war into the present day, which would make an attack by his forces subsume into the minor transgressions committed by both sides. A decade was not long enough for the peoples occupying each side of the disputed border to forget the injustices inflicted by the other.

An attack against Eritrean traders would be looked upon as an act of the Ethiopian military, regardless of the lack of evidence. And for sowing the seeds of the subsequent unrest, Dabir would be handsomely compensated.

It was warmer than it had been in Afar; a line of sweat trickled down the back of Dabir's neck despite the wind stirring through the jeep. He knew that, next to him, the driver also felt the heat, as did the two men in the back, but all of these men had grown up in this place; the heat was something to be considered and then forgotten. Like killing. Done and then forgotten.

Rahm spoke a single, unnecessary word to let Dabir know they were emerging from the foothills, but Dabir had known exactly where they were, knew they would head due north for another mile before turning west, the sun rendering them almost invisible against the topography of the land behind them. In less than an hour, more than two dozen people—women and children among them—would be dead and Dabir and his men would vanish like ghosts. A day later, and more than a hundred miles away, a half-dozen bodies—the Rashaida who now aided him—would be dumped into a hole in the scrubland, where in all likelihood they would spend a thousand years rotting without anyone knowing they were there.

Dabir and his men were ghosts—in many ways like Mr. Standish himself, who disappeared like vapor every time he left Addis. Had Dabir truly believed in spirits he would have thought that Standish fit the bill. It was a skill that Dabir envied, and one that caused him to expend whatever resources he had in order to track the man, for he knew that eventually Standish would consider the mercenary's usefulness expired. On that day, Dabir would find himself dumped into a hole in the desert too.

It was for that eventuality that he planned. And the reason he smiled, despite the blood that would be on his hands soon enough, was that for the first time Standish's trail had not utterly vanished with him.

December 5, 2012, 7:43 P.M.

Brent had been at it for hours, going through more than a hundred case files and plotting the interesting bits over the Poincaré map developed by Richards's team, although the legend by which to interpret his work was to be found only in his head. It was an arrangement that vexed his army handler, as it left her little to do beyond answer his questions—which had grown less frequent over the last few hours—and try to stifle the yawns that came in inverse proportion to the professor's queries. Brent had to respect, though, that she had not once hinted that maybe they should call it a night.

"What did you go to college for?" he asked, catching her eyes at the moment their top lids touched the bottom. He kept his smile to himself as those lids snapped open, guilt as the motivator.

"Premed chemistry," Madigan said, rubbing her eyes with her palms.

"So what made you join the army?"

He asked the question as he scanned one of the team's reports.

After years spent reviewing documents, looking for patterns or for something that stood out from the pattern, he could do it on autopilot. It allowed him to listen to Amy Madigan talk herself to alertness.

"Student loans." She stifled another yawn, took a sip of lukewarm coffee, and said, "After a year I started to get worried about having to spend the rest of my life paying for my undergrad degree—especially when I knew medical school was coming."

He looked up from the papers and offered the weary captain a wry smile. "That's what the National Guard is for, isn't it?"

She chuckled at that.

"Don't underestimate the power of a good recruiter," she said.

Brent shuffled the papers and then set them aside. He reached for his own coffee cup and took a fortifying drink.

"But what made you stay? My guess is your four years was up a while ago. The army would have paid for your schooling and you could be working in a private lab anywhere in the world."

"First, thanks for the crack at my age." When Brent gave her a confused look, she added, "My four years wasn't up *that* long ago." He offered a chastised look as Madigan leaned back in her chair, stretching her legs under the table. "I was about to leave. I'd been accepted to medical school and was ready to say good-bye to Uncle Sam."

"Then what?" Brent asked after she'd lapsed into silence.

"Then I met Colonel Richards, and he offered me a spot on his team." She paused and waved a tired hand in the air, taking in the room and perhaps the larger facility. "Well, you've seen this place."

"Some of it," Brent said, thinking back on some of the things he'd witnessed in his short time in residence. "Yeah, I guess I can see why you chose to stay."

That acknowledgment elicited a smile from Madigan, but

apparently she was too tired to pursue the conversation, so when she again lapsed into silence, Brent pressed on once more.

"So has it been worth it?" he asked.

"It's rarely a good idea to entertain 'what ifs.' I believe I'm where I'm supposed to be."

Brent fancied himself a good observer of people; it was part of what allowed him to turn his sociology expertise into consulting positions. And so he noticed Amy Madigan's hand move absently to the cross hanging from the chain around her neck—a symbol, and a gesture, that spoke of a religious upbringing carried through to adulthood. It was a bit of knowledge he would file away for a later occasion should such information prove valuable. He'd already committed a great deal to that particular mental file cabinet—such as the fact that Amy Madigan was more attractive than the average army officer.

As if picking up on that thought, she said, "So is there a Mrs. Michaels?"

She'd asked just as he'd taken another swallow of coffee, and while the question certainly dovetailed with his thoughts, he still found himself fighting to keep the coffee from going down the wrong pipe. What made the inquiry even more interesting was that she would have read his file—would have known he wasn't married.

"Nope," he said, his eyes watering only slightly from the coffee. "There's no Mrs. Michaels."

She offered a raised eyebrow in response. "That's surprising at your age."

The comment pulled a laugh from the professor. "I really don't think forty-five puts me past my prime," he said, a bit more defensiveness in his voice than he'd intended. When he saw her smile, though, it made him not mind having been baited as much as he might have. "I guess I just haven't had time to find the right woman."

"Too busy hopping around the globe doing consults?"

"Variety makes the real job more palatable."

"You don't like teaching?"

"Don't get me wrong," he said. "I love teaching." When all that greeted him from Amy Madigan's side of the table was silence, he said, "What other job lets me take a consult on a moment's notice? Or go fishing whenever I want?"

It was the type of response that often came across as charming, but rather than a lowering of Amy's guard, Brent saw a clinical look take roost in her expression.

"One of your consults was Admir Naheem, wasn't it?"

"Yes . . ." He paused before continuing but suspected that the fact that she'd asked the question meant she had the necessary security clearance to learn the details. "I'm sure you already pulled this from the file, but Naheem had spent almost a decade stirring tensions along the Nigerian border."

"How did you decide that he was responsible? I mean, the Nigerian border with Cameroon has been a hot spot for decades. What made you realize that Naheem was inciting violence along the border in order to build support for a seizure of the presidency? After all, it might have been just cyclical ethnic activity."

Brent returned a thoughtful nod before responding.

"Granted, on the surface that's what it looked like," he said. "But part of what I do as a sociologist is to look at possible causal factors and then rule out the ones that don't account for what I'm observing."

"And I'm guessing you have a good system for doing that?"

Instead of answering her, Brent arranged some report pages into a folder, then lifted it from the table for her perusal. "I'm sure you've noticed that Africa accounts for almost half of your reports over the last two years."

She nodded.

"And from what I can tell from reading over your older reports, it looks as though that number of events is a substantial escalation."

Another nod.

"So my first impulse is to try to figure out what's going on over there that would influence an area stretching from Egypt to South Africa. To do that, I start with looking at the obvious questions, things like economic factors, regional politics, any groups or individuals with the resources and reach to carry this type of influence." He shrugged and added, "Even the weather."

Madigan's eyebrows went up.

"Western Africa accounts for more than half of the industrial farming on the continent. Now, let's say there's a dry spell that drastically reduces the region's crop." He let that hang there until he knew she'd picked up on his train of thought. "Whatever your trigger is, it has to either be something of comparable scale to the area it affects or—"

"Or it has to be designed," she finished.

"Exactly," Brent said.

Madigan tipped her chair back and pondered his words for several moments, and when she looked back at the professor he could tell she had it.

"And you couldn't find anything obvious—anything natural—in Nigeria to account for the escalation in violence, so you suspected manufactured unrest," she said.

"It was the only thing that made sense at the time." He tossed the folder on the table and yawned before continuing. "Once your vetting process leaves you with people as the probable cause, what I do becomes a mix of detective work and psychology. Meanwhile, you just hope you end up getting it right."

"Which you did with Naheem," she offered.

He returned a wry smile at the acknowledgment. "I got lucky on that one," he confessed. "There were at least half a dozen military or political leaders who could have been responsible for it. Sometimes it just comes down to a feeling."

Again, Brent saw her processing what was essentially an admission that the man they'd flown in and were paying handsomely for a consult had admitted to guesswork as a viable mode of analysis.

"And that's your system?" she asked.

"Pretty much. What I'm feeling is that whatever this is—whatever your team has been tracking over the last few years—it's big." When her eyes narrowed at the ambiguousness of his answer, he said, "Remember, part of the system is calculating what can impact a large area. But you have to be careful not to have tunnel vision about the size of the area you're investigating."

She didn't answer, nor change her facial expression, so he continued. "In looking at these reports my initial impulse is to focus on Africa—to try and find that big thing sending ripples across the continent. But tunnel vision can be crippling." This was one of those occasions when he felt like a professor absent a classroom. The difference in this case was that Amy Madigan seemed much more interested than his average student. "Let's take it out of Africa. Your reports document increases in political, economic, and social unrest across Europe and Asia as well as the Western Hemisphere. If I take each one of those individually, I might be able to convince myself that the causes for each were local in origin. Taken as a whole, though—"

"There's something outside of the respective systems that's influencing all of them," she interrupted, continuing his thought for the second time in minutes.

"The domestic issues alone are anomalous," he said. "And so we're talking about something working on a global scale."

"Which means it's man-made," Madigan ventured.

Brent shook his head. "Not necessarily. Think about something like El Niño. That's a natural occurrence that could conceivably be large enough to act as a catalyst for something with global ramifications."

That sent Madigan into a contemplative silence. When she emerged from it, she said, "But doesn't El Niño mean that the science of sociology is little more than guesswork?"

Brent chuckled and shook his head. "One of the misconceptions out there is that sociology is just psychology on a grand scale," he said. "And while there's an element of truth in that—I mean, I can't count the number of theories that exist on the nature of crowd behavior—it's a lot *more* than that. At its most basic level, sociology is the study of anything that impacts a particular people group on a large scale. It's really as simple as that."

As he watched Amy Madigan take that in, he found himself pondering his own words. Because if he'd learned one thing over the last forty-plus years, it was that few things were that simple.

———

"I thought you said you'd be home for a while," Phyllis said.

She wasn't angry; Canfield knew she didn't get angry. Instead, her manner was all nervousness, an unsure flightiness that annoyed him. Even when she sat still she never seemed to hold her position for long, her body engaged in half starts that looked like spasms, as if she would decide to get up and then change her mind the moment she began to rise. Sometimes he'd found himself wanting to shout at her, to order her to sit still, but in their twenty years of marriage he'd never once raised his voice to her. At times, he wished she *would* get angry. He thought he might like that more than the long-suffering shell of a woman she'd become.

"I thought I would be too," he answered.

He folded a shirt and stacked it on the rest of the clothes in his suitcase. With half of his life seemingly spent in the air, he could pack for a trip in under ten minutes. His plane left tomorrow morning for Kenya. He would make it to bed after Phyllis was asleep, and his car would pull onto the street before she awoke. It made things easier that way.

In truth, leaving on another trip so soon irritated him too. The last two years had done much to damage a marriage already hurting beneath the cumulative effects of all the things that worked against any lengthy union. So much so that even with the project scheduled to conclude in less than a month, he suspected the damage was of the irreversible kind. A man could not spend the better part of two years estranged from his wife and come back to the status quo; nor could a man keep the kinds of secrets he'd been forced to keep from Phyllis without establishing a necessary distance. That distance, he knew, did not contribute to his wife's mental well-being. He knew enough about depression to understand that he was not its cause, that it had a biological foundation. However, he also knew his frequent absences—his disengagement—did not provide an environment in which she could thrive.

"Look," he said with a sigh, "I'm sorry I have to leave again so soon. But it's a short trip. I leave tomorrow and I'm back on Monday."

At that, the corner of her mouth went up in something like a grim smile. With a fluttering hand on her chest she sat on the bed next to his suitcase—watched as he added a last pair of pants, then as he found spots for socks and underwear.

"How's your ankle?" she asked.

Canfield looked down at his Dolce and Gabbanas. He lifted his right foot off the floor and gave it a few rolls. "Feels fine," he said. "Thanks to you."

In reality, the ankle hurt a great deal. It took more effort to keep the grimace from his face as he demonstrated the positive effects of his wife's care than it had required to keep him from limping in front of his boss. The last thing he needed right now, though, was Phyllis seizing on an opportunity to demonstrate her usefulness.

Soon afterward she left to see about dinner. Canfield continued packing and it didn't occur to him for a while—until after the customary ten-minute exercise had turned into thirty—what, beyond the regular stresses of his job, was the true source of his disquiet. As he adjusted the items in the suitcase for the tenth time, it came to him that in regard to Project: Night House, little separated him from Dabir in terms of his usefulness after December 21. He wondered if his boss would consider him just another loose string to tie up once that fateful date passed.

Canfield considered that for a time, until the smell of steak found its way to him from the kitchen. Then he shut and zipped the suitcase, filed this new line of thought away for future consideration, and went to help his wife finish fixing dinner. He was careful not to limp.

December 6, 2012, 9:11 A.M.

Brent thought that after forty-eight hours a person could make just about any place feel like home. However, in the case of his current job, he didn't consider his temporary office a home so much as a refuge. Once one stepped into the hallway, anything could happen. While he didn't have sufficient clearance to grant him access to every area under the investigative unit's control, he'd walked into three different rooms in which things he couldn't begin to understand were transpiring. And while the strange nature of this team and their interesting pursuits teased the researcher in him, he knew that going off task would keep him in Washington longer than necessary. Abby couldn't arrange coverage for his classes forever.

Brent had papers spread out over the desk, copies of the originals so he could mar them with his own notes or draw lines between different sheets. For the last couple of hours—after a handful of parameter-building questions to Captain Madigan—he'd bounced between the growing stacks of papers and a computer model with ever-increasing data.

That left Madigan doing next to nothing. The part of Brent that loved to dive into a complex problem didn't realize he'd shut her out until, after entering some numbers into a proprietary computer program, he glanced up to see her with her chair tilted back, eyes on the ceiling. He thought that if he gave her a few more minutes, she would either fall asleep or the chair would tip too far back for her to catch it.

"You have time for a question?" he asked.

"You're kind of catching me at a bad time," she answered without moving. "Lots going on over here. Really busy."

"We were talking about Ethiopia—about the satellite readings that drew you there."

She nodded. "Like I said, the disturbances we saw didn't seem to have a seismic signature, which is why we went to investigate."

"And got shot at."

"And got shot at," she confirmed.

Brent leaned back, thinking.

"What's on your mind?" Madigan asked.

"How do you hear about most of the incidents you investigate? At least the ones you've included in the data set."

"We get some off the wires," she answered, righting the chair. "Some we hear about on CNN or MSNBC. Some of them we don't hear about until the colonel gets one tossed down the chain." She paused for a moment. "Of course, the colonel has at least one friend just about anywhere you could name. So he might get a hint of something before it blows containment."

"Okay," Brent said.

"What?" Madigan asked.

"I'm not really sure." He shuffled the papers on the desk, his handwritten notes marking every page. After a few seconds he gestured to the laptop. "This computer program is designed to look for those patterns we talked about—those things that could account for changes across a wide region. To see things that someone might miss because the connecting pieces seem incidental."

"You do realize," she said, "that with all the data you're putting in there, we're going to have to confiscate your computer once your consult is done, right?"

The question stopped him cold. He hadn't considered that understandably delicate issue. But to take his laptop? He tried to determine if Madigan was joking with him, but her face remained impassive. And so, because he could do nothing else, he chose to believe things would work themselves out.

"What's interesting," he said, "is that well over ninety percent of the incidents your team has investigated have been covered by one media outlet or another."

Madigan seemed to parse that before saying, "You know there are only about five people in the world without a cell phone, right? And seeing as most of those phones have cameras, just about anything that goes on in the world winds up on the Internet. And from there it's a quick walk down the hallway to a legitimate news outlet."

Brent smiled even as he shook his head. "Believe me, this is a pretty high number. You have to factor in that some of the things you and your team have researched barely have even local significance, much less national or worldwide. Which is why I asked how you decide what to investigate. If you're pulling your list from existing news sources, then the number would be skewed high."

"But if a lot of these incidents come to our attention via other sources, then your number needs another causal factor?"

"My thought exactly," he said. "So what do you think the percentage is?"

Madigan frowned as she considered the question.

"If I had to make a guess," she ventured, "I'd say at least forty percent of our workload—or at least the stuff we thought was connected enough to include in the data set—comes from either internal referral or through one of the colonel's contacts."

"And if you tack on an additional, let's say, twenty percent of leads that came in outside of any news outlets but that were big enough stories to get there anyway, you still have a lot of stuff that didn't deserve coverage but got it anyway."

"Which means?" she prodded.

"I have no idea," Brent said with a shrug. "Just thought it was interesting."

His response produced a smile from Madigan. "We say that around here a lot."

"From what I've seen already," he said with a chuckle, "I believe it."

A silence fell over the room as Brent's eyes returned to the computer screen.

"I'm still finding this all a bit weird," he said. "Yet there doesn't seem to be anything about it that I would describe as paranormal. It's all percentages and connections."

"And the rest of it isn't?"

"Well, I suppose you're in a better position to know that," Brent said. "But cars that won't start when they're parked in front of a hardware store? Strange things floating around in jars? I heard Rawlings say that your team investigated a haunting at a base in New Mexico last year—and the results were inconclusive? Doesn't sound like legit science, Captain."

"I defy anyone to define *legit* science," Madigan said. "Believe it or not, Dr. Michaels, almost everything we investigate ends up having a rational, scientific explanation."

"And the stuff that doesn't?"

"That's the fun stuff," she answered with a grin, one that was impossible for him to keep from mirroring.

"How do you reconcile the 'fun stuff' with your belief in God?" he asked, pointing to the tiny cross that hung from a chain around her neck. "Aren't you supposed to reject anything that seems to have a paranormal connection?"

Madigan sighed, shifting in her chair. "There's a lot to unpack there, Professor. First, you keep using the word *paranormal*. Just because we can't explain something right now doesn't mean it has anything to do with the supernatural. Yes, we investigate some strange things, but weren't most things that we now accept as legitimate science once looked upon as maybe something just short of magic?"

He conceded the point with a nod, yet she wasn't finished.

"I've been with this team for five years, and in all that time I haven't seen anything—not one thing—that I don't think can be explained. Eventually."

"What about the others?" he asked. "Do any of them approach things from the other perspective?"

"A few," she said. "Rawlings more than the others. Of course, he's convinced he has latent telekinetic abilities, so I'm not sure I'd put much faith in his opinion."

"What about Richards?"

"The colonel?" Madigan said. "I think with the colonel it depends on the day."

"And what kind of day do you think I'm having today?" came the man's voice from the doorway.

Brent saw Madigan's eyes widen but also witnessed a hint of a smile.

"That depends, Colonel," she said, "on whether or not you've seen what Addison has going on in the lab right now."

The colonel opened his mouth to respond, but instead he turned on his heel and started off in the direction of the lab. Brent thought he caught a look of worry on the man's face before he disappeared.

———

When Colonel Richards had popped into Brent's office, and before Madigan's warning had sent the man hurrying to check on Addison, he'd intended to let the professor know that as luck would have it, Brent would have the chance to witness the team at work in the field. Even more important was the possibility that the thing requiring investigation would soon be included in the team's data set.

As a general rule, explosions and fires at a Texas oil field—even those bearing the hallmarks of domestic terrorism—did not attract NIIU attention. Such an event lacked the strangeness—and there was no better term—associated with most of the team's assignments. But the investigative unit had come to understand that within the province of this investigation, seemingly normal events seemed poised to gather up into some abnormal whole.

They'd taken a plane to Lamesa, then loaded into two black SUVs for the trip across the scrubland. Brent had been impressed with the C-250, which came complete with a small room outfitted as a field forensics lab. It added yet another layer to his increasingly complicated understanding of this team: soldiers, ghost hunters, scientists, and cops. And at this point, he had no idea which role they embraced most.

The SUV in which he sat was trailing the other one, and Brent wondered how the driver could see through the cloud of dust kicked up by the lead vehicle. Still, even if they'd gone off the narrow asphalt road that cut through the flat terrain, the professor knew that little but grassland stretched out for miles in any direction, which made him feel relatively safe. Colonel Richards occupied the front passenger seat, with Rawlings behind the wheel. Sitting next to Brent in the middle seat was Madigan, whom Brent decided had been assigned to him. The third seat, as well as the space behind it, was filled with a variety of equipment, most of which the professor couldn't have hazarded a guess as to its purpose. The only piece of info he knew for sure was that the large spiky thing that Rawlings had wrestled into the back amid a stream of curses was named Spike.

They'd been driving for perhaps a half hour and Brent was about to engage Madigan in conversation, if only to break the military-style silence, when the dust cleared enough for him to spot their destination.

According to the briefing he'd listened to on the plane, Hickson Petroleum was a small oil field among the giants spreading their claims over the Trend, where more than ten billion recoverable barrels of oil waited beneath a surface spanning twenty-five hundred square miles. In fact, it was one of the smaller companies with a claim to drilling rights, which to Brent made it an odd choice as a terrorist target.

Soon they'd passed through the security checkpoint at the main gate—a checkpoint that included Homeland Security personnel—and were exiting the vehicle. When Brent stepped from the air-conditioned cab, the outside air felt more like Houston than Washington, only more arid, as if the brown grass of the Llano Estacado had sucked all the moisture from the air. But any attention he might have given the climate vanished when his eyes found the husk of melted, blackened metal that rose like a sore from the scarred earth. Had he not known what it had been, he doubted he could have posited a guess that came close. Now it looked like some avant-garde sculpture, or a Greek column that some giant had hurled in a fit of rage.

"My guess is the fire burned somewhere near two thousand degrees," Rawlings said. Brent hadn't heard the man come up beside him.

"That's nothing," Petros remarked. "Remember that Russian submarine that went down in the Bering Strait in 2004? The fire in the engine room reached twelve thousand degrees." The man studied the disfigured oil rig, impressive in its own right. "Talk about a difficult body recovery," he said, and it took Brent a while to figure out that he was still talking about the doomed Russian sub.

Despite the fact that Brent had been with this unit for three days, it occurred to him that he knew little about anyone besides Madigan and Richards. Most of what he'd gleaned about the others had come from the mission reports, which vacillated in detail depending on who wrote them. Still, what he'd witnessed firsthand seemed to verify his impressions from the reports—namely that Petros was the team's facts man, and Rawlings was the guy who believed that if he did this job long enough, he'd finally find something interesting. A thrill seeker. A man who had witnessed things that would sate the adventuresome appetites of most men but who himself remained dissatisfied. Of the two, Brent couldn't figure out with whom he connected most.

Brent moved away from the men, his feet kicking up dust as he made his way closer to the drill rig. The fire must have been impressive; he could imagine the thick black smoke it must have produced, the confusion it caused for the men trying to find safe passage to the gate, the ones searching for friends who were close by when it exploded.

An occurrence like this one still bothered him despite everything he'd learned about tribal behavior. For regardless of societal advances over the last several thousand years—advances which had established rules of law and the recognition of individual rights—humans could still revert to actions indistinguishable from mob rule or predator behavior. Under normal circumstances it would have been an academic exercise, but in the face of mangled metal that was once an oil rig, theory became something else entirely.

Behind him, the team separated and began to perform their tasks, leaving Brent to wander around an enormous fenced-in area. Other than the ruined oil rig, his eyes found other areas that appeared to have been targeted and he studied these for a while. He had little to offer here, suspecting Colonel Richards had included him so that he, an outsider, could get a feel for how the team worked, as well as the methods they employed. Meanwhile, he would attempt to use that knowledge to try to develop a working theory about something he wasn't sure he believed.

But he found that the twisted metal and reminders of lives lost mostly served to depress him, so he turned his attention to a spot just past the gate, to the only place in sight that not only offered a break from the carnage but also a respite from flatness.

Hickson Petroleum was practically in the shadow of the escarpment—the line of rock, red dirt, and weather-savaged greenery that separated the Llano Estacado from the more habitable areas to the west. The escarpment reminded Brent of what he loved about Texas, namely a topography that spoke of both independence and loneliness. His focus stayed there for a while as the team spread out over the oil field and as Colonel Richards, standing only yards away, spoke with someone from Homeland Security, and while Spike remained in its place in the back of the SUV that had ferried it from the airport.

He couldn't have pinpointed the exact moment the thought began rolling around in his head. One minute he was taking in the scenery, and the next thing he knew, an idea beyond his field had made itself known. And once he realized it, he came close to dismissing the notion, for criminology wasn't his area of expertise. His province was group dynamics. Or in those cases in which he practiced at the individual level, it was to examine how an individual could be influenced by larger factors. But was the idea he'd been pondering that far removed from sociological theory?

Sociology was the study of human behavior as influenced by any number of causal factors. In that respect, was it far removed from behavioral analysis? Even so, it took the passage of several minutes before he could put voice to what had arranged itself in his mind.

"This was more about creating a panic than about doing any real damage," Brent said. Standing there by himself, and with the others engaged in whatever it was they were doing, he had no idea if anyone heard him, and yet he'd spoken the words more for himself than for anyone else.

He didn't turn but he could almost feel Colonel Richards break away from the Homeland Security agent, and in a moment the man was next to him.

"What makes you say that, Dr. Michaels?" he asked.

Brent didn't answer right away. He took a deep breath, allowing the dry air to fill his lungs, his eyes playing over the escarpment.

"If I'm a terrorist, I'm going after as big a bang as I can for my trouble," Brent said. "Instead, they pick the target closest to a convenient escape route. Not only that, they choose a target that would produce the least damage even if they'd succeeded in blowing the entire thing." He paused, hands on hips, looking out across the oil field.

Colonel Richards followed Brent's gaze, the two men surveying the escarpment. After a time the colonel said, "As far as I can tell, that's the only chance whoever was behind this had to get out of here unseen. Doesn't that make this the only possible target for a terrorist action?"

Brent considered that. After all, he'd already admitted to himself that he was out of his element. He could posit theories for anything requiring an analysis of group dynamics, but generally the FBI would fly in to develop a behavioral profile. Still, even in the face of the colonel's question, the thought would not subside.

"Even with the escarpment, the risk of pulling off something like this in a wide open area is far too high to go for something small scale." Brent didn't say anything else for half a minute, and Richards didn't press him. "A terrorist action, domestic or otherwise," he said, turning to meet the colonel's eyes, "almost always has an ideological purpose." He gestured to the ruined oil rig. "Nothing about this speaks to that. This was about adding weight to a message already delivered—a tweak of an established agenda. An agenda hinted at in Africa, Western Europe, Russia, Venezuela, South Korea, and a dozen other places your team has been over the last two years."

Colonel Richards took a half step back. "So what are you telling me, Dr. Michaels?"

Brent could sense the dual nature of the inquiry. On one hand, the colonel was enjoying having brought the professor there to see this event that would be added to an already extensive data stream. On the other hand, the question was genuine. The problem was that Brent had no idea what he was telling the career military man. In his estimation, only one force existed that was capable of extending its influence as far as this one seemed to spread, and it was the very government the colonel worked for.

Finally, Brent shook his head. "All I know, Colonel, is that if I look at everything you've given me and conclude that it's all related, then you have to be ready to accept whatever findings I come up with." He didn't vocalize his belief in the possible involvement of the U.S. government. He'd let the colonel do that heavy lifting himself. And when he looked at Richards, he found nothing that hinted at an established ideology. In fact, when the colonel answered him, what Brent found was a complete absence of judgment.

"Dr. Michaels, in case you haven't figured it out yet, that's precisely what we do."

———

December 6, 2012, 10:05 P.M.

Despite all the travel required of him over the last few years, two things never ceased to amaze Canfield. The first was that he could be just about anywhere in the world in twenty-four hours.

The second, and almost diametrically opposed to that, was that there were certain portions of the world that required a significant act of will to reach.

Garissa was one such place. One of the larger cities in the North Eastern Province of Kenya, Garissa had a large enough population to make the presence of a single westerner unworthy of notice but not large enough to warrant any decent roads leading to it. He'd landed in Wajir, opting for a smaller airport—one restricted to prop planes—than a landing in Nairobi would have provided. From Wajir, he'd hired a local to take him the 198 miles south to Garissa. He'd traveled the route once before, perhaps eight years earlier, and this most recent trip proved much less eventful than the previous one, when flash floods had turned the dirt road into a mud pit that caught and held tires. This time a small herd of hirola with a collective reluctance to relinquish the road proved the only obstacle.

Garissa was an odd blend of industrialism and decay, beauty and squalor. In certain parts, the houses were freshly painted, colorful awnings shaded the doorways to shops doing brisk business, and construction crews raised office buildings and hotels. In other spots, though, the buckling infrastructure common to the continent was evident: packed-earth streets littered with trash; whole neighborhoods of decrepit structures with rusting metal awnings propped up by pipes and wooden poles; merchants leading donkeys pulling two-wheeled carts, navigating their way around mud holes, large rocks, and debris.

Canfield, who had visited dozens of cities just like it, hardly noticed anymore. He was there for business and would be gone from the place in an hour. One thing that pleased him, however, was that this particular piece of business involved an old friend.

"It's nice to see you, Matt," Canfield said.

He leaned against a small writing table in the other man's hotel room—a room Canfield had paid for—enjoying the air-conditioning after a long ride through the arid land, the lowered windows of the truck the only ventilation.

"You too, Alan," Matt Ragsdale said.

It was hard to guess the man's age by looking at him. A lean, rugged-looking body spoke of someone in his midthirties, while a lined, weathered face suggested a man approaching fifty. Canfield, who was forty-two, and who knew that Matt Ragsdale had graduated from Duke a year ahead of him, understood that two decades on this continent bore responsibility for the inability to pinpoint his age. This place chiseled the fat from the bone, but exacted a price for such work.

Ragsdale sat on the room's single bed, a green duffel bag at his feet. He'd opened it before Canfield had arrived. Amid the jumble of items in the bag lay a handgun.

"How long's it been?" Ragsdale asked.

"Eight years," Canfield said.

Even that long ago it had been hard for Canfield to reconcile his old college friend with the man he'd become. At Duke, Ragsdale's ambitions included law school and, perhaps later, politics. Against that background, the man's work as a guide, poacher, and sometime mercenary was difficult to process. Still, it was obvious this life suited him.

"Are you still toting tourists around?" Canfield asked.

"That and leading a safari every once in a while."

And poaching, Canfield knew. In Kenya, it was difficult to spit without it landing on a game preserve. Making a two-hundred-mile circle out from Garissa would capture more than half a dozen of them. His friend Ragsdale earned a good living taking protected game and sending it over the border to Somalia.

"Why are you here, Alan?" Ragsdale asked. "Not that I'm not grateful for the free room. But I imagine this isn't just a social call."

"No, it isn't," Canfield said.

He understood that what he was about to ask of his old friend was a risk. Van Camp Enterprises had teams to take care of this sort of thing. But those teams seldom operated in this part of the world, and a team from the States was more difficult to get in and out without someone noticing. This operation required something of a local touch.

"How do you feel about Ethiopia this time of year?" he asked.

9

December 6, 2012, 8:45 P.M.

By the time Colonel Richards extended the invitation to dinner, he, Brent, and Madigan were the only ones left in the Pentagon's subbasement. After they'd arrived back in Washington, the rest of the team had gone home. But Brent had wanted to press on, with Madigan's social life—if she had one—a casualty of his desire to finish the consult and head back to his own little part of Texas.

The colonel kept a modest home in Arlington, on Twelfth Street North, just minutes from his office. He shared the four-bedroom home with a woman who could have been a middle-aged angel for the warm smile she'd bestowed on Brent when he stepped through the door, as well as for the sumptuous dinner that was served him.

From what he could gather, having the colonel home this early was an uncommon occurrence, and for some reason she seemed to think that Brent had something to do with it. And as he assumed that was why she'd gone to the trouble to make ribs, he wasn't going to dissuade her of that notion.

"This certainly beats the burger I probably would have grabbed on the way back to the hotel," he said to his hosts. He loaded a section of ribs onto his plate and then reached for the mashed potatoes and corn. Emily, sitting at the opposite side of the table, smiled.

"Emily might just be the best cook in Virginia," Richards said, which might have been the most personable thing Brent had heard him say over the last few days.

"What do you mean *might*?" Emily needled.

Brent sampled the ribs. "Your wife's right," he said. "What do you mean *might*?"

Nodding, Richards said, "Point conceded."

While pouring the wine, Emily asked with a knowing smile, "So tell me, Brent, what's it like working with Jameson's team?"

"It's . . . interesting. Definitely a different environment than I'm used to."

"You're only saying that because of the eyeballs," Richards remarked.

"Those might have been the tipping point, sure."

"The eyeballs?" Emily asked.

"Something Rawlings is working on," the colonel explained.

"Ah," Emily said. "That makes sense."

The lighthearted talk continued throughout dinner. Then, as Emily began clearing the table, Richards leaned back in his chair, released a sigh that spoke of contentment, and said, "So how's your research progressing, Dr. Michaels?"

Brent, who was still getting used to the idea of the colonel engaging in easy conversation, reached for his wineglass and took a sip of the cabernet. After setting the glass down, he replied, "Slowly, Colonel. While it's easy to find minor connections between most of the events you've included in the data set, it's difficult to know if those connections are meaningful. Even the trip we made today.

Although portions of it look as if they track with the rest of your mission reports, everything could be little more than conjecture."

"Well, that's always a possibility. It wouldn't be the first time one of our theories turned out to be unfounded."

Brent's eyebrows went up a little. "Wait a minute. Maddy said you were convinced there's something to this."

"I am. But none of this is an exact science." He frowned then. "Maddy?"

Brent didn't realize the reason for the colonel's reaction right away, and when he did he found himself hoping that he hadn't gotten the captain in any trouble.

"After sitting at the same table for three days, I got tired of calling her Captain," he said. It wasn't until the colonel's lip curled into what passed for a smile that Brent knew he and Maddy hadn't broken some item of military protocol.

Richards stood and gestured for Brent to follow him. He led Brent into the family room, where the colonel settled onto the couch. Brent took the chair near the fireplace, where a flame burned low over blackened wood. The colonel thumbed the remote, and the large wall-mounted television came to life.

"Background noise," Richards explained. "Unless I'm reading a book in here, I have to have the TV on."

Richards set the remote down but didn't continue the conversation that had started in the dining room. Brent, though, felt compelled to chase the topic to its conclusion.

"Colonel, as much as I appreciate your offering me this job, I have to tell you that I can't remember a research project where I've felt less confident about a deliverable than I do about this one." He leaned forward in the chair, elbows on his knees. "A project like this should take years to complete, and that's if it's possible at all. And I'm not certain it is." He thought that if he was going to anger the military, it would be best to do so on the front end, before expectations got too high.

But instead of anger, Brent's statement pulled a sigh from the colonel.

"Dr. Michaels, that's exactly why you got the job. Most of the other academics we considered would have taken the money and, if they couldn't find anything, they would have made up something. After looking at your profile, I figured you were the sort of man who would give it to me straight."

"Only because I'm afraid you'd shoot me if I lied to you."

His response produced a chuckle from Richards, but then Brent saw the man's eyes move past him, drawn by the television.

"What do you think of this 2012 business?" he asked.

Brent shifted his position until he faced the TV. On the screen a news anchor delivered his teleprompter-supplied oration while beside him a large monitor showed footage of an ancient temple in South America. Richards grabbed the remote and raised the volume.

". . . exactly what will happen on December twenty-first, 2012, but that isn't stopping a lot of people from preparing as if it's going to be the end of the world."

The picture cut to a reporter at a discount store, putting a microphone in the face of a man standing in line.

"You just don't know," the man said. "Probably nothing is gonna happen, but with all the stuff goin' on in the world right now, man, I wouldn't be surprised. I mean, you just don't know."

The picture cut back to the anchor.

"Researchers who study the Maya, though, *do* think they know. And they say that the only thing they're expecting will happen on December twenty-first—" he paused, aimed a smile at the camera— "is that it will be cold here in Washington."

With a shake of his head, Richards hit the mute button. "With all the things people have to worry about today, you'd think they would be smarter than to waste their time on this kind of nonsense."

Brent looked from the TV to the colonel, and it took Richards a few seconds to catch the bemused smile on his guest's face.

"What?"

"I just think it's ironic," Brent said. "You traipse all over the globe investigating things most people don't believe in and yet you dismiss this other thing out of hand. I would think the 2012 phenomenon would be right up your alley."

That pulled a smirk from the colonel. "Dr. Michaels, we started investigating 2012 a decade ago," Richards confided. "It took us a week to see that there's nothing there. The Maya created a calendar that runs out next month. If the ancient Maya were still around today, do you know what they'd do? They'd start the calendar all over."

Brent thought he'd finished, but then the colonel said, "People have always bought into doomsday scenarios, and this one has the added benefit of being based on something that's actually true. The Mayan Long Count calendar really does end this month. And what makes this one even more virulent is that the pervasiveness of the media allows these nut jobs to talk to each other."

It was the first time in their brief association that Brent had witnessed the colonel getting worked up about something.

"Yet I imagine with the length of time you've been at this job, you've seen a thing or two that doesn't have a ready explanation, am I right, Colonel?"

Richards nodded. "You've heard us talk about our allegiance to the scientific method. Well, believe every word of it. It's the only solid launching point for what we do." He glanced at the television, then back at Brent. "But I've seen too much to close the door to the possibility of supernatural causes for certain phenomena."

Brent was a bit surprised: a career military man who accepted the idea that science might not explain all?

"So I suppose you brought in the man of reason on this one in order to balance out your man-of-faith tendencies?"

The colonel laughed. "A man's made up of both, Dr. Michaels," Richards said once the laughter had eased. "And while I might have a few more doors opened to some of the less scientific methods of inquiry, I can assure you that nothing trumps the science."

"Which doesn't rule out the possibility that these people"— Brent gestured to the television—"are right about the world ending in two weeks. Personally, I don't believe it, but can a reluctant man of faith completely rule out the possibility?"

Instead of a return to laughter—or even a smile—Richards's face turned serious. "Putting faith in foolishness makes one a fool." He glanced once again at the television. "All this sort of thing does is stir up needless panic. And that's the last thing we need right now, knowing the kind of thing we're investigating."

Emily, carrying a tray with coffee, cream, and sugar, chose that moment to join the men. After setting the tray on the coffee table, she took a seat on the couch next to her husband. She placed a hand on his knee.

"Do you need decaf tonight, sweetie?" she asked the colonel. Then she winked at Brent, who returned something approximating a smile.

———

Arthur Van Camp believed that opportunity found its greatest fulfillment in chaos. He preached that truth to his senior executives, forcing it down the ranks as a kind of secret vision statement. And he demanded that all the members of his staff understood and practiced this truth: the man who kept his head while everyone around him panicked was the man who won. As a result, he considered himself something of an expert on chaos. He could see it coming long before others sensed it; he could get inside it, study it, learn its patterns, and determine how to leverage it for his own gain. Perhaps it was this intimacy with the unpredictable that caused him to keep his office in an order bordering on the clinically obsessive.

He owned three properties in Atlanta, all in Buckhead. He'd paid $25 million for the sprawling estate he seldom visited anymore. He didn't need nine bedrooms or sixteen fireplaces. Since his wife died he'd been spending the majority of his time in the penthouse suite of the Ashbury. All four of Ashbury's penthouses belonged to him and had long ago been made one unit. At ten thousand square feet, it was still much more space than he required, yet he couldn't argue with the view.

The penthouse office was spare in its design, its furnishings consisting of a desk, a single chair in addition to the one belonging to the desk, and a narrow bookshelf holding the more rare and expensive volumes of his considerable collection. A fireplace had been built in the east wall, where even now a fire was burning. Two paintings hung on the wine-colored walls: a Matisse on the north wall and a much less valuable landscape above the fireplace. The latter, painted by his wife before she fell ill, was the one his eyes went to most often.

At the desk, Van Camp scrolled through a spreadsheet showing the financials for the month, each of the industries that made up his business empire neatly arranged under its own tab by his accounting team. He paid the men and women who compiled these reports a great deal of money, to ensure both accuracy and loyalty, and because he hired only the best for what he considered to be a critical function in support of his business interests. And it was because he knew that his employees were the best corporate financial team ever assembled under a single umbrella that he wondered if any of them had attained a sufficiently global view to find the patterns in the figures—how a trend across one of his many business lines affected, or was reflected in, the trends of the other lines. If that were to happen—if one of his employees came to him and demonstrated an understanding of the bigger picture—Van Camp didn't know if he would give that person a substantial raise or have him killed. He leaned toward the first option while retaining the right to exercise the second.

He finished with the spreadsheet and leaned back in the leather chair, feeling his muscles argue against the more relaxed position. The numbers he'd reviewed reinforced what he'd already known: the plan he'd set into motion years ago was, almost miraculously, coming down the home stretch in much the fashion he'd designed. While he seldom touted his own skills—his business savvy—he recognized the magnitude of what he'd accomplished, even as he understood how precarious the whole thing was, for any one of a hundred factors could shift beyond optimum and ruin the entire thing. Were that to happen, he didn't know if any of the exit strategies he'd devised would serve to protect him from the fallout, nor was he convinced that this mattered.

He was eight when he heard the Sunday school lesson that would play a major role in setting the course for his life, though he wasn't aware of it at the time. Even at that young age, Van Camp had held an appreciation for money—a respect enhanced by the financial state of his own family, which saw him showing up for Sunday school attired in the hand-me-downs of some of his wealthier classmates. And so when his teacher commented about King Solomon's great wealth—that he'd been the richest man in the world—a seed fell in fertile soil.

He'd studied the calculations: how much money Solomon might have had were he Van Camp's contemporary, and while the sum seemed astronomical, it was not impossible. A part of him understood the foolishness of risking an empire rivaled by few men for a chance at realizing the fulfillment of a silly childhood wish, of attaining a wealth even greater than Solomon's. But silly childish wish or not, he knew it was this very goal that had burned in his blood for decades, which had informed his education and lurked in the background of every decision he'd ever made. To deny it now, even though it could cost him everything, would be a kind of betrayal.

And his interest in non-maintainable systems—the entropic nature of free economics—was the key. While his wife had lived, his ambitions had been tempered by her influence; then, he was content to slow-grow his wealth, although the childhood promise remained as ever. However, with her declining health forcing him to come to grips with what life would be like without her, his focus on exploitative strategies shifted. Instead of taking advantage of the opportunities the system produced, he pondered manipulating the system to produce what he desired. In essence, fashioning chaos. The idea was to manipulate chaos and receive a greater payoff rather than wait for chaos to arrive and *then* prosper from it.

The picture his wife had painted, the one hanging above the mantel, might have argued otherwise, but this night he avoided looking at it.

December 8, 2012, 10:33 P.M.

After a mission—whether one assigned to him by Standish or one he'd selected himself—Dabir would spend a good portion of the next several days in prayer. Allah was a god who brooked little disobedience, and the Koran was a difficult text. Weren't there competing theories regarding several important theological points, all espoused by men a great deal smarter than he? If these learned scholars could debate among themselves, how could a simple man like him make sense of all that the book seemed to require?

So in Dabir's opinion, it was all about interpretation. The Koran provided a guideline for the faithful, a blueprint regarding how to live. The thing about blueprints, though, was that they could be altered as needed. This thought steeled Dabir for his next assignment from Standish, which seemed a simple thing—much less dangerous than he'd expected. In fact, it was similar to one of the smaller excursions Dabir might have assigned himself just to keep his spoon in the pot: a research team from South Africa, a three-person crew conducting tests along the Afar Depression. Standish had even supplied exact coordinates.

Dabir was unsure about taking part in another mission in this area so soon after the ill-fated venture against the American military unit. However, he knew the lack of policing in this region made the assignment safe enough. Few people would even know about the previous attack, and among the ones who did, few would care beyond the fact that the altercation had not produced bodies to be pilfered or left any cargo behind. The Americans would not have left anything in the desert.

Because of the small scale of the night's activities, Dabir had brought with him only three men, some of those who had accompanied him from the beginning, and whose work he knew well enough that he need not doubt they would do as instructed.

Guiding a vehicle at night through the northeastern Ethiopian desert was akin to paddling a small boat over a vast lake. While the lake lacked the monstrous waves of the ocean, an occasional swell might make things difficult. In the desert, the sand ever expanded beyond the range of the jeep's headlights, with the metaphorical far shore retreating a step ahead of the glow. But every once in a while the earth would dip below them, or a patch of scrub would manifest from the darkness, forcing them to proceed with caution. At some point, when Dabir would have his men cut the headlights, making them reliant on the GPS, they would have to slow even more.

As they progressed to the target area, Dabir mulled over the information he'd obtained. Catching Canfield in the airport had been luck, he knew. He did not congratulate himself for this success beyond accepting credit for the ambition to learn the identity of his benefactor. But having the resources and talent to put a new name to the face was an accomplishment worthy of celebration. The trick now was to learn everything he could about Alan Canfield, other than of course the man being employed by Van Camp Enterprises.

Dabir smiled to think that much of his investigative work so far had been financed by Canfield's employer.

The driver pulled Dabir's attention to the GPS. They were two kilometers from the targets, who according to the message Standish had sent, were camped near the rift, very close to the southeastern Eritrea border. Dabir, who had spent his childhood on the other side of this border, knew the area well—enough to know that proceeding in a straight line would be foolish. Between the jeep and the research encampment lay two ravines large enough to swallow the jeep whole. The largest of these fissures stretched for almost forty kilometers north to south. Dabir and his men were approaching the encampment near the southern end of the ravine, yet the obstacle required that they make a circuit southward. Dabir thought they would come up on the research team from the southeast. With any luck they would find the men sleeping. Afterward, they would send the photos to the necessary email address and Dabir's account would increase by a considerable factor.

———

Dabir's face did not change expression as he studied the scene through the night-vision binoculars, though inside his stomach roiled, for this could be nothing other than his own execution narrowly avoided. They'd come in with the lights out from half a mile, then walked the final two hundred yards. He'd known they'd arrive on a rise of rock and dirt and suspected that a research team would make camp below, where the rise afforded some protection against the wind. Were they sleeping, Dabir and his men would have slipped down and finished their business quickly.

What played out, however, in the panorama of the binoculars, was a betrayal, an announcement of the end to a business partnership. At first he wondered what he might have done to warrant the abrupt change, but then he realized this situation found its impetus in the botched attack on the American military unit.

Shuul was at his elbow, tugging at the fold of Dabir's shirt, causing the binoculars to jump, the scene to shift. Pulling them away from his face, he glared at the other man until Shuul backed off. Replacing the binoculars, Dabir continued his survey. Three trucks, perhaps a dozen men, equally split between white and black skin. A team not native to the region; the clothes on the black men were of Ugandan design. That in itself was sloppy, unless of course the clothes were a misdirection. There was no way to know.

He watched for a while longer, even as he felt the growing unease of his men behind him. After the encounter with the Americans, he leaned toward a more cautious operation, and caution required knowledge gained through patience. The men around the three trucks were alert but not tense. They did not talk, but neither did they take pains to disguise their movements. It told Dabir that these men had the confidence of superior numbers and of having their enemies' agenda. Once more he scanned the group until he halted with the binoculars trained on a man standing by the driver's side of a Hummer. He watched as the man reached into the truck, pulled out a bottle, and drank from it. He made no effort to hide the activity, and that, along with the quality of the rifle he held in his hands, identified him as the leader—and not a careful man.

Satisfied, Dabir moved away from the ridge, back to where his men waited. He quickly went over his options. He could leave now, disappearing into the darkness and removing what money he could from his account before Standish/Canfield made that impossible. Or he could kill these men prior to disappearing. The benefit of this choice was that it would buy him more time to secure what funds he needed. The downside was the probability that some, if not all, of his men would die in the assault—perhaps even himself.

His three associates gathered around, faces expectant. All of them were with him when they assaulted the Americans; each knew the portion of fault that was his. Yet each of them would follow Dabir over the ridge if he ordered them to.

He had a decision to make.

———

Dabir had waited two hours before initiating contact, and during that time he found himself growing to appreciate the patience of the team that waited to kill him.

The waiting, though, was over.

He'd sent two of his men down the slope toward the scrub that Dabir had chosen as their best cover. In truth, his men relied on their dark clothing and skin to reach their places without attracting the enemy's eye. Dabir watched as each man found his spot, halfway down the hill and flanking the men who still looked for Dabir's team to come from the west.

Dabir used the binoculars to confirm they would not be caught off guard when he began the assault. Then he waited another ten minutes before commencing the attack.

Part of the money he'd accumulated over the years had gone toward the purchase of several items whose purpose made engagements like this easier. And so when he launched the SL-2500 rocket toward one of the trucks, he took pleasure in knowing that his enemy's bosses had financed their own demise.

The truck went up with a single concussive blast, and Dabir saw the man next to it, the one he took for the leader, tossed through the air like a child's doll. Next, the air became filled with the reports of his men's guns, cutting down whoever they could. Others dove behind the remaining vehicles for cover.

Dabir signaled his associate to open up with the NSV they'd dismounted from the jeep. It wasn't until the first salvo had taken out another three men that those left standing began to return fire, and despite the fact that they'd been caught off guard, there were marksmen in their midst.

The first of the rounds struck the ridgeline where Dabir sat, likely following the now-dispersed rocket trail. They were close enough to cause him to pull back. Among experienced combatants, the element of surprise seldom granted more than a temporary advantage, and he suspected it was now spent. Nonetheless, the enemy occupied a bowl, with Dabir's men positioned on the rim of that bowl.

He shuffled forward on his elbows, raising the rocket launcher to his shoulder. It took him but a second to acquire a target, one of the two remaining vehicles pulling away from the kill zone. He led the truck but didn't anticipate its sudden acceleration and came close to missing it. Instead of hitting the engine as he'd planned, the missile turned the cab into an inferno.

———

Excepting the failed assault against the Americans, Dabir made it a point not to leave one of his own behind. Shuul would travel with them back to Hadar, wrapped in a blanket in the back of the jeep. His brother would collect the body, as well as the money Standish/ Canfield provided for such an eventuality. Dabir would say a blessing for the dead man and then he would leave the family alone to grieve.

Dabir sat down and used a knife to cut away his shredded pant leg from the knee down. The grenade that killed Shuul had also sent shrapnel into Dabir's leg. Not a life-threatening injury, but in the desert, even a simple cut could worsen in a short time. From the first-aid kit in his pack he pulled out alcohol, antibiotic ointment, and bandages. The process took only a few minutes. When he'd finished he stood and made his way down the hill, joining the two men who stood near the remaining, relatively intact Hummer, admiring the vehicle despite the countless holes, shattered glass, and human remains.

While Dabir had been working on his injury, his men had been gathering the dead men's weapons, money, and any identifying paper work. Dabir flipped through it all, stopping at one item. It was a passport belonging to the man Dabir suspected to have been the leader. He guessed the passport to be a fake. Still, Standish/Canfield would know.

Dabir crossed the darkened desert and stopped at the man's body. A quick scan revealed that while his men had already taken the rifle, they'd missed the knife. Dabir knelt and removed it from its sheath and held it up to the moonlight. The blade flashed beneath it.

Despite the worsening throb in his leg, he leaned over the dead man and placed the passport on his chest. Then, using the knife as a pushpin, he slammed it first through the passport and then through the body cavity.

Standish would see; he would know. By then Dabir and the money would be gone.

He had the men gather what weapons they could carry, and then they started the walk back up the hill.

December 9, 2012, 6:13 P.M.

"Certainly not our finest hour, Alan."

In the eight years of his drawing a paycheck from Arthur Van Camp, he could not recall ever seeing the man angry, and with fluctuating markets, changes in global dynamics, and the numerous situations that arose when managing a company employing more than twenty thousand people, ample opportunity for an extreme emotional response often presented itself.

Perhaps, though, Canfield had simply overlooked the man's anger. For while Van Camp didn't raise his voice, Canfield could sense the anger seething below the surface. He would have preferred shouting or insults or even the Akbal carving thrown at him rather than the disgust Van Camp exuded.

"The fortunate thing is that it's next to impossible for anyone to trace this back to us," Canfield offered, knowing the inadequacy of the response. What had just happened in Ethiopia had forced Van

Camp to expend resources to do something he seldom did: keep
something *out* of the news.

"We have in-house resources available for this kind of thing,"
Van Camp said. "Not only did you select an outside vendor, you
chose one you have ties with." Something must have struck him as
humorous, because he released a small chuckle. "You trampled all
over the company Conflict of Interest policy."

Canfield felt the corner of his lip curl. He considered a joke under
these circumstances a positive sign. Even so, the proper response
remained the penitent one.

"The team was otherwise engaged, sir," Canfield said, although
he knew his boss was aware of that. Hitting Hickson Petroleum had
made a noticeable impact in the market—noticeable if one knew
how to look at it. "Even had I considered postponing the mission
until the team was available, my thought was that using them on
foreign soil was a bad move. They don't know the language or the
terrain. And then there are the logistics of getting them in and out
without setting off an alarm bell somewhere." He paused, releasing
a deep sigh of his own. "Matt is—was—exceptional at this sort of
thing. I thought he could handle it."

"And now you have a dead friend, as well as a former business
associate who will likely disappear like smoke. I assume he's cleaned
out the account."

Canfield nodded.

"A tactical error, Alan," Van Camp said. "That's not like you."

Van Camp drew in a breath and released it slowly. When he settled
back in his chair, Canfield knew a good portion of the man's anger
had dissipated. He knew how his boss operated: Van Camp looked at
the entire body of work; he never made a rash decision. Simply put,
Canfield bore the lion's share of responsibility for the current state
of Project: Night House. Van Camp would not overlook that.

"You're right, sir. It won't happen again."

Van Camp drummed his fingers on the desk, appraising his vice-president of Business Development, who sat stoically staring back at him.

"I should hope not," he said. "The question now is, what are we going to do about your rogue employee? Dabir, is it?"

"I'm not sure there's much we *can* do," Canfield admitted. "As it is, he has no idea who I am, who he's been working for. All he knows is that I tried to terminate our contract. With the money we've paid him—and what he cleaned out of the account—it's unlikely we'll hear from him again. So my suggestion is to leave him be." At Van Camp's frown he added, "Our only other option is to start turning over rocks in Ethiopia, Djibouti, Eritrea, and who knows where else. Doing that will draw a lot more attention than if we were to just let him be."

It was the logical choice—the only choice really—and his boss could appreciate that.

"Very well," Van Camp said. "Let's consider the Ethiopian operation closed. Perhaps we've spread ourselves too thin anyway."

Canfield didn't answer, but he felt the tension drain from his body.

"You look tired, Alan. Is everything alright at home?"

Canfield affected a weary smile. "Just fine, sir. I'm sure it's just all the travel."

"Of course it is." Again the appraiser's eye.

When Canfield left his boss's office, it was with the feeling of having had a huge weight lifted. He knew, though, the temporary nature of that state. Twelve days remained for him to accomplish a great deal. If he failed, the next meeting he'd be having with Arthur Van Camp would be of an entirely different nature. And that truth spoke to the other emotion rising to the surface—one he seldom allowed himself to entertain: anger. For it was becoming increasingly clear that the endgame he'd laid out for himself was now subject to alteration.

Over the last couple of years, as he'd led Project: Night House from one milestone to another, he'd approached the endeavor as a career advancement strategy. That mind-set made it easier to get through some of the more sordid elements of the project. Now, however, he was beginning to realize that, like Dabir, and the earthquake project at Afar, and the mining operation in South Africa, and any of a dozen other initiatives that Van Camp had called a halt to, Canfield might find himself on that list as well. After all, if Night House succeeded, the man who had pulled it off would undoubtedly be the most dangerous of loose ends. Rather than consider that unpleasant thought more, he decided to go home.

He pulled into the driveway just after eleven p.m. and could see no lights on in the house. Phyllis wouldn't have waited up for him. He stepped through the front door and set his briefcase on the hall table, then moved quietly to the kitchen. There, he turned on a light and began scrounging around in the refrigerator for the makings of a sandwich. He sat at the small kitchen table, letting go the stresses of the day. In fact, so thoroughly did the list of things he had to accomplish drain from his mind that he decided to head up to bed rather than spend the next few hours in his office. Setting his plate in the sink, he switched off the light and went upstairs.

Reaching the bedroom, he saw the shape of his wife in bed. In the darkness, eased only by the moonlight spilling through the window, he thought he saw a wineglass on the nightstand. He shook his head as he started to undress. If she was drinking to help her sleep, it meant she wasn't in a good place. He resolved to go to the office late tomorrow, to spend some time with his wife. Maybe he'd make breakfast. They hadn't taken a walk around the neighborhood in a long time.

As he slid into bed he moved close to her and gently kissed her cheek. The action took him closer to the nightstand on her side of the bed—the one with the empty wineglass. Next to the glass lay an open pill bottle.

December 10, 2012, 9:54 A.M.

When Richards walked into the room, Brent could sense a different tone than he'd witnessed so far, even before the colonel opened his mouth. Maddy must have sensed it as well, because her face lost its smile.

"Problem, Colonel?" she asked.

Instead of answering, Richards tossed a few stapled pages on the table between the captain and the professor. Maddy reached for it, reorienting it so she could scan the text. In only a few moments she looked up, her eyes carrying either surprise or worry—Brent couldn't tell which.

"What is it?" he asked.

"It's a threat update," the colonel answered. "We get one daily."

Brent reached for it, assuming that if he wasn't supposed to read it, Maddy would break his hand. He read the first few lines, essentially bullet points of various hot spots around the globe. It went on for three pages, and if the first entries were an indication of things, then the overall state of the world was much more precarious than Brent thought. He looked up at the colonel.

"Since you get this every day, I'm assuming there's something abnormal in this one?" he asked.

"The second entry," Maddy said, reaching across the table and tapping the one in question.

Brent read the few lines with greater care than he had the first time through. "A tribal skirmish in Tablisi?"

"It's in a part of Afghanistan that doesn't see that sort of thing," Maddy explained. "One of the more stable regions in the Middle East."

Brent digested that but still failed to see the significance. "So the odds are low for something like this. But it's Afghanistan—is this really that surprising?"

"In addition to being one of the cultural and economic beacons in the country," Richards said, "Tablisi is also home to a large oil refinery."

"And I'll give you three guesses as to the only industrial casualty of this tribal skirmish," Maddy finished.

It took precious few seconds for Brent to track with them.

"So this was designed to destroy the refinery," he said.

"We don't know that for certain, Dr. Michaels," the colonel said.

"But your experience would indicate that it's probable," Brent pressed, to which Richards returned a nod.

And with that verification, Brent's mind went somewhere else, engaged in a mental review of all the information he'd compiled from the paper work, from his talks with Maddy, and from his one off-base excursion with the team. He didn't know how much time passed while he parsed these things; only that Richards and Madigan hadn't moved when he emerged from it.

"Here's the problem I'm running into," Brent said. "Do I see a pattern? My answer is a definite maybe. But it's only a maybe because I have a very hard time believing in global patterns. Because if this *is* one, it's not a natural occurrence. No, this is organized by someone." He paused, fixing the colonel with a look. "And that's the part I have a problem with. There's not a person in the world who carries this kind of influence. Not the president. Not Bill Gates. I don't care how much money a person has, there are just too many factors involved for it to be possible."

Richards took it all in, his lips pursed.

"If this was a smaller system—let's say a university—how would you read the data?" the colonel asked.

"In that case, I'd say absolutely there's some kind of organized system at work."

"And the only thing that makes you doubt that is the expanded parameters of this system?"

Brent aimed a wry smile at the colonel. "It's not that simple, Colonel. When you expand the parameters that much, you just can't read the data the same way."

"Why not?" Madigan asked.

She glanced at the wall on which a projector displayed the same global map the colonel had shown Brent on his first day. Except this map contained a number of new colors in its legend, as well as several symbols that seemed to demonstrate patterns which, mathematically speaking, were not random events.

"The scientific method is what it is, regardless of the size of the thing we're studying, right?" the captain said.

One of the things Brent had come to appreciate about Maddy was the way she drilled a thing down to its most basic level.

"Yes and no," he answered. "When you conduct an experiment, you must have a controlled environment, with all factors accounted for. That's the only way you can accurately analyze a result. With something like this"—he pointed to the map—"there's no way to catalog everything that might affect your outcome."

"Come on, Brent," she said. "Leave that sterile lab stuff back at the university. In the real world, science is messy. Sometimes you have to think with your gut." She glanced at the colonel, perhaps to see if she'd overstepped her bounds, but Richards gave a nod as if agreeing with her assessment.

Brent raised his coffee cup and took a sip, his eyes back on the map. Because of the setting, and with two uniformed officers in the room with him, Brent thought this seemed more like a session on war strategy than it did an exploration of scientific data.

"Dr. Michaels," Richards said, "before we called you, I had a feeling there was something going on that we needed to investigate. Even in a world as obviously self-destructive as this one, we recognized an abnormal upsurge in violent events—as if everyone in the world decided to lose their minds at precisely the same time."

"Like the world is trucking toward crazy a good deal faster than normal?" Brent asked.

Next to the colonel, Madigan's cheeks colored.

"That's one way to look at it," Richards agreed. He gestured to the map. "Now that I see what you've done here, how you've managed to take our reports and translate them into something like this, I'm more inclined to believe there's something here that's worth looking into."

Brent took in and released a deep breath. But even as the exasperated breath left him, he felt a thought tickling the back corner of his brain. It wasn't until he glanced back at the map that the thought started to take a more solid form. With the color-coding system Brent was using to distinguish the variables of each incident in the data set, the map held a variety of hues. Some, like the blue, had significant representation, while others, like the emerald green, hardly made an appearance. This was Brent's way of weighing the probability of an incident occurring under known sociological conditions, the impact of the incident across a number of fronts, and other measurable elements. With each incident he analyzed, the more patterns he found. And the faster he interpreted the patterns, the faster he was back at the university sharing this new knowledge with impressionable minds, not to mention the bonuses of a fatter bank account and another notch on his résumé.

What bothered him, though, was something that began with the team's visit to the ruined oil field. On few occasions could he remember having the chance at a tangible exploration of a data set. As a general rule, all he got to see were the facts and figures. Now, as he studied the map again, he saw that his experience in the Spraberry Trend was shifting his focus. Walking the oil field he'd asked all the pertinent questions—the ones specifically related to that one event. This approach differed not just in degree but in kind from the one he practiced in the office, and so he wondered if he was missing something important by looking at the *who* instead of the *why*.

"They're nudges," he said, more to himself than to Richards and Madigan. But when he looked up to see two sets of eyes asking the same question, he offered an explanation. "Sometimes you can get so wrapped up in looking at something that you never realize you're not asking the right questions."

"Meaning . . . ?" Madigan asked.

"The majority of what we see here are minor events," Brent continued, referring to the map. "On a global level, most of these are insignificant, with little impact on anything beyond their geographical boundaries. In fact—" he paused to catch the colonel's eye—"my guess is that if there's someone or something behind this, they would be shocked to learn that anyone has even started putting any of the pieces together."

Colonel Richards absorbed that and seemed to understand that Brent had just paid him and his team a compliment.

"So what are you getting at, Dr. Michaels?"

"Are you familiar with *curling*, Colonel?"

"The weight-lifting exercise or the Canadian sport?"

"The latter," Brent said. "Once the first guy releases the stone, the other guy stays in front of it, brushing the ice, changing the speed and direction. It's subtle—just slight alterations in angle and velocity. But if it's done right, the stone will stop just where you want it to."

"You're saying there's a defined endgame," Richards said.

"Up to this point we've been looking at what might be causing all this," Brent said. "Like they are symptoms of something else—something happening behind the scenes. And that's left us open to the possibility that the cause or causes might be natural phenomena."

He glanced at the map, his eyes landing on the single blue area along the Texas-New Mexico border.

"But what if these aren't symptoms? What if these are the tools?"

The professor was gratified to see that neither Richards nor Madigan seemed ready to dismiss this new idea out of hand. Rather, both appeared thoughtful, even a bit intrigued.

"How do you propose we begin to look at the *why* rather than the *who*?" Richards asked.

Brent had been waiting for the question, because he had a good idea as to how to explore this new line of inquiry. "Colonel Richards, how do you feel about taking a field trip?"

———

In the midst of all that was swirling around in his mind, each thought clamoring for Canfield's attention, the one thing he kept returning to was the sandwich. Even though his wife occupied a bed in the ICU just steps away, and Van Camp's admin had left him two voice mails already that morning, and he'd received a message from the Shackleton team, and he could barely function because he hadn't slept in more than forty-eight hours, he couldn't get the sandwich out of his mind.

He'd arrived home last night and made a sandwich. He'd sat at the kitchen table with the sandwich and a glass of water, and relaxed. He couldn't stop playing this small sequence of events over and over again in his mind. Without the sandwich, perhaps he would have gone upstairs ten minutes sooner. And those ten minutes might have made the difference between Phyllis needing to get her stomach pumped and then being released, or having a machine breathe for her.

Of course, Canfield knew how foolish such thoughts were. The sandwich did nothing but provide a convenient outlet for the guilt he didn't know where to place. In the grand scheme of things, ten minutes meant nothing. She could just as easily have taken the pills when he left for the airport. The fact that she hadn't, that she'd waited until he was on his way back home, was out of his control. He'd never been much good with guilt, and one of the things he'd learned from studying at the heels of Arthur Van Camp was that crisis mode was not the time to indulge an untested strategy.

The last few hours had reminded him how much he'd learned from the man. Anger was one of those things. He shook his head at the thought, because he'd often wanted Phyllis to show that kind of intense emotion. And now that it didn't matter anymore, he suspected she would have welcomed something similar from him— something to show her that at least a form of passion still remained in their relationship.

Rising from the chair near his wife's bed, he put his hand briefly on hers and then walked out of the room. He had all the information available about his wife's condition: she was unlikely to emerge from this sleep, and even if she did, the brain damage was likely extensive.

The doctor who'd spoken with him said his best guess was that she would have been without oxygen for anywhere between twelve and sixteen minutes when the ambulance arrived. He pushed the thought from his mind. They had his phone number if anything changed. He would accomplish little by sitting idle in a chair.

Canfield was on the phone before he made it to the elevator, ignoring the sign that prohibited cell phone use.

"Hello, Catherine," he said, his voice holding an unusual iciness. "Please tell Mr. Van Camp that I'm on my way in. I know he's not expecting to see me today, but there are some things I need to take care of."

He abruptly ended the call, then reached out a hand to push the elevator's down button. Recognizing the anger was the first step; the next came in deciding what to do with it.

December 11, 2012, 12:19 P.M.

At some point during this last connecting flight, Brent found himself wondering how a simple consult had turned into something much larger. When the question first arose, he didn't have an answer. Now, with the plane taxiing to the terminal, and with the tans and whites of Mazar-e Sharif visible through the oval window, the question still lacked that answer.

Even so, he had to admit that he was enjoying himself. While he liked teaching, there was something about fieldwork that raised his energy level. It gave him the same feeling now that it did when he was the young sociology hotshot with a new journal article published nearly every month and more requests for consults than he could keep up with.

In fact, his last trip here, seventeen years ago, was for one of those consults—his first for the U.S. military. In the wake of the Soviet withdrawal, when tribal warlords fought with each other to fill the leadership gap, Brent had been hired to analyze the "temperature" of the country, as the general he was working for put it. This meant that the general wanted Brent to establish the odds of the country devolving into a protracted civil war or finding some lasting détente. At twenty-eight, Brent had thought it a jewel of an assignment, one that would open doors for him. Now, at forty-five, he understood the hubris involved in thinking that one could, in a few weeks, analyze the dizzying number of factors that had served to shape the alliances and relationships of this land for thousands of years. He'd finished the consult and turned in his report, and as luck would have it, some of what he'd predicted turned out to be true. But he—and perhaps only he—knew the guesswork infused in every line.

He couldn't help but smile at the memory. Because if Colonel Richards was correct, then making sense out of the elements of his current project made Afghanistan look like a walk in the park.

When the professor shared his thoughts with Richards, the colonel had agreed that it deserved looking into. But he'd also rightly ascertained that sending the entire team to Afghanistan for what was, ostensibly, an interview was a waste of resources. Maddy had drawn the short straw once again, yet Brent had to admit that he wasn't displeased by the arrangement. After all, there was something exhilarating about traveling to an exotic location with a lovely woman.

"So where are we meeting your guy?" Maddy asked him.

"Balkh," Brent answered. "Hopefully Abby will have worked out the exact spot by now."

"Abby?"

"An associate," Brent explained, raising his phone to his ear.

"Hello, doll," Abby said after the first ring.

"Here's where you tell me you were able to arrange the meeting," Brent said.

"Sure, because while my day job is to maintain office equilibrium—an office, I might remind you, that I'm increasingly the only one in—by night I organize clandestine meetings between hard-to-find foreigners and wayward university professors."

Brent smiled. "I value your skills more than you realize."

"In that case, I can tell you that one Oman Tzahibi will meet you at your favorite restaurant at three p.m. local time."

"My favorite restaurant?"

"He said you'd know," Abby said.

Brent, again, had to smile, because the fact that Oman expected him to remember the name of a restaurant he'd frequented for three weeks seventeen years ago spoke of one of those sociological differences he was paid handsomely to understand. The name of the place hung just on the verge of recollection. What he could recall, though, was how to get there.

"That's perfect, Abby. Thanks."

The plane had reached the terminal and Brent heard the sounds of the plane shutting down, of the stairs striking the side of the fuselage. And through the phone he heard what sounded like Abby's perpetual typing.

"Excellent. I'll go ahead and add this little gem to the already sterling performance appraisal that you'll just have to put your signature on before sending it up the chain," Abby said.

"You do remember that I can replace you in a heartbeat, right?" he said.

"Oh, sweetie, there are few women in the world who are as good at what they do as I am. Don't you ever forget that."

"Don't I know it," he agreed.

They spent the next few minutes talking shop, and when Brent hung up, he saw that Maddy had retrieved both of their carry-on bags.

"Is everything set?" she asked.

"As long as I don't make a wrong turn."

Ignoring her confused look, he took his luggage and started

down the aisle. He and Maddy were the last passengers to exit the plane, a connection out of Tikrit that stretched the limits of what might be called a commercial airliner. It would have been easier to take the team's private jet, but with no equipment to carry, and because a military plane often attracted the kind of attention that was best to avoid in this part of the world, they'd opted for commercial travel, complete with Maddy in civilian clothes. It was Brent's first experience seeing her out of uniform, a sight that had made the long trip more enjoyable than it might have been.

He reached the doorway, the Afghan sun hitting him full in the face, and started down the steps. Immediately he felt a transformation of sorts occurring, as if each step brought back memories that he hadn't pulled out for review in more than a decade. By the time he reached the tarmac he was smiling again, despite the cold that sent a shiver down his spine, even through the heavy coat he'd bought in Washington before boarding the plane. A northern Afghan winter was something a visitor felt with the entire body. The mountains that dominated much of the country's interior rimmed Mazar-e Sharif to the south, and the winds funneling down from the peaks dropped the mountain iciness onto the city before picking up any last vestiges of warm air and carrying them across the plains toward Uzbekistan.

Standing next to him, Maddy didn't even attempt to conceal the shivers.

"Have you been here before?" Brent asked as they hurried to the terminal building.

"Only in the summer," she said, her chin tucked down into her jacket.

In less than ten minutes, Brent had arranged for a driver to take them to Balkh, and soon afterward the two Americans occupied the back seat of a Honda Accord and were leaving the provincial capital on the A76. Almost a suburb of Mazar-e Sharif, Balkh held the distinction of being one of the oldest cities in the known world. As Brent understood it, much of what would become the major civilizations in the Middle East found their ancestors born in this area. And as these civilizations grew and thrived, Balkh was a hub for the trade of goods and ideas. With such a history it seemed understandable that the complex sociology of the region eluded even the best minds in the field.

Maddy remained quiet during the fifteen-minute trip to the old city. Brent had briefed both her and Colonel Richards regarding what he expected to accomplish, and there was little to do besides let the thing play out. Brent couldn't help but wonder how Oman might have changed since the last time he saw the man. He was a decade older than Brent, and the professor knew that a man balancing his own concerns amid powerful tribal leaders vying for leadership in a shattered country would have aged poorly. He thought it a miracle that Oman had survived at all.

"What are you really hoping to get from this guy?" Maddy asked, as if sensing his thoughts.

Before replying, Brent watched as Balkh's ancient ruins came into view, a site that provided a lot of tourism dollars for the city.

"Like I told you, when I was here last I was working on sketching out a relationship tree between the various factions vying for political power. Part of doing that is talking to the right people. Oman was definitely included in that group. By the time I met him, he'd been working for various tribal leaders for more than a decade and, in the meantime, building his own little empire."

He glanced over at Maddy. Seeing the puzzled look on her face and intuiting her question, he said, "You're right. It's unusual for someone playing powerful men against each other to survive long enough to see any profit from it."

Brent paused and shook his head, remembering the man

who had helped him better understand the relationship dynamics between tribal groups.

"The man with information will always be a step ahead of those without it," he said.

And then they were in Balkh, the driver pulling off the A76 and onto a concrete road that would take them straight to the city center. Laid out much like Washington, with concentric circles passing through spoked streets, Balkh was a simple city to navigate, which was why Brent wasn't concerned about finding the restaurant where he would meet Oman. Anyway, the meeting wasn't for another two hours. Surely he could find the restaurant by then.

———

He chalked it up to his being a university professor. After all, weren't most teachers at that level possessed of a self-confidence that bordered on narcissism? When the driver had let them out at the ruins of Masjid Sabz, Brent decided that Maddy needed to experience some of the more interesting things in the city. They'd started with the mosque, navigating through the ancient structure with its signature green dome. They'd moved on to Bala-Hesar and then one of the bazaars that showcased goods both local and from abroad. By the time they finished, only fifteen minutes remained for them to locate the restaurant. Maddy, who had assumed that Brent knew where he was going, did an admirable job holding back any biting comments.

They reached the restaurant only five minutes late, and Brent mentally kicked himself when he saw the name, Azeen's, spelled out in English below the Dari Persian. When Brent and Maddy stepped through the door, the professor lost his vision to the restaurant's dim interior. It took several seconds for his eyes to adjust, and when they did he found that Maddy had taken a half step past him and positioned herself in front of his right shoulder. While he appreciated her willingness to risk danger on his behalf, it irritated him that she thought he needed a bodyguard.

"I thought we were supposed to be keeping a low profile," he whispered.

"We are," she said over her shoulder, her eyes scanning the room.

"Then how come I feel like Whitney Houston to your Kevin Costner?"

Maddy didn't respond, but Brent thought he saw the corner of her mouth turn up.

The restaurant was half full and to Brent's eye held only locals. It took him a few passes but eventually he saw the man he'd come to meet sitting along the far wall, where the shadows fell most prominently. He doubted the choice of seats was accidental. He also noticed the additional members of the dining party—three men in local dress and with gun-shaped bulges that their long, baggy shirts couldn't quite conceal. When his eyes locked with Oman's, the other man smiled and waved him over.

The Afghan rose from the table as Brent approached, and when the professor drew near, Oman grasped both of Brent's elbows and pulled him close, depositing a kiss on his cheek. "How are you, my friend?" Oman asked with genuine warmth.

"I'm well, Oman," Brent replied. "Thank you for agreeing to see me on such short notice."

The Afghan waved that off, his eyes moving from Brent to Maddy, then back to Brent. "I haven't seen you in more than fifteen years, and now you pop up and say you need a favor. If our friendship wasn't enough to convince me to listen, my curiosity alone would ensure my presence."

When he finished, he looked at Maddy again. Brent understood what was going through the man's mind. While Oman was more progressive than many of his contemporaries, there was still something in the Afghan mind-set that resented the idea of women on equal footing with men. Politeness would never allow Oman to express his displeasure with anything beyond his eyes, but the displeasure remained nonetheless.

"Oman, this is my associate, Dr. Amy Madigan," Brent said. "She's helping me out with a little project I'm working on."

The Afghan let his eyes linger on Maddy for a few seconds while the captain stood silent under the scrutiny. Brent saw that she knew better than to offer her hand. Oman would have taken it, but then their meeting would have been brief.

"It is a pleasure," Oman said, then motioned for the Americans to sit.

With everyone seated, including Oman's three associates, who occupied the table adjacent to them, the Afghan offered both of them a wide smile before turning his focus to Brent.

"I have followed your career since we last ate together," he said. "It is gratifying to see a friend doing so well."

"Much of my success is due to the work I did here," Brent said. "And you were very important to that work."

Oman waved off the praise, though Brent could tell the man was pleased.

"I simply offered a few words. I am happy you found them helpful."

It turned out that Oman had already ordered for everyone. A pair of waiters approached the table, placing heaping trays of lamb and *qabli pulao* between them, as well as the flatbread that Brent had grown fond of during his last stay.

"I don't think I've eaten this since our last meal together," Brent said. He offered Oman a grateful nod and served himself, knowing the Afghan would wait until he did so. Maddy served herself last, and while she demonstrated a knowledge for the way of things in the country, Brent could feel the heat rising next to him.

They spent the next half hour eating and exchanging pleasantries, with Brent noticing that the men at the next table did not eat but kept their eyes on the door and the other patrons. When last he'd eaten with Oman, the man had been alone. The presence of three hired men signified a change in status, which made Brent grateful he'd agreed to the meeting.

After a suitable time, Oman leaned back and set a hand on his stomach. "I'm assuming you did not come all this way just to share a meal with a simple trader like myself."

Brent pushed away his plate and chuckled.

"The food is definitely good enough to have traveled so far," he said. "And you are *much* more than a simple trader."

Oman smiled. "Perhaps. So what can I do for you, my friend?"

"Oman, what can you tell me about Tablisi?"

As the man took in the question, Brent watched the smile drain from his face, replaced by a thoughtful expression.

"It is a city like many others in this part of the country," Oman said. "A bit more affluent but not as far removed from Balkh as one might think."

When he did not seem prepared to provide anything else, Brent said, "I'm interested in the fighting that occurred there a few days ago. Is there anything you can tell me about that?" He understood the ambiguousness of the question, yet he also knew that Oman knew what he wanted.

Oman's response was to lean back in his chair, his eyes never leaving Brent's. Then, with a shrug of his shoulders, he said, "What would I know about the politics of a distant city?"

"As I recall, you knew everything about everything when I was here last. I wouldn't have expected that to change." He fixed Oman with a look that recognized the other man's superiority in these matters. "I need to know what was behind the unrest. From what I've been able to gather, there was no warning—nothing that signified an escalation in tribal hostilities."

It was a fine line Brent was walking: the acknowledgment that he needed help but without coming across as weak. Weakness was not something Oman would respect. Assisting a worthy associate, however, was acceptable. Even so, the Afghan made him wait for an answer. He gestured to one of the men sitting at the next table. He whispered something in the man's ear that sent him from the restaurant. Brent suspected it was all show but kept his silence. Then, with this interaction concluded, Oman returned his attention to Brent.

"This is a dangerous business, my friend," Oman said. "Why are you concerned with a small disturbance in a city far from your university?"

Brent was no military operative; he had no training in extracting information from a source without revealing too much. No doubt Maddy would have been able to handle it better, but he could only work with the tools in his possession.

"Because I'm convinced that whatever is behind the incident in Tablisi is also responsible for a number of similar events around the world. I need to know what made the Pashtuns destroy the oil refinery."

When the professor had first worked with Oman to gain an understanding of the various factions in the country, he couldn't recall a single instance when Oman displayed hesitation or unease. Unable to discern what he now saw in the Afghan's expression, Brent waited for the man to make himself clear, even if that meant an end to their meeting.

Instead, Oman did something unexpected. After a time during which he seemed to be weighing his options, he motioned for his associates to leave. He waited until they exited the restaurant before turning back to Brent.

"One must be careful who he trusts," Oman said. "Even among those on his payroll."

Brent nodded, waiting for Oman to continue. And when he did so, his words were absent much of the Afghan cultural baggage, evincing instead a Western sensibility.

"Foreign money floods into the tribes," he said. "This would make them do whatever the providers of the money deem necessary."

Brent sensed Maddy tensing next to him. He placed a hand on her knee beneath the table, but Oman's eyes had already moved from the professor to the captain.

"You are military, are you not?" Oman asked. Before Maddy could respond, he added, "Your carriage bespeaks the discipline of the U.S. armed forces. And you have a gun concealed in a shoulder holster beneath your jacket."

His eyes shifted back to Brent.

"For months I've watched the money come in; watched as once-ignoble men achieved wealth and a following to which they are unworthy. I have extended resources to discover who funds them and what their objective might be."

The Afghan stopped, and Brent saw him scan the room as if, in the absence of his protectors, he wasn't sure how to separate ally from foe. Once his attention had returned to Brent, he said, "I have learned that they are careful. They spend their money so no one can trace it back to them."

"And what is their objective?" Brent asked.

Oman shrugged. "From what I can see, it is the same as that of the Soviets—destabilization."

This seemed to fit with what Brent had uncovered from the research done by the NIIU. Still, he needed more. Something that would add weight to his theory. But he didn't know how to ask the question that hovered just beyond reach. He decided to turn the question back on Oman.

"Destabilization?" he asked.

"So it would seem to this simple trader," Oman said.

It was then that Brent stumbled on the question, and he was careful to harness his emotions before asking it.

"Can you give me a name?"

Years ago, when Brent spent time and money prying information from this man—information that he used to craft a report that put into English the words of a local—he never saw him display the level of insecurity he did now. Had Brent not known otherwise, had he not sufficient experience with the Afghan to recognize the repercussions of the question, he would have thought Oman was shutting him down. But because of his familiarity with the culture, he understood that Oman was fighting a battle against his instinct, and anything he revealed from this point on could impact his very survival. And so it was with gratitude that Brent saw the Afghan's face set in resolve, taking a last look around the near-deserted restaurant.

"The name whispered in certain circles—the one on the lips of those who perform acts that no one would perform unless enriched by foreign dollars—is Standish."

As soon as Oman released the name, he seemed to close in on himself, telling Brent that he would get no further information from him.

They finished their time together in near silence, each of them knowing what the meeting had exacted from the local man, with Brent unable to provide a suitable reward.

December 11, 2012, 10:13 A.M.

Canfield could scarcely understand why he was on a plane headed toward Antarctica, to a research vessel anchored off the continent's lonely islands, when his wife lay comatose in a hospital bed. Yet he knew that his presence at her side would do nothing for either of them. Phyllis was somewhere he couldn't reach her, and all that remained now was guilt—and the growing realization that his own future was less than secure.

He blamed himself. What made him think that Arthur Van Camp, a man who ran his businesses with a meticulousness bordering on the obsessive, would allow him to live once the project concluded? Since leaving the office, after assuring Van Camp that he could manage the project despite his wife's condition, he'd had time to think. And the topic that occupied his thoughts was self-preservation. How did one extricate himself from an operation involving untold numbers of deaths, and walk away clean? He suspected it couldn't be done—not without having someone else on whom to place the blame. That was why Van Camp had assigned the project to Canfield, why he'd been insistent about leaving no paper trail. If at some point the house of cards Canfield had built fell, Van Camp could reasonably avow that it was all the work of a rogue employee.

The chief problem, as he saw it, was that his hands were too dirtied for him to walk away, perhaps turning Van Camp over to the authorities. Without a paper trail, the possibility existed that he would be unable to prove that the orders came from above.

For the last two hours, as the Learjet took him to the southernmost endeavor under the Project: Night House umbrella, he'd pondered his exit strategy. The more he thought about it, the more he understood that only one way existed, the first step of which was seeing his assignment through to completion. If Night House succeeded, he had a chance, slim as it might be. That meant hurrying completion at Shackleton, escalating operations in the Middle East, continuing to stoke the end-of-the-world fervor, and making sure that news crews were there to cover it all. Canfield had much to do in the few days remaining.

Which was why he muttered a curse when his phone rang, and again when he saw the number on the display. Calls from the field were allowed only when something was amiss.

"Standish," he said.

As he listened to the heavily accented voice on the other end talk of a meeting between two Americans and a local Afghan trader, his mood darkened. Then the informant gave the names of the foreigners, and Canfield found things escalating beyond his ability to control them.

When the military unit forced the shutdown of the Afar project, Canfield had paid it little mind. But when that same team showed up to investigate Hickson Petroleum, he knew it was no coincidence and so began to investigate Colonel Jameson Richards's small group of scientist soldiers. And now that they'd sent two of their number to Balkh, Canfield realized he had to act—although he didn't recognize the name Brent Michaels as belonging to the unit.

As Canfield imparted his instructions to the man in his employ, he understood that he was opening a door he would never be able to close. All he could hope for was that his cost/benefit analysis would, in the end, come back in his favor.

He ended the call and initiated a second, intent on delivering a message Stateside as well.

———

Since the next flight out of Afghanistan didn't leave until the following day, Brent decided to use the time remaining to explore Mazar-e Sharif along with Maddy. They walked together past the food stalls set up near the shrine of Hazrat Ali, pausing now and then to look at the wares. Maddy seemed to have let go of the tenseness she'd held since their leaving the restaurant and the Afghan contact. At one point during their walk Brent stopped and purchased two fruit shakes, one of which he handed to Maddy, and the two of them found a bench that offered a view of the mosque over an expanse of well-kept lawn. Maddy sampled the shake and gave an appreciative nod.

"That tastes good after how spicy that lamb dish was," she said.

Brent smiled, taking a sip of his own. "Most of the food here is pretty spicy, but there are a few places in town that will whip you up a burger if your stomach won't take any more."

Maddy chuckled and resumed sipping the shake, her eyes taking in the enormous, ornate mosque. They sat in silence for a while, enjoying the day despite the looming threat that his research seemed to be pointing to.

"So what can we do with a name?" he finally asked.

Maddy considered that and offered a shrug in response. They

watched a young girl pass by on a bicycle, Brent amazed that her long garments remained clear of the chain. When they lost her around a corner, Maddy glanced at him.

"I'm not sure," she said. "I've already sent the name on to the colonel so he can run it through CODIS, Interpol, and a few other databases. If we're lucky, we get a hit. But even if we do, there's no telling how useful it will be."

She paused as a group of people walked past them, heading toward the mosque for evening prayers. A man and his wife with two young boys in tow. The man offered the foreigners a nod and smile as he passed.

"I wasn't sure how useful this trip was going to be," Maddy confided. "I mean, what were the odds that you would know a guy with intel related to our investigation?"

Brent thought about this and decided that Maddy was right. Oman was the only card he had—although knowing what he knew about the way the Afghan operated, Brent had considered it a definite possibility that he would know *something*.

"To be fair, I'm not completely convinced that whatever it is we're investigating is even real," he said. "Coincidence is a genuine presence in systems analysis."

"Which makes coming here something like a step of faith, doesn't it?" Maddy asked.

Her question pulled a smile from Brent because it was quite the opposite to what he'd proposed to her boss just a few days ago, when he'd suggested that he was the man of reason to Richards's man of faith.

"I don't think so. Tenuous link or not, this is a legitimate avenue for investigation. No faith involved." Then he finished the last of his shake before catching Maddy's eye.

She frowned at his comment, which evoked a feeling in him that suggested he was growing very fond of this woman. And he may have been wrong but he got the impression that the captain had feelings for him as well. Granted, his experience with Amy Madigan extended back a scant few days. For all he knew, the way she interacted with him wasn't much different from her interactions with other consultants brought within the sphere of the team. Except that he guessed that was not the case, as evidenced by what she said next.

"Look, I don't know why I'm telling you this," she began. "When I joined this team I was at a certain place—a place that made it difficult for me to accept a lot of what our research hinted at. . . ." She trailed off and glanced at Brent, and whatever she saw in his expression must have encouraged her to continue. "You've already noticed the cross I'm wearing. I have no idea what kind of upbringing you had, but mine was pretty religious. Church three times a week; we would have gone more if the doors had been open."

"My father was an atheist," Brent said, "but my mother was very devout." He laughed at the memory. "My mom dragged us to church whenever she could. My father didn't seem to mind too much."

Maddy smiled at his recollection, which while not an exact match for her own, showed he could at least relate to what she was trying to say.

"This job can be a challenge at times," she said. "My background tells me there are only two reasons things happen: God and science."

"That's funny. Usually I hear people arguing God *or* science."

"What I mean is most Christians are okay with giving scientific answers to the easy questions. It's the other stuff—the stuff without a ready explanation—where we often throw up our hands and say, 'I don't know. I guess God did it.'"

"And you don't buy that?" Brent asked, wondering what peculiar brand of Christianity the captain practiced.

"No, I don't. I think God is responsible for *all* of it. I also think that science can explain all of it." At Brent's raised eyebrow, she added, "Like I said a few days ago, I've seen a lot during my time on this team that runs the gamut from strange to truly frightening. But nine times out of ten we find a good reason that things happen like they do."

Brent grunted. "And the one out of ten?"

"Just means we haven't worked hard enough to figure it out."

Brent leaned back against the hard surface of the bench, trying to put some distance between himself and the conversation. Even so, he had to point out what he saw as a flaw in her argument.

"What about miracles?" he asked. "If you had such a religious upbringing, you must believe in miracles. Aren't they, by their very definition, unexplainable?"

"Sure," she agreed. "But I think there's a big difference between making a few loaves of bread feed five thousand people and finding a six-foot-diameter circle in the middle of the Amazon where anything made out of copper floats. See, eventually we figured that one out. Who knows? Maybe because of our work in a decade or so they'll be manufacturing airplanes that use half the fuel they do now."

"Wait! You found *what* in the Amazon?"

"That's not important," she said. "All I'm trying to say—" She stopped, seemingly looking for the right words. Finally she shrugged and offered him a weak smile. "I don't really know what I'm trying to say. I guess I'm just trying to let you know that things aren't as chaotic as you might think. The ground we walk on is pretty solid; it's the only way we can deal with the stuff that isn't."

Brent mulled that over and he thought she was right—she didn't know what she wanted to say. Still, he thought she'd said it pretty well anyway. The professor found himself very much intrigued by this woman. Of course it didn't hurt that she was more attractive than most, if not all, the women who had crossed his path.

The sun had lowered while they talked, and the streets that had, just minutes before, teemed with people were now nearly deserted. Brent gazed at the mosque, where the devout now prayed to a god who was foreign to Amy Madigan. He wondered how she reconciled the fact that in the end few people deviated from the beliefs of their parents. As the sun finished its descent, he gave some thought as to how he himself fit into that paradigm.

A moment later, he pushed from his mind such weighty thoughts of differing ideologies, stood, and offered a hand to Maddy. Then the pair started off in the direction of the hotel where they'd planned to dine together.

———

The restaurant was attached to the hotel and catered mostly to tourists in its offering dishes without the spice so favored by the locals. The proprietor had led them to a booth, speaking passable English and making it very clear that the Americans were welcome in his restaurant. Brent had selected a pasta with vegetables, while Maddy chose a hamburger with all the fixings. Neither of them had ventured further into the conversation begun on the bench, and Brent now sensed some reticence in her. He knew, though, that as a general rule people seldom broached the topic of religion in polite conversation. At least that was his experience.

He allowed the silence to linger, pleased it was not of the uncomfortable variety. On the contrary, the two of them sat and ate like old friends, content in both the meal and the company.

Finally, Maddy broke the silence, bringing up the business that had brought them to this foreign city.

"So what will you do when we get back?" she asked.

After wiping his mouth with his napkin, Brent said, "Good question. Although I'm not entirely convinced this is a global phenomenon, I think we've uncovered enough data to head that way.

I think the thing we have to start looking at, beyond who is behind this, is *why* the escalation?"

"What do you mean?"

"Well, the incidents in your data set start a little over two years ago, right? But up until about nine months ago they were spaced pretty evenly. Then *boom*." He shook his head. "In my experience, when you see an escalation like the one we're tracking, there's an endgame that's approaching sooner rather than later."

Maddy absorbed that and then smirked at Brent. "So in addition to figuring out what's going on, we now have the added concern of doing it on a timetable we don't know anything about."

"Pretty much," Brent said.

Despite the ludicrousness of the situation, Maddy laughed and Brent couldn't help but follow suit. Engaged as he was, he hardly noticed the dark truck that rolled past the restaurant's large front window. From where he sat he could see the tail end of the vehicle in his peripheral vision, but almost as soon as he registered seeing it, he let it go. He had no idea what was happening at the table, this easy rapport with a woman he'd known for such a short time, yet he recognized an opportunity when he saw one.

But then he saw a cloud pass over Maddy's face and he frowned, wondering what he might have said to shut her down. It took a moment for him to recognize that she was looking past him. He glanced over his shoulder to see what had caught her attention, which left him unprepared as Maddy lunged forward and shoved his head down onto the tabletop.

Brent heard a repeating popping sound, then lifted his head enough to see Maddy rising from her seat, gun in hand, firing toward the restaurant's front door. She shouted at him to keep his head down, but Brent chanced a look behind him. He counted three men, one of them on the floor and not moving, and more shadows near the front door—perhaps reinforcements for those already inside.

He noticed then that the restaurant patrons were nowhere to be found.

As a professor and researcher, Brent had been in a precarious situation or two, but none resulting in the firing of actual bullets. Consequently he had no idea what to do. His first impulse was to throw himself to the floor beneath the table, hoping that whatever played out in the air above him would wind up in his favor. But in the instant he had to decide, he could see that Maddy alone wouldn't be able to handle all the assailants pouring through the front door.

It was in that moment that Brent saw the proprietor—the man who had welcomed them with warmth and kindness—emerge from the kitchen wielding a pump-action shotgun. The man took one look around, leveled the weapon, and fired toward the door. He managed to squeeze off a second shot, and Brent saw one of the assailants go crashing down.

He and Maddy had taken cover in the booth, where she returned fire against a better armed enemy. When he looked the other way, he saw the proprietor's shotgun lying on the floor. He caught Maddy's eye, and while she couldn't possibly understand his intent, she seemed to intuit that he was about to do something foolish. But before she could put voice to it, Brent launched himself out of the booth, keeping low as he navigated the gap between the booth and the kitchen's double doors. Running from the booth, he thought he had his feet under him, but somewhere along the way he stumbled and fell, landing atop the dead proprietor as bullets cut a trail past his ear.

Brent snatched up the gun, turning and aiming it at their attackers. The reinforcements had followed behind the initial trio, taking positions in the hall between the entrance and the dining area. The only experience Brent had with a gun was skeet shooting, so he used the same technique and fired a shot in the direction of the enemy. Despite all the chaos, he saw the man who was moving into the dining area collapse under the shot. Before Brent could chamber another round, another man took his place and aimed his weapon at him. Brent dove to the floor, using the proprietor's body as a shield. Peeking above the dead man, he saw a number of lifeless bodies in the doorway yet still more coming in.

He glanced over at Maddy, his eyes finding her just in time to see one of the enemy's bullets find its mark. Then Brent watched as the captain, who had come out from behind the table, reeled back and fell onto the seat.

As he saw her go down, everything shifted into slow motion, as if he'd stepped away from himself to view the scene from a vantage point safe from gunfire and the sights and sounds of carnage. One moment he was staring at Maddy's fallen form, and the next he was looking at their attackers, four men advancing into the room. He raised the shotgun with arms steadier than he would have thought possible. He quickly lined up his shot and squeezed off a round that, while missing the man's chest at which he was aiming, succeeded in taking out the legs. A bloodcurdling scream filled the room.

Turning, Brent saw movement from the booth—Maddy pushing herself upright and facing the men closing in on them. Even as he readied the shotgun to fire again, he watched her raise an arm, hesitate for a second, and then fire. The attacker toppled over, dead. Spent by the effort, she brought her arm down and the gun dropped to the floor.

To Brent's amazement, the two remaining men, their paths obstructed by fallen comrades, backed down the hallway and exited the way they'd come. As Brent struggled for breath he heard the sound of an engine, followed by the screech of tires. In the silence that followed, when he was certain that no enemies lurked anywhere in the restaurant, he lowered the gun and pushed himself to his feet. He rushed to the booth, his ankle protesting with each step he took.

Maddy had collapsed again, lying still on the booth seat. Brent set his weapon down and reached for her. He wedged a hand beneath her shoulder and eased her up, and then realized that the wetness he felt on his hand was her blood.

Far off in the distance he heard the wail of sirens.

——

When the call came in, Richards found himself in one of those situations in which he did not have an immediate response, as if the news conveyed to him from thousands of miles away was meant for someone else. What urged him forward was decades of training, of acting within defined parameters while the particulars sorted themselves out. The first order of business was to contact General Smithson, to have a marine unit dispatched from Kabul, some three hours away by road from the hospital where his charges had been taken. Even considering a rapid response, as well as a probable chopper insertion at Mazar-e Sharif, Richards suspected a good ninety minutes would pass in which Maddy and Dr. Michaels would be subject to a follow-up assault. He thought that unlikely, as terrorist cells seldom moved against their targets without the element of surprise, but he disliked having his people in a position where he couldn't protect them.

Once he'd secured Smithson's promise of a company to support the Afghan security now surrounding the hospital, he placed a call to the U.S. embassy in Kabul, hoping a representative would have time to catch a lift with the marines before they headed out. He had to make certain a diplomat was en route, because while Maddy was cleared to fire in-country, Dr. Michaels was not. And terrorist attack or not, the local authorities could make things difficult for a foreigner accused of killing a native.

In spite of the circumstances, his one consolation was that with two phone calls he could organize a defensive operation from half a world away. What angered him, though, was that he couldn't get anyone to tell him if Maddy was even alive. All Dr. Michaels had told him was that she was unresponsive going into surgery—and that there'd been a great loss of blood.

Richards had never lost a member of his team, not in the decade since he'd created it, and the thought of losing Amy Madigan was something he just couldn't bear. In the absence of anything else he could do this far away, he chose one of the few courses of action available—an accounting of his team, to tell them what had befallen one of their own. It wasn't a conversation he was looking forward to. Rawlings, Addison, and Bradford were in the building, working in the lab. Snyder was in transit from McDonough, and Petros had taken a personal day. He would get them all together before he gave them the news.

In less than two minutes he had both of his off-base personnel on their way in, with a minimum of grumbling from Petros. Richards thought he heard the soldier mumble something about the theater, which he found a bit surprising but didn't press under the circumstances.

When he hung up he breathed a deep sigh, then sat down and did something he did not do well: he waited. And in an office without windows, dug out from the hard, rocky ground that made the construction of a building in this area as much an act of will as of logistics, Colonel Jameson Richards could not know that as a man on a personal day stepped off a Washington curb in possession of theater tickets he would now be unable to use, and as the man slipped behind the wheel of his Porsche and cranked the ignition, that act ended his life.

The car went up as a fireball, rising more than two stories, its sideways motion shattering the glass of the curbside ticket booth, killing both the ticket taker and a woman out walking her dog, and sending pieces of the incinerated Porsche for a block in every direction. Safe in his subterranean office, Colonel Richards could not hear the sounding of a dozen or more car alarms, or understand that war had just been declared on his team.

———

Dabir was not one to grant superiority where such was not warranted, so he refrained from giving the airport protocols in his country more due than they deserved. What he did concede, however, was that American security was not as untouchable as he had been led to believe. In the short time since he'd exited the plane and passed into the portion of the concourse beyond the security line, he had counted four instances in which he could have wreaked havoc on any plane taking flight that day. The information was of little use at the moment, but who knew when such knowledge would prove useful?

As he made his way past the funneled bodies—thick yet nowhere near as concentrated as an Ethiopian bazaar on a normal day—what impressed him the most, beyond the cleanliness of the place, was how much he stood out against the lighter skins of everyone around him. The result was that he felt far more exposed than he'd ever felt before. That feeling faded, though, when he realized that no one was paying him the least bit of attention.

Unlike his country, averting one's eyes seemed to be the norm here, even from those who showed more than a passing interest. In these cases, when Dabir met their questioning eyes with his own steady gaze, eye contact was quickly severed, with the Ethiopian convinced that the ones who had noticed him would forget before they reached their departure gates.

Of primary concern was money. Dabir followed the universal currency exchange signs and soon was in possession of sufficient funds in American dollars, enough to secure for himself transportation and temporary lodging. And food. He hadn't eaten in almost a day and he'd always wanted to try a hamburger made in America. He knew what the knockoffs in his country were like and couldn't help but wonder how the genuine article compared.

After he'd worked his way through the line, paid what to him was an exorbitant price for a meal, and located a place where he could sit and eat, he found himself disappointed. The American hamburger lacked the spice of those served in his country. But rather than belittle the food, he remembered that familiarity was a powerful thing. He suspected, with a measure of pride, that realizations like this one were what made him an exceptional soldier. He was one of those outside-the-box thinkers highly prized by Standish.

Canfield. He had to keep saying the name to himself, to continue substituting the real name for the assumed. For that was why he was there.

Once he cleaned out the widow account, adding it to what he'd accumulated over the last year, he had enough to spend the remainder of his days somewhere free of worry. Yet he knew, even before he spent a year on a pristine beach and let the thing gnaw at him, that he would never be happy until he saw Standish—Canfield—face-to-face one last time.

His intel said the man worked for Van Camp Enterprises, which meant he would spend the bulk of his time in Atlanta. As logic would dictate, he owned a home in a high-end section of the city. That was another thing that amused the Ethiopian: a man who could wield such influence and produce such devastation in a country not his own could allow himself to be wholly unprotected in his country of residence. Dabir knew the American counted on anonymity to protect him, but he himself was proof that luck could send the entire arrangement crumbling. With a well-timed tail to an African airport, he had uncovered Canfield's secret.

Now Dabir had to decide which course to pursue—whether to expend resources studying Alan Canfield or the company for which he worked. At first blush, Van Camp Enterprises was a monster corporation. CEO of one of the largest media enterprises in the world, Arthur Van Camp also had a hand in an impressive number of unrelated concerns. And yet Dabir had never heard of the man.

As much as he wanted Canfield, Dabir decided that much of what he needed to know began and ended with Arthur Van Camp. He pondered this as he finished his first American-made burger, and he hoped, indeed prayed, that whatever he wound up accomplishing in this country would not disappoint him nearly as much as this simple meal.

December 11, 2012, 9:15 P.M.

The Southern Ocean beat mercilessly against the Shackleton Ice Shelf, its massive waves coming with foam-tipped crests, striking the monstrous frozen platform that stretched for more than two hundred miles before turning southeast and degenerating into an arc of malformed ice with fissures ripped by the elements, hemming a bay filled with icebergs once married to the shelf. The ice shelf was in the death throes of a geologic formation not long for this world, if only in the stress fractures spider-webbing their way through its surface and the bergs newly calved to the sea.

Farther inland, where the glacier that formed the ice shelf narrowed, the effects of whatever natural forces had decreed its demise were most evident, strangling the shelf, shattering its brittle bones. The estimates were that the shelf would retain its shape—its place—for roughly thirty years. A wink in the period by which the growth of mountains was measured, but an eternity in the life of the average researcher.

And it was those three decades Canfield counted on. Without them, the time and expense exhausted by this project were wasted, and while Mr. Van Camp had money to spare, a project like this one was pricey enough to warrant extreme care.

Canfield stood on the flat ice, gazing straight ahead, the dim light rendering everything beyond him as shadows, including the ice that stretched for miles in three directions. The Shackleton Shelf covered more than twenty-three thousand kilometers, which meant that, even if it were a perfectly clear day, he wouldn't have been able to see the ocean from where he stood.

Looking to his right, though, he could hear the expanse of sea-water assaulting the shelf. Twenty yards away, an Ashok Leyland truck with a mounted DTH drilling rig bored a hole in the ice, forcing the bit down a quarter mile; the operation was illuminated by fluorescent kits that gave off no heat. What they were about to do required depth, which was why Van Camp had spent the money to have the hydraulic motor modified to push the bit through the deep, compressed ice. Other parts of the unit had also been adapted to the job, as well as to the environment in which it performed, such as the white surface that camouflaged the truck's presence on the ice, including its tires. Even a refrigerant system had been set up to expel heat-stripped air around the cabin, masking the warmth inside. All to avoid detection from those satellites Van Camp's money and influence were unable to reroute.

From Canfield's spot on a slight rise, he could make out the locations of eight more units. The units were arranged in a straight line and spaced twenty-five yards apart. For the last four months they'd been working their way across the shelf's surface—drilling, lowering charges, and filling the holes again, all the while progressing northward. Of all the projects on the Van Camp docket, Canfield thought this one the riskiest. It was also his idea, which prior to his recent change in goals made him more than concerned for its success.

In a perfect world, Canfield would have been there every moment, and that may have shaved two weeks off the project time. But with his other responsibilities sending him around the globe, he'd been forced to leave the supervision of the shelf to others. And it wasn't until this last week—when they were nearing completion of an endeavor that would qualify as perhaps the most ambitious project ever attempted on earth—that he'd felt nervous.

The wind had picked up over the last hour and he could hardly hear it when his foreman, a journeyman and pipeline supervisor named Ricker, said something to him over the radio. Canfield brought the radio closer to his ear and asked the man to repeat himself.

"We're finishing up the last one, Mr. Standish," the man said. In the background Canfield could hear the roar of the rig, the scream of the bit ripping through thousands of years' worth of ice.

"Excellent," he shouted into the radio. He waved a gloved hand across the distance before realizing Ricker probably couldn't see the gesture. But the other man, a white blur almost missed against the whiteness around him, raised his hand in response.

Canfield had selected Ricker for the simple reason that he was the best in the world at what he did, one of only a few who could take on a project of this magnitude. The problem was that as a former marine accustomed to thinking of everything in tactical terms, Ricker was bright enough to know that what they'd done there could have only been initiated for one of two reasons: scientific research or war. And the cost of the equipment—Ashoks with state-of-the-art drill rigs, crawlers with 800mm auger drillers, and the monstrous blast-hole drill—was far too expensive for all but the most well-financed of science expeditions. Not to mention the amount of explosives they'd buried beneath the ice, which were they lumped together in a single location and detonated, would leave a crater the size of Rhode Island. Canfield knew that Ricker understood all of this, which was why he had to consider the man yet one more loose end in a long string of them.

The foreman stood by one of the drill units, watching as the operator put the hydraulic cylinder in reverse and started to thread the line out of the fresh hole. Not far from Canfield, a white helicopter sat idle on the ice shelf. The chopper would carry him back to a research vessel working its way around Bouvet Island. He turned toward the helicopter and flashed a light, and immediately the pilot brought the bird to life.

Canfield lifted the radio to his lips. "Great work, Max. When the last charge is set, get everyone back to base camp. I'll have the plane there at nine o'clock tomorrow morning. Does that give you enough time to finish breaking down?"

Even across this distance, he could see the man's shoulders shake with laughter.

"I'd have the camp down in fifteen minutes if you had the plane here now," Ricker said. " 'Cause there's a hot shower calling my name the second we get back to the boat."

"I'll make sure there's a clean towel and a bar of soap waiting for you," Canfield returned with a chuckle.

He watched for a few moments longer, until the drilling rig finished its egress from the new hole and a pair of men began removing the bit and attaching the cable and payload to be lowered to the bottom. Then he turned and headed toward the helicopter.

Once there he placed a call to the research vessel, to the team waiting to clean up the camp. Once the call was made, and he knew that he would pass the second chopper in the air, he offered the endless ice outside the window a tired smile, knowing that Van Camp would appreciate his heeding his last dressing down. He was using company resources for this one. And once the deed was done, no trace of the drilling operation—or its men—would remain.

———

For more than an hour after arriving at the hospital, Brent was unable to locate a single person who spoke English. He'd finally given up, allowing the nurses, and the doctor who looked at him for less than ten seconds, to poke and prod. Their treatment of him was a good deal more gentle than the prodding he'd received from the Afghan authorities. The professor didn't necessarily blame them. When the police—with an ambulance close behind—arrived at the restaurant, they found a half-dozen dead men, a gravely wounded American woman carrying a gun, and a foreign man who could do little but babble and point. Thinking back on it, Brent was grateful they hadn't shot him on sight.

Once they wheeled Maddy in for surgery, all he could think to do was call Colonel Richards. For despite his barely knowing the man, Brent found it a comfort to talk to someone who assured him that all was under control and that he, Richards, was in charge, even from thousands of miles away. Later, he felt a whole lot better when a lieutenant with the marines showed up. According to the soldier, American forces were surrounding the hospital just in case the enemy was planning a repeat attack, though everyone thought that to be unlikely.

Brent had explained the events leading up to the attack, doing his best to leave out anything he thought Richards might prefer to remain classified. But since the lieutenant and his men were operating on specific orders to protect the army captain and her civilian traveling companion, anything more than the basics wasn't required.

Brent's ears were still ringing from the shotgun, as well as the rounds fired in his direction, and somewhere along the way he'd twisted his ankle. Yet he couldn't complain, given how Maddy looked when they wheeled her away. He tried his best not to think about it, because each time he did his stomach knotted up.

"How are you, sir?" the lieutenant asked as he extended a plastic cup of water to the professor. Brent noticed the name Templeton on his shirt.

"Just fine," Brent said, accepting the cup with a grateful nod. He hadn't realized he was so thirsty.

He suspected he should say more to the man who'd choppered in from Kabul on his behalf, but nothing came to him and his eyes remained on the door through which Maddy had disappeared.

"Dr. Michaels, I've spoken with the local police and explained what I could, and while they're not happy about it, it looks as though they're deferring to us for the time being."

"That's good to hear," Brent said.

The lieutenant followed Brent's gaze to the gray windowless doors. "I'm sure she'll be alright, sir," Templeton said. "I hear Captain Madigan is pretty tough."

Brent couldn't help but smile, because in his assessment, Amy Madigan was indeed tough. Still, the lieutenant didn't see how much blood she'd left in the restaurant. "Thanks," he said.

The lieutenant nodded and walked away, leaving Brent to his own thoughts.

———

"I want that blast report yesterday!" Richards snapped.

The large briefing room was now a war room, teeming with officers. What had begun as a quiet investigation by his team was now a multi-branch operation between the army, air force, and Homeland Security. Although grief-stricken about the recent tragic events, Richards glanced around the room and was filled with pride, admiring the level of professionalism on the faces of his team. Even

Snyder, who had spent more time with Petros than anyone else in the unit, maintained a look of resolve as he pored over the first of the reports taken from the blast site. Richards knew they would have time to grieve later; if they began now, they wouldn't do right by Petros—or Madigan.

"We picked up traces of PTEN," Snyder said. "The blast radius indicates whoever did this used a lot of it."

"If they used PTEN, we're talking about someone organized," commented one of the Homeland Security techs, a smart-looking woman in her twenties who sat nearby working on a laptop. "And if they had enough PTEN to create an explosion that large, then they either had tons of money or a serious support system, or both."

"Okay," Richards said, "so we have a professional hit on an army officer in Washington, and a brute-force attack on another officer in Afghanistan. Who could strike both of them in less than twenty-four hours, and why?"

"If they're even connected, Jameson," said General Smithson. "Not only do you have to take into account the distance, the methods are different enough to give me pause about suspecting one person or group."

Richards couldn't blame the general for his skepticism. Were Richards not involved in investigating just such a far-flung series of unique events, he wouldn't have bought it either. At some point he would need to pull the general aside and fill him in, but he harbored doubts about divulging that information to such a large and diverse group. Besides, he agreed with the Homeland Security tech's assessment: any one person or group that could pull this off, and that could orchestrate everything the team had catalogued so far, was well positioned to infiltrate at least one of the groups assisting him now. Any man or woman in the room could be watching and listening for someone else. Richards scanned the room, aware of the paranoia, which only made it easier to indulge it. He looked back at General Smithson.

"You have to trust me on this one, Frank," he said, and despite the differences in their ranks, Richards's long tenure in this building allowed Smithson to take a measured look at the colonel's face and then nod.

"Alright then," said Smithson. "It looks like we have our work cut out for us."

Richards saluted the general and returned to his work, barking out orders across the room.

Armed Forces Global Threat Assessment

December 11, 2012

- Richland, Washington: Shipment of caesium-137 lost in transit to Columbia Generating Station.

- Seoul, South Korea: China to conduct six-day naval exercise in Yellow Sea.

- Odessa, Texas: Destruction of oil rig at Hickson Petroleum. Responsible party unknown.

- El Paso, Texas: Ciudad Juarez's Ruiz cartel kills three police officers in cross-border attack.

December 12, 2012, 7:52 P.M.

For an hour Canfield had held his wife's hand, almost like an experiment to see if heat would transfer between them, but her fingers remained cold to the touch, as if he were holding the hand of a statue. He ran a thumb along the taut skin around her knuckles as he talked quietly to her. The talking was something he performed out of duty, for he wasn't certain whether he wanted her to awaken. Still, it was one of the duties he felt compelled to hold on to, having abandoned so many others over the course of just a few days.

He thought it incredible how such a short period of time could so alter a man's life—how it could grant him a completely new perspective. He'd come to realize that he was indeed his own man. Up until he'd learned that Van Camp would likely seek his death once the ice shelf fell into the ocean, he could tell himself that it was the job, and the influence of a powerful man, that had turned him into someone who could kill with impunity. After all, he seldom left anything to chance. That was why the drill team couldn't have been allowed to return to the States. The chances of even one of those men going his entire life without telling someone how he'd participated in separating an ice sheet from a continent were longer than he wanted to bet.

Now, with the artifice of company loyalty stripped away, leaving only self-interest as motivation, he knew the calculated brutality was his alone. He knew when he'd stood on the windswept Antarctic ice and ordered that the drill team be eliminated, the decision belonged to no one but himself. And he would know it too when he took Van Camp's life.

And in speaking to his unresponsive wife, Canfield wondered if he was avoiding taking into consideration the new tactical error he had made. He'd made the mistake of allowing his newfound freedom—the headiness that came with commanding his own fate—to cause him to overstep. Worried about the investigation by the NIIU, he'd struck a devastating blow. However, would the deaths of some of their own cause this odd little military unit to back off, or would it breathe new life into the investigation? Had he let the team alone, would they have been able to put together enough of the pieces to make sense of the whole? At this point, he would probably never know.

———

Brent wasn't sure how he'd managed it, but he convinced one of the soldiers on guard duty to go to his hotel and retrieve his laptop. The professor suspected the man chafed inwardly at running an errand for a civilian, but then it got him away from the hospital for a while, so it was a win for both of them. Brent felt mildly guilty that he didn't want the laptop so much for his ongoing research as he did for entertainment. They got the Internet in Afghanistan too, and he could find any variety of shows to keep him entertained while he waited for Maddy to wake up.

The captain had come through surgery well. The bullet wound, while horrible looking, showed a strike between her shoulder and sternum, staying clear of the heart. In fact, had it not severed an artery, she could have had the round removed with as little hassle as getting a few stitches. As it was, the severed artery would have killed her had it taken another fifteen or twenty minutes to get to the hospital.

He'd been in to check on her and to show her that he was in good health, and then he let her rest, promising to pop in again in the morning. That left him in a hospital lounge, surfing for something interesting to read to pass the time.

At some point he wound up on CNN, where he perused both the U.S. and international news sections, which now that he'd worked with the NIIU for a while he couldn't view except through a lens crafted by this consult. It left him seeing ghosts everywhere. After searching a number of news stories, he was about to click on Sports when the video articles did their programmed JavaScript shuffle and moved an interesting looking one to the top. Curious, Brent clicked on it and found one of those Mayan end-of-the-world stories that had so irritated Richards.

He supposed the consult was the reason he hadn't given more thought to the Mayan 2012 phenomenon. He'd become so involved in this job that a once-in-a-lifetime event with significant sociological implications was passing by him untracked. Almost a year ago he'd considered soliciting a research grant to study the 2012 phenomenon through the prism of Y2K, which was the closest parallel to the forthcoming event. He could have put together a pretty important paper about how far-reaching apocalyptic prophecies influenced the global psyche. It might have been interesting to study the lessons learned from Y2K as they related to the current situation.

He edged the volume up a touch on his laptop. The reporter, a silver-haired man with a serious expression, was standing uncomfortably close to a crowd of people in full riot mode. The text at the bottom of the screen identified the place as Stuttgart. As Brent watched, a group was pelting a line of police with rocks, bottles, and anything else within reach. The police were taking the brunt of the assault using their clear riot shields, and Brent could see that they were close to advancing against the angry mob.

Brent tried to focus on what the reporter was saying, even as the images on-screen pulled at his attention. Part of the draw was the fact that his field gave him an understanding of crowd dynamics, and in studying this one, he could see the fuel for an encounter that would escalate beyond police control.

The camera angle changed, making it clear that the confrontation was playing out against the backdrop of a bank. In light of this, some of the reporter's words found their way past the professor's filter: *stock exchange, credit,* and *bleak.* It was a moment before Brent noticed the man watching the screen over his shoulder.

"Stocks have been erratic for months," the marine said—not the soldier who'd retrieved Brent's computer but another from their unit. The man gestured to the rioters. "Most of these people are probably short-term investors worried they're about to lose all the money they've sunk into companies they shouldn't have invested in."

The comment caused Brent to give the marine a second, closer look. He might have been all of nineteen. "You know a bit about investing?" he asked.

"Yes, sir. My father was a day trader before he retired, so I usually have a good feel for what's going on."

Brent nodded and glanced back at the screen. "In that case, what's going on here?"

"That's a good question, sir. And I'm not sure there's a real good answer. From everything I've seen, most of the stocks that have dropped over the last six months are pretty solid investments. And yet people are short-selling and the prices are dropping." He shook his head as if puzzled by what he was watching. "It's like people are panicking without anyone yelling *fire* first."

Brent considered the marine's words but didn't respond, and not long afterward the man left. It took several seconds before he realized that something was troubling him, yet he couldn't pinpoint what it might be.

He closed the laptop, stood, and stretched, and then went in search of coffee. When he found the dingy pot in what looked like a break room, he poured himself a cup and stepped back into the hallway. The thing that bothered him still had a hold on some part of his brain, and as Brent sipped at the bitter brew he sensed the subversive thought slowly wiggle its way toward the surface. As it began to take form he understood that it had everything to do with the crowd of rioters, which he'd already analyzed using the Le Bon model. It was typical Convergence Theory. Yet that wasn't all of it. There was something about watching that crowd develop into a dangerous organism for, if the investment-savvy marine was correct, no easily discernible reason that seemed to track with his earlier thoughts.

Brent took another sip of coffee, returned to his laptop, and sat down. He was about to continue on to the Sports section from which he'd been distracted when the idea chose that moment to reveal itself. The next moments were a blur as Brent scooped up the laptop and, leaving the cup of coffee on the floor by the chair, pushed past the two marines guarding the recovery room door.

Maddy was awake when he barged in. Without so much as a greeting, and as if this were just another brainstorming session back in the NIIU offices, he said, "I've been overlooking something. We've been tracking a tremendous expending of resources over a period of two years to produce a desired outcome. But aside from the fact that whoever's doing this has a wide reach, everything we've seen has been pretty subtle."

"You call the obliteration of an oil field subtle?" Maddy asked. Still in the insufficient hospital gown apparently ubiquitous to hospitals worldwide, she made a few adjustments of her attire for modesty's sake.

"Comparatively speaking, yes," Brent said. "When you're dealing with sociological change, there are two things you have to consider. The first is gradual change over time. How do small influences alter the social framework over a prescribed period?"

"Which is what we've been following."

"In an accelerated fashion, yes. Usually the kinds of changes we've seen would take decades to manifest. But if we can accept the original theory—that this is an artificially induced state—then, yes, what we're looking at falls within the gradual family."

"And the other family is . . . ?"

"A polarizing event. It's also referred to as a catastrophic event, but I think that's a bit much."

"A polarizing event?"

"Right. In our recent history, think 9/11. A single event that alters the landscape for everything—from security to foreign policy to the stock market."

He waited to make sure that Maddy was tracking with him.

"Y2K was a big one too," he added. "Something that quickly entered the worldwide collective consciousness, which caused people to change behaviors, which affected what people bought and sold, if they went to church or not. Even though Y2K ended up being nothing, it doesn't change the fact that up until the clock struck midnight, people were prepared for the worst."

Brent saw the captain taking in everything he'd said. Over the last eight days he thought he'd come to know her pretty well, and he knew she wouldn't dismiss his new theory out of hand—except that he hadn't yet arrived at the big reveal.

It didn't take Maddy long to do the heavy lifting.

"So you're anticipating an imminent polarizing event," she said.

"I am."

The silence that settled over the room had a chill to it. It matched the one moving up Brent's spine, despite that he'd been privy to the information prior to its delivery. What warmed him, though, was Maddy's response, which indicated a willingness to accept the professor's new theory as the truth.

"But how do we recognize this event before it happens?"

Brent shook his head. "I have no idea. That's the part that I need your help with."

"I'll do what I can—you know that."

"There's one more thing," he said.

With some pain, Maddy shifted slowly in the hospital bed and met Brent's eyes.

"I mentioned Y2K."

"Yes. What about it?" she asked.

"Y2K was a polarizing event that never materialized," Brent said. "But the interesting thing about it was that it also contained elements from the gradual school. After all, everyone knew the year 2000 was coming."

Maddy took that in and, after a few moments, responded with a nod.

"Just imagine what would have happened if 9/11 had happened on December thirty-first, 1999."

"Global panic," she said. "Chaos."

"I think someone learned from Y2K. Someone watched the way the world reacted and realized that should something like it happen again, there would be money in it." He paused, took a deep breath. "But the real money comes if Y2K actually happens."

Following the bread crumbs was a lot to ask of anyone. Even

Brent wasn't sure he bought all of it, and he was the one versed in theory. What he did know was that it felt right.

Maddy then raised the question Brent had been hoping she would raise.

"But there is no Y2K right now. Nothing for a polarizing event to piggyback on, right?"

Even as she spoke, Brent kept his eyes on her, almost willing the captain to put the pieces together, as if she were a student listening to one of his lectures.

"Wait a minute," she said, her eyes widening. "You're not saying . . ."

"If I'm right, we have less than nine days."

———

Arthur Van Camp seldom ventured outside the range of a convenient gun—one that he could pick up at any moment. With his position of power came a list of enemies of varying degrees and means, and while he doubted the eventuality of its use, he nonetheless kept it close.

He held the gun in his hand, feeling its weight. The Ruger P85 was a heavy gun—a brick, really. But he liked the solidness of it. It was the first time he'd removed the gun from the desk drawer in at least a year, and he didn't know why he felt the need to do so now, except that having it in his hand made him feel better than he had when he'd walked in that morning.

He'd spent some time in the office at his apartment before giving up and having his driver thread him through Atlanta's morning traffic to the massive house in Buckhead. The painting over the apartment fireplace refused to let him work without sending accusatory vibes in his direction. Still, he'd tried to sip his coffee and muscle his way through a few reports. In the end, his wife's painting forced him from his workspace.

As he placed the Ruger back in the drawer, he chuckled at the thought. When she was alive, she'd served as his sounding board, listening, withholding judgment, providing necessary insight. He missed that more than anything. But now, as she tried to speak to him through one of the few things he had left of her, he wouldn't listen. He wondered, as he picked up the most recent stack of financials, if that was what Alan was doing.

He thought there were things Alan wasn't telling him, and that was his own mistake. He'd selected Alan because of his stellar track record, his ability to maintain a cool head despite the nature of any conflagration that raged around them, and for the man's expendability. Van Camp's mistake, as he now saw it, was allowing Alan too much freedom. Such a loose reporting structure left the company vulnerable should Van Camp's man in charge of Project: Night House find the stresses of the position too much to bear.

Yet there were reasons for the current arrangement, and the need for that phrase that politicians tossed around: plausible deniability. Without the proper checks in place to make certain that Alan was acting within the established policies of the company, Van Camp would be able to tell a prosecutor, a grand jury, or whoever else might ask that Alan had acted outside of the scope of his duties, and that the man having access to company funds sufficient to finance such an endeavor was an oversight Van Camp would correct. He hoped it never came to that; he hoped it in the same fashion he considered the use of the Ruger in the drawer.

The problem was that Alan wasn't returning his calls. To be fair, Van Camp had left only two messages, and Alan had a number of irons in the fire. But he also knew Alan had stopped by the office recently, taking two appointments and then leaving.

He understood the stresses the man must be facing, considering his wife's condition. He of all people did not begrudge Alan the time he needed to get his head straight. However, everything they'd worked for over the last two years would culminate in a matter of days. Alan's crisis at home had come at a most inopportune time.

Among the standard reports on his desk were a number of papers that, when not in his immediate possession, resided in only one place: the large safe in the Buckhead home. Along with the files he'd procured a 1945 Mouton from the wine cellar. Of all the wines in his possession, the Mouton was most suited for the upcoming occasion. After securing the two items and then spending a few minutes with the key members of his staff, Van Camp left the house, leaving his staff wondering how much time would pass until he returned.

The file in front of him now—the one he hadn't reviewed in months, as the contents were firmly fixed in his memory—was a skeleton really. A combination of his first hasty notes and a subsequent fleshing out of the plan. Most of it preceded Alan's involvement, although several key features bore the man's mark. Among these was the Antarctica project.

Shackleton concerned Van Camp more than any other element, for the concrete reason that, at this point, he should have had the detonator in his hands, the one that would separate the ice shelf from the continent. According to the figures Alan had gathered, the result of such an activity would be catastrophic to the financial sector. Van Camp Enterprises stood to make more than $43 billion by this man-made "act of God," from a mixture of stock speculation, anticipated changes in commercial fishing patterns, and above all, a heightened interest in national security.

There was also the human element to consider. According to every model they had run, the separation of the ice shelf would produce a tsunami that would potentially strike China's coast. The researchers who had worked through the available data put the odds at forty-three percent. Not included in that scenario was the number of small islands—some of them inhabited—that fell inside the affected area. There was a part of him that did not think it inappropriate to offer a heartfelt prayer for those souls, or to ask his wife to speak in his stead. And should she choose not to do so, he would deal with it on his own.

Right now he had to consider the possibility of a different kind of tsunami, one that Alan had the potential to unleash. If that were to happen, Van Camp would find a way to deal with that too.

December 13, 2012, 1:09 P.M.

The thing about Tucson, Albert thought as he crawled out from beneath the 1972 Charger, was that it wasn't always hot. That revelation had come as something of a disappointment to him. After all, he'd selected Arizona because it was supposed to be hot. He wanted a heat that, without the proper sunglasses, would bake his eyeballs in their sockets. A heat that made breathing uncomfortable, that let him fry the proverbial egg on the sidewalk. But now, in mid-December, the temperature got down to the mid-forties at night. When he woke up in the morning he didn't want to have to put on a jacket to retrieve the newspaper from the end of the driveway. He wanted air-conditioning blasting 24/7 in defiance of a merciless sun. What he got, instead, was sweater weather in the morning and a pleasant breeze in the afternoon.

Albert had had a lot of time to think since the helicopter lifted him from a place colder than anything he'd imagined and ferried him to a small island, where they'd loaded him on a plane and sent him to Miami. Miami was warm; he should have stayed there. But something about the desert appealed to him.

He was forty-six and had spent thirty of those years in some of the coldest spots on the planet, drilling holes deep into frozen ground. For three decades his world was composed of bitter cold and screaming metal. He supposed that after a while, the body's ability to retain heat vanished like a battery that would no longer hold a charge.

He grabbed a rag and rubbed the oil from his hands as best he could. The Charger was one of three cars in his yard—the front yard, so that he was sure to tick off the neighbors—and the one that he loved working on most.

After they'd pulled him from the ice sheet, he'd taken to thinking about the direction his life had taken, how he'd contented himself with bearing up under the assault of the elements on the chance that he would be part of something big—something that would result in his never having to work again. Flying over icebergs with a mangled leg did much to put things in perspective for a man. He was almost grateful for the mishap that had severed some of the muscles in his calf, leaving him with a permanent limp. A clarifying moment, he called it.

He tossed the rag onto the hood of the car and thought about what to do next. The Charger needed a good deal of work still, but nothing like dropping a new engine into it last week. Everything from this point on was a walk in the park by comparison. In truth, anything short of getting an auger drill working in sub-zero temperatures was akin to a picnic.

He heard the screen door open.

"Albert," his wife called. "Someone's on the phone for you."

He raised his hand in acknowledgment. Since relocating to Tucson two months ago, he'd fielded the occasional call from his former company. They wanted him back in the field, and with the understanding that most of his former mates were now working for someone else, the money they'd dangled in front of him had been substantial. Still, nothing they'd said—or promised—had been powerful enough to present a serious threat to his airborne epiphany: that money didn't matter if you were too cold to enjoy it.

He took in a deep breath of air that, though cooler than he'd imagined, was a good deal more palatable than what he'd inhaled in Alaska or Antarctica. Then he went inside. She'd left the phone lying next to the cradle and he scooped it up.

"Yeah?"

"Albert?" came the voice from the other end. "Is this Albert?"

The thing that struck him right off was that, whoever owned the voice, it wasn't someone who worked for Sheffield Petroleum.

"It is," he said. "And you are?"

"Albert, this is Ruth. I'm Ben's wife. Ben Robinski?"

"Oh sure," Albert said. "How is old Ben?"

There was a pause on the other end of the line and Albert thought the phone might have cut out on him. They'd been having problems with the phone service the last few months. In some ways, it reminded him of growing up in Adelaide. They'd lost service a lot there.

"That's why I'm calling, Albert," Ruth said. "I haven't heard from Ben in months."

Albert took that in, along with the worry in the woman's voice. "Well, I wouldn't worry about it. From what I remember, the job we were on was supposed to last until the end of the month. You should hear from him anytime now."

His attempt at encouragement was greeted with silence.

Finally, she said, "I've called fifteen people. You're the first person to even acknowledge my husband was on a team somewhere."

Albert was a man accustomed to dealing with simple things. It was cold outside so one wore a coat. The drill broke so one fixed it.

But women were complicated, hence he seldom engaged them in conversation. He'd gotten lucky in that his Andrea wasn't complicated. She liked the same simple things he did.

"Look," he said. "I don't know what to tell you. I ain't with the team anymore because my leg was ripped up in one of the drills. But I remember Ben talking about you all the time. He'll come back, you'll see."

"Albert, if there's anything you can do to help me find out where Ben is . . ."

Through the phone he heard what sounded like crying.

"Sure," he said. "I'll make a call or two, alright?"

After several seconds of silence, Ruth thanked him, gave him a number where she could be reached, then said good-bye.

Albert hung up the phone and turned around to see Andrea staring at him.

"What was that about? Not another woman with her eye on my Albert, is it?"

He grinned. "So what if it is?"

They spent the rest of the afternoon addressing that question, and somewhere along the way, Albert forgot about Ben Robinski.

———

They were cleared to head home.

Maddy, her wound bandaged and her arm held in a sling to keep from aggravating the injury, hadn't argued when Brent removed her luggage from her free hand and carried it along with his own to the chopper, where he helped her climb aboard.

Now they were waiting again, but rather than the single unit of marines surrounding the hospital, in the neighborhood of a thousand officers occupied the base, providing Brent and Maddy with what the professor thought was sufficient protection to guard against a second attack.

When they first arrived at the base, a doctor removed the bandages applied by their Afghan counterparts and gave the army captain a thorough examination, using equipment not available to indigenous medical personnel. According to Maddy, who relayed the results to Brent, the base doctors had conceded a grudging respect for the work of the locals.

They would take a military transport back to the States—an enormous Airbus that Brent could see through the windows of the waiting area. He hoped that he and Maddy wouldn't be the only passengers.

Maddy, who seemed to have intuited Brent's thoughts, said, "It may go back empty, but it'll return fully loaded. It won't be a wasted trip."

Feeling fidgety over the events of the last twenty-four hours, Brent had taken to pacing the room. Now he stopped and glanced over at his traveling companion. The captain was sitting down with her head tilted back, eyes closed.

"You can stop doing that," he said with mock gruffness. "The only one allowed inside my head is me."

Maddy smiled but didn't open her eyes.

"It takes you ten steps to cross the room," she said. "And you've been pacing for so long that I've gotten used to the rhythm." She opened her eyes and straightened her head. "Since you started, you've only stopped twice. The first time was at five steps, which would have put you right in front of the windows, at which point you said the same thing that everyone who sees an A400M for the first time says: 'It's big.' Not very original."

At Brent's frown she offered a wink.

"The second time you stopped was just now, again at five steps, which means you were watching out the window again."

Brent nodded in acknowledgment. Then he crossed his arms and said, "Okay, so you knew I was looking at the plane. How did you know I was thinking about what a waste it is to fly something that big across the ocean just for the two of us?"

Maddy gave the professor a smug look. "You drink a lot of soda, but I haven't once seen you throw a can in the trash—always the recycle bin. I've seen you hold onto an empty can until you can find a bin to put it in. Then there's your paper usage. You use almost all of it—even the margins once both sides are full." She chuckled. "A guy who will carry around an empty Mountain Dew can with him for an hour would definitely have an issue with the amount of fuel it's going to require to get us home."

Brent had no response for several ticks of the loud clock hanging on the wall next to a battered vending machine. Then he released a genuine laugh and, once he was done, shook his head.

"The observational skills of a true scientist," he said.

"No, the observational skills of a bored woman who is just a little buzzed on whatever painkiller they gave me before I left," she answered.

Brent slipped into the seat next to her. "How are you feeling?" he asked.

"Pretty good, actually."

For the last day—except for the time spent developing his new theory, sharing the details with Colonel Richards over the phone so his team could begin researching while they were in transit—Brent found himself thinking a lot about Amy Madigan. An experience like the firefight had a tendency to create an emotional bond where one might not have normally existed. Yet he believed it to be more than that. For some reason, the army captain was insinuating herself into his thoughts—and he didn't know if he liked that or not.

She'd gone quiet, and Brent thought she might be falling asleep, so it surprised him when she spoke again.

"Why did you choose your father's path instead of your mother's?"

Brent didn't understand the question right away and wondered if the medication Maddy mentioned might now be kicking in. Then it came to him, and when he understood what the question referred to, he fielded dueling responses: irritation, and gratitude that she cared enough to ask.

"I could ask you the same thing," he said. "Except that we both know the answer."

When she returned a puzzled look, he explained.

"You're a Christian because your parents were. It's all you knew when you were a kid."

It looked as if she was about to object, but Brent cut her off.

"Has it ever occurred to you to wonder why the odds that a person embraces Christianity depend almost entirely on where that person is born?" he asked. "If you're born in Saudi Arabia, the chances of your embracing Christianity are next to none, but it's pretty certain that you'll practice Islam. It's the same no matter where you go. That's social dynamics. Religion is more cultural than mystical."

He hadn't meant for any of this to come out with the edge he suspected it had, and he gave Maddy an apologetic smile, even if he wasn't sorry for his beliefs.

"It just seems pretty telling that all over the world people practice different religions, and all of those people think they have it right. It's the height of arrogance to claim that your religion is the right one and everyone else is wrong."

Maddy smiled. "You haven't answered my question. Even if you're right, and a person's faith depends on where they were born and grew up, why did you pass on it?"

Brent had to concede that he hadn't answered her question, even though he thought he'd made a pretty good argument for a logical dismissal of not just Christianity but any faith. He felt a wave of combativeness rising in him, the same as when one of his believing family members raised the topic. There hadn't been a single instance in which he felt he'd lost a religious debate. But now, in a foreign country and in the company of Amy Madigan, he realized he didn't want to have an argument. Instead, he wanted her to understand.

Just then a soldier entered the waiting area, and seeing a civilian and an officer from another branch of the military, he hesitated and then offered a cordial nod before slipping coins into the vending machine. A candy bar fell, was scooped up, and the man was gone.

In the intervening silence Brent looked over at Maddy, only to find that she'd again closed her eyes. He almost used that as a cue to let the matter drop, but he found that he didn't want to do that.

"I think I was eight," he said, glad to see Maddy's eyes open when he spoke. "My father was watching a program on PBS—one of those where a cameraman and some guy who's an expert in something spend a few weeks with a tribe native to somewhere that seems really far away when you're in third grade."

"I like those," Maddy said with a nod.

"My dad did too," Brent said, smiling at the memory. Then he frowned and looked her in the eye. "Did I tell you my father was a sociologist?"

She shook her head. "No, but it was in your file."

Her response gave Brent pause as he wondered what else might be in that file, but he shook it off.

"I remember sitting down on the couch next to him and watching it for a while. And the thing I remember about the show was a ceremony the cameraman got to shoot. It was an elevation ritual. Normally it's a pretty private affair, yet for some reason this tribe let this British team in and they taped the whole thing. There was some witch doctor guy with a very large knife, doing what, at eight years old, I couldn't imagine a human being doing to another."

He saw Maddy shiver at the thought.

"And when I glanced up at my father, he was looking at me, like he was waiting for the question."

"What question?" Maddy prompted.

"Well," Brent said, "nothing I'd heard in church prepared me for what I saw that day—what some guy with a bone necklace and scars down both cheeks did to a bunch of kids. And the thing I kept thinking was that the kids weren't much older than I was." The professor shook his head at the memory.

"So my dad explains what's going on, how this is a ritual designed to appease whatever god these people worshiped, and for a kid raised in the Baptist church, let me tell you, it was quite an eye-opener. But do you know the most vivid memory I have from watching that program?"

Maddy did not and signified so with a single headshake.

"My father's arm around me the whole time. The man loved me, I was certain of it. And once I realized that, it was like I had the green light to sift through things on my own."

The professor might have said more, but his seat afforded him a view of the plane and he saw the propellers begin their spinning, which would carry him and Maddy over the ocean. Ten seconds later, a private entered the waiting area and signaled that it was time for them to board.

December 14, 2012, 9:33 A.M.

Alan Canfield knew all about lines. For years, as he'd navigated his way up the ladder at Van Camp Enterprises, he'd measured success by recognizing which lines he could cross and which ones he best respect and leave alone. Although the last few years had done much to blur his respect for lines, in each instance he'd justified his actions, resetting the lines with the authority granted him by his position. However, even he knew that what he'd set in motion crossed a line impossible to uncross, speaking some profound word of finality on the stakes of the project.

One did not murder an American military officer, and attempt the same on another, without repercussions. At this point he knew the cleanup operation in Balkh had failed, though he thought it might give the NIIU pause. And he also knew something he hadn't before the attack, namely that only one of his targets was military. The other was a civilian consultant.

Nonetheless, the deeds were done, which meant that he had to intuit how things would unfold from that point onward. He harbored no delusions that the attacks would dissuade this team from their investigation. On the contrary, what he'd hoped to accomplish was the refocusing of their investigation on standard terrorist targets. All he needed was for them to remain occupied for eight more days. After that, they could navigate their investigation to the doorway of Van Camp Enterprises for all he cared. For if Canfield could pull it off, the CEO of the company, the one responsible for the entire operation, would be dead.

What he couldn't do was continue his absence from the office for the intervening time period. To that point, he could chalk up his failure to return his boss's calls to the extraordinary number of things on his plate, including his wife's condition. Under normal circumstances few employers would begrudge a subordinate the time necessary to deal with such a grave family issue. However, Arthur Van Camp was not most men, and the duties assigned to Alan were of paramount importance.

Still, absolution was not what Canfield sought. Instead, he hoped for a general sense of disappointment from Van Camp. Disappointment was acceptable. It did not intimate suspicion.

The elevator deposited Canfield on the forty-third floor, where it was a short walk to his office. He failed to acknowledge his administrative assistant, who seemed surprised to see him but who quickly donned the proper sympathetic look in honor of Canfield's wife. Once in his office he closed the door and set the file he was carrying on his desk. Before sitting, he went to a file cabinet, inserted a key, and found a bottle of bourbon secreted beneath a collection of old documents. Unlike Van Camp, who was allowed to keep his liquor in the open, Canfield had to partake on the sly. He uncapped the bottle and poured some into the ice-filled Styrofoam cup he'd brought with him. He took a long sip. Then he crossed to the window and looked down on the city below. While his office offered a magnificent view, Van Camp's offered a much better one.

And the successful completion of Project: Night House was the key to that better office. With that thought in mind he left the window and went to his desk, sitting and opening the topmost file: a brief dossier with a photo attached.

Colonel Jameson Richards had a wife named Emily and a daughter who lived in Seattle. Her name was Molly.

In the next file, Captain Jim Rawlings. Divorced and with custody of a son, who was seven.

David Addison was married with no children, while Sylvester Bradford had five children with his wife—Connie was her name.

Captain Amy Madigan had a sister in Vegas. Other than her sibling, she had no immediate family that he'd unearthed, although she did visit a grandmother in a retirement home in Cleveland a few times a year.

Dr. Brent Michaels, the sociologist who was on the verge of bringing the whole operation down on Van Camp's head, had no immediate family. In fact, beyond his university job, Michaels didn't seem to have any attachments at all.

Canfield studied the rest of the names on the list, minus one Anton Petros. It was possible that what he'd done so far would buy him the time he needed, but he couldn't count on that. He had to be prepared, which meant knowing the enemy. The problem with that was there were a growing number of people fitting that description. And he didn't know if he could identify all of them.

He lifted the Styrofoam cup and took another drink.

———

A tranquil domestic household did much to make a man forget about life's ills. Albert wasn't sure where he'd heard that little nugget, but he couldn't argue with it. He couldn't remember a moment in the last twenty years in which he'd been more content than he was now. Who'd have thought it all came down to heat and a good woman? He said as much to Andrea as his newly awakened wife snuggled in the crook of his arm.

"It's because people overthink things," he explained. When relaxed, the South London accent—almost lost after so long living among Americans—really came out. "Keep it simple. That's what I always say."

Andrea tipped her head so she could see his face. "I love it when you let your accent have its way."

He grinned at the mirroring of his own thoughts. It was true; were he to meet up with his mates, they would give him a brutal ribbing, tell him he'd been Americanized.

"I was thinking the same about you, love," he said.

She snuggled in closer, and after a few minutes he thought she'd gone back to sleep. He tried to follow suit and had almost succeeded when her question brought him back.

"Who was the woman on the phone yesterday?" she asked.

Drowsy as he was, it took a moment for Albert to remember what his wife meant.

"Someone named Ruth. Said she was married to Ben—one of the men on the Antarctica job."

"And . . . ?" Andrea pressed.

"And what?"

"Well, what did she want?"

"She said she hasn't heard from him since he left for Antarctica. I guess she's worried about him."

"I don't blame her," Andrea said. "If you were gone for three months without a word, I'd be out of my mind with worry."

"What makes you think you're not already out of your mind?" he said, then kissed her on the top of her head.

"I'm in Arizona with a man who has three broken-down cars in the front yard. Of course I'm out of my mind."

He laughed, closing his eyes to resume what he hoped would be a quick jaunt back to sleep.

"So are you going to call?"

His eyes popped open again. "Call who?"

"How would I know? I heard you tell this poor woman you were going to make a call or two."

"Oh, that," Albert said. "Alright then. I'll do that later today."

This time he didn't close his eyes. Twenty years of marriage had granted him the ability to feel it in her body before the words left her mouth. Even so, she almost lulled him into a sense of complacency by holding it in for a half minute or so, until he began to think it might have been a false alarm.

"If I were that poor woman—"

"*Alright,*" he said. With a grunt he removed his arm from beneath her head and got out of bed, grumbling all the way to the kitchen. He had to wade through the mountain of papers, note pads, and various other items on the kitchen table before he found the address book.

In thirty minutes he'd ascertained quite a bit. One was that few people liked getting phone calls before ten in the morning. Another was that none of the real friends he'd had on the Antarctica job—no offense to Ben Robinski—had been heard from either. And a third was that regardless of the fact that he'd submitted a workman's comp claim to the number he'd been given, he had yet to receive a red cent.

"What kind of operation do they have running here?" he asked himself as he sat on the wobbly chair between the table and the refrigerator.

———

Until that morning Brent had always thought of himself as a coffee snob. He usually bought the more expensive darker blends, and while he appreciated the drink's ability to pick him up when he needed it, he was no addict. That morning, though, it performed only one function: fuel.

When the plane landed last night, he suffered through a mercifully short debriefing at the hands of the colonel and accepted a ride to his hotel, where he collapsed into a dreamless sleep until Richards called to wake him. Maddy, having been cleared by the base medical staff in Afghanistan, was able to fight off the colonel's request that she be transported directly to the hospital and instead slept in her own bed.

Looking across the table at her, in uniform but still sporting the sling, he saw that she looked as tired as he felt. He took another sip of the bitter brew.

In one sense, the room's atmosphere reminded Brent of the coauthoring sessions he'd undertaken back when he was trying to get his name out there, collaborating on a book with a well-known name and scholar in order to enhance his own career. He'd work until he couldn't mumble a coherent word, then collapse for a few hours before rising to do it all over again. In this case, though, the room also contained a somber air—the specter of their fallen friend.

"What I don't understand," Rawlings said, "is how people can let themselves be led around by the nose."

Although Brent had given Richards an overview of his new theory—that some entity was nudging the world into panic for the purpose of profiteering from it—they'd done little groundwork. Most of the energy spent in this building over the last few days had gone into investigating the murder of Anton Petros. The professor understood the need to do right by the man, but the part of him that saw the big picture knew that their time should be focused on the broader investigation.

"What I mean is, why do people take everything they see on TV as gospel? Some newsperson says something and everyone just eats it up." Rawlings paused as if considering his own words, then shook his head and said, "And it's not just television. I can't believe the number of people who read something on an Internet message board and buy into it without any critical thought."

Brent kept a sardonic chuckle to himself. "People have a need to think that something bigger than themselves is going on." When Rawlings answered with a puzzled look, Brent added, "For most of human history, people had gods to believe in. It gave them the assurance that something existed that transcended their own small, pathetic experience. Since World War II, though, God's slowly been taking a backseat, and that's leaving people scrambling for something else to latch on to."

"What does God have to do with World War II?" Maddy asked.

"Nothing." Then he paused and said, "Or maybe everything. Who really knows? What I'm trying to say is that World War II saw the juxtaposition of two events that have shaped the American collective consciousness. The first was the move toward secularism—humanism, scientific inquiry, that sort of thing. The second . . . well, that *is* tied to the war."

Brent enjoyed an audience, which was why he'd ended up teaching. As he looked around the table now, he saw some of the same interested expressions he could pick out among his students back at the university.

"The bomb," he said.

"What? You mean nukes?" Snyder asked.

"The Manhattan Project," Brent said. "If you look back through the history of the presidency, you can argue that the Manhattan Project was the event that solidified the federal secrecy concept." At registering the non-grasping faces around the table, he said, "I'm sure most of you are aware that the project was such a secret that not even the vice-president knew about it, right? In fact, the level of infrastructure that had to be created to keep it all quiet was a pretty big accomplishment, logistically speaking."

"Right," Rawlings said. "But what does that have to do with the gullibility of the American public?"

"Everything," Brent said. "Think about it. For more than a hundred and fifty years people went about their lives assured—probably naïvely—that the government was acting in their best interests. At the same time, they had the secondary assurance that even if the government took a misstep, they could count on providential design. Then all of a sudden you get something like the bomb, along with professors and scientists telling you that God is dead, and you're left wondering if everything you've ever been told is a lie."

He saw a few lights go on.

"I guess that would be a scary place to be if you're not used to it," Maddy mused.

"Is it any wonder people see conspiracies everywhere?" Brent asked. "Or that some people can buy into just about anything someone says?"

Maddy frowned at that.

"I would think it would be just the opposite," she said. "Wouldn't never knowing who was telling you the truth force you to think critically?"

Brent was smiling and shaking his head before she'd finished the question. "Most people don't want to do the heavy lifting. They just want something to believe in."

In the silence that followed, Rawlings jumped to the logical conclusion.

"So this polarizing event you mentioned—that has to be something like a terrorist attack, right?"

Brent understood the underpinnings for that line of reasoning.

As a military man, Rawlings was wired to think that way. And in truth, something like 9/11 made the most sense to him too.

He'd discussed it with the colonel that morning, before the rest of the team arrived. And the big problem with the idea was that, according to the colonel, there was no chatter on any of the terrorist networks that would indicate an imminent attack. Brent shared that with Rawlings now.

The man frowned. "A domestic act wouldn't show up on the terrorist hotline."

Brent didn't know enough about how those hotlines worked to form an opinion, so he took Rawlings's statement as the truth. Still, he didn't think another Timothy McVeigh lurked out there, waiting for a signal to unleash hell. For one thing, by his understanding, no domestic group had ever shown the ability to conduct operations overseas to the extent necessary to account for the number of events in the data set. Americans had a leg up in a lot of things, but seeding terrorist cells throughout the world was not one of them.

"Look, I don't think the methodology the government uses to locate prospective terrorists before they strike will work here," he said. "You have to think differently. Think like some rich guy who wants to make an anonymous statement on December twenty-first."

"It would help if we knew who the rich guy was," Maddy said. "Or rich *person*, so as not to be sexist."

"We've already been down that road," Brent said. "You're the one who said that investigating stock rolls was time-consuming. And we don't have a whole lot of time."

Maddy didn't answer. On the flight back from Afghanistan they'd discussed how to develop a short list of candidates, and Maddy had suggested a canvassing of the stock market to find any individuals or entities who had experienced unusual growth. She quickly dismissed the thought, though, as she considered the logistics of such a thing in the eight days that remained.

Brent, who wanted to err on the side of caution, said, "That doesn't eliminate the need to find some way to develop a list of rich men—or women—who have the wherewithal and general meanness to ravage the world for profit."

"Meanness casts a wide net," Maddy said. "But throw tremendous wealth in there and we should have a short list."

"So let me see if I have this, Dr. Michaels," Colonel Richards said. "We have eight days to not only find out who is responsible for manipulating puzzle pieces all around the world to produce a profit, but also to uncover some pending event that will cause massive destruction and probable deaths if it's allowed to happen. Does that about sum it up?"

Were this his first experience with the man, Brent would have withered beneath the sternness of both the colonel's words and eyes. However, ten days spent in his orbit had given the professor a better understanding of the man, enough so he could locate the slight trace of humor in the man's words.

"That's it in a nutshell," Brent agreed.

The colonel harrumphed and offered a headshake. Then he sent his eyes over the rest of his team, as well as the civilian who had been brought on for a short consult but who it seemed had fused, at least temporarily, into the group.

"Maddy, I need you to work Homeland Security and get them to leverage the SEC. They can go through the stock records a lot quicker than we can. And tell the HS guys we want Level 4 security on this."

Maddy nodded and the colonel moved on.

"Snyder, did that explosives report come in yet?"

"Yes, sir. The chemical signature of the PTEN traces back to a production facility in Vancouver." He riffled through some pages on the table in front of him, finding one with a section circled with a highlighter. "They had a shipment go missing three months ago. They suspected the driver was in on it but couldn't prove anything, so they canned the guy."

"Did the shipment cross the border?"

Snyder nodded.

The colonel pursed his lips a moment and then said, "Ask Homeland Security to put some pressure on the driver. See if he can give us a name."

Brent could almost feel the man's distaste for having to ask for assistance from Homeland Security, but even Brent understood that the military's ability to conduct investigations on civilians was minimal. Only HS had the clearances and the reach to push Richards's agenda.

"The rest of you," Richards said. "I want you to turn over every stone you can think of and find this polarizing event. If it's going to happen in eight days, I refuse to believe that we can't find it. You can't hide something that big."

After a last look around the table, Colonel Richards dismissed everyone and then stood and left the room.

December 15, 2012, 9:14 A.M.

As Dabir navigated the busy sidewalks of downtown Atlanta, he did his best to keep from succumbing to the urge to consider the sights and sounds through the eyes of a tourist. Unlike most of his countrymen, he had the benefit of having traveled a great deal, including his schooling in London, but even he was not immune to the sheer size of the city, the diversity of its people, the loudness of it all. In many ways it was like one of the many bazaars in his part of the world, except on a much grander scale. The chief benefit was that a place this size granted him the anonymity he needed.

Indeed, it was not just the size of the city that lent him that veil. He'd found that as he strode the sidewalks, people there didn't bother to look at him, even if he passed close by. Feeling like something of a ghost, he stopped and hailed a cab.

One of the truths of any major city was that within it one could find a pocket of virtually any people group. It hadn't taken him long to find his people, or to solicit the name of someone who could facilitate a business transaction.

Exiting the cab two blocks away from his destination offered him the opportunity to familiarize himself with this part of town, as well as avoid revealing the destination to anyone checking records for the taxicab company. While the Eritrean community in this southern metropolis paled in comparison to those in other large American cities, it gratified him to see how they had claimed a portion of the city for themselves, preserving culture and community amid a sea of influences.

The business he sought was nondescript, occupying the corner of a two-story building that ran the length of the block. When Dabir had received its name, he checked it against the Yellow Pages at the front desk of his hotel, but did not find it listed. He suspected that was because no one searching for a pawnshop would come to this neighborhood unless they lived there. And anyone who lived there would know of the pawnshop.

Before entering he took a few additional steps to glance down the cross street, only to find it an alley that met a crumbling concrete wall some fifty feet away. A battered green dumpster sat flush against the wall of the building, and Dabir saw a trio of men huddled in the far corner, where the concrete wall and the next building met.

Finally he entered the shop. There was only one other customer, a man combing through a bin of used DVDs. Looking past him, Dabir saw the proprietor. He was in Western dress, and except for the clothes could have been lifted from any street in Dabir's more familiar world.

Dabir went to the counter and addressed the man in their common language.

"Honored sir, I come on the word of Mahmud, who says you are able to supply that which others cannot."

The shopkeeper didn't respond but instead called out to the

other customer and ordered him to leave at once. Without a word of complaint the man hurried away, exiting out the front door. It was only after the door had swung shut behind him that the shopkeeper returned his attention to Dabir.

"And you would have?"

"A Taurus 627," Dabir said with no hesitation.

The shopkeeper ran a clinical eye over Dabir, who was dressed in a new pair of jeans and a plain white shirt. "Eight hundred," he said.

Dabir's eyes narrowed at the markup for a weapon that, had he the necessary paper work, he could purchase for $450. But had he the necessary paper work, he would not be reliant on this man.

"Done," Dabir said, and the man on the other side of the counter showed only mild surprise. "I trust you have it in stock."

The shopkeeper returned a slow nod but did not move from his spot. He would not produce the gun until his customer handed over the agreed-upon sum.

But rather than reach for his wallet, which courtesy of Standish/Canfield, contained more than enough to meet the man's terms, Dabir placed his hands on the countertop and leaned in closer.

"There is something else," he said. "I require a CheyTac M100."

At this request the shopkeeper took a step back. He studied the man in front of him and then shook his head. "I have nothing of that quality here."

"Then you will have one sent," Dabir said, his tone firm.

At some point during the exchange, the power had shifted from shopkeeper to customer.

After a long pause, the man nodded and said, "I can have one in three days."

Dabir considered that, wondering if he could wait that long. "I would prefer two," he said with something close to a smile.

"I will do my best, but I am dependent upon my suppliers for such an order."

Dabir nodded and then asked him the price, knowing the man would weigh his desire for profit against his instincts for self-preservation, and in doing so advance a figure that would benefit them both.

"I can have one here for seven thousand dollars," he said.

Dabir thought he could accomplish the feat for five thousand, but he did not say as much. The man deserved to profit from his work. Dabir would not hold that against him. He fished his wallet from his pants and paid for the gun he would take with him, leaving a deposit for the other.

———

In Albert's opinion, the fact that he hadn't worked on the Charger in almost forty-eight hours was his wife's fault. Had she not badgered him into making some phone calls, he might have remained blissfully ignorant of the things that now bothered him about the Antarctica job.

Albert had a penchant for dismissing from his mind anything with the potential to disturb his otherwise tranquil lifestyle. A jury summons? Lost beneath the mountain of mail on the kitchen table. A planned dinner with the couple down the street, whom his wife was keen on striking up a friendship with? Forgotten in favor of a trip to the hardware store. The fact that he hadn't yet received a workman's comp check? Barely worth noticing.

The problem was that the more calls he made, the more this thing took on too solid of a shape to dismiss in favor of the Charger. For Albert's concern wasn't only about the whereabouts of Ben Robinski but the issue of his missing checks. Now that his wife had forced him to give the matter his attention, he couldn't just forget it. Instead, it would nag at him relentlessly—that is, until he got to the bottom of things.

The big issue was that, while Sheffield Petroleum was a monstrous corporation with holdings all over the world, with drilling operations in nearly every geographical area where it was possible to set up a drill, the people he'd spoken with insisted there was no crew in Antarctica, nor had there been in quite some time. To make matters worse, it seemed no one had ever heard of Miles Standish, the man who'd recruited Albert. It was the sort of wall that Albert didn't know how to climb. He'd expected a runaround on his compensation checks. That was only natural. But to have the company refuse to even acknowledge he'd worked for them? That was an entirely different matter, and a puzzling one at that.

The impasse forced him to do something he rarely did: he cleared enough of the junk away from the computer to reach the power button, and as the machine booted up he repeated the process until he had unimpeded access to the keyboard. It took almost five minutes before the ancient machine reached a state where he could access the Internet. Then he spent the next half hour searching for information about the company, specifically an employee directory. Soon he came across an interactive map that listed all their active drill sites. Albert noticed Antarctica didn't have any blinking red dots on it. What he couldn't find was a company directory. After thinking for a moment he returned to the search engine and entered the name Miles Standish. He was elated when the computer came back with several references to the mysterious Mr. Standish.

"Now we're getting somewhere," he said.

It took him only a short time to realize that the Miles Standish the computer had located for him could not possibly be his man, seeing as this one had died in 1656. And that he had something to do with the pilgrims.

With a sigh Albert pushed away from the computer.

Up to now he'd given little thought to the Antarctica job—a job that, for him, was cut short as he was forced to evacuate for medical reasons. On some level he'd understood that the whole thing was a bit off, even if the mechanics of it were simple: drill a shaft, drop a charge. He just hadn't given much thought as to why Sheffield Petroleum needed a few hundred miles' worth of shafts, as well as enough explosives to sink the continent. Consequently, once the chopper pulled him off the ice, he'd rid himself of such questions.

In retrospect he wondered if the reason none of the Sheffield people seemed to know about the Antarctica job was because it had been a secret one, not on the list of official projects. That would explain a lot.

The problem was how to approach a company as large as Sheffield Petroleum with any hope of earning a helpful response. He gave that some thought yet nothing jumped out at him. He decided such weighty cogitation required the proper fuel, so he stood, stretched, and went to the refrigerator for a beer. It was as he was downing the first sip that the thought came to him.

"Andrea, what's the name of our congressman?"

"Cooper," she called from the living room.

"Cooper," he said to himself. "Okay then. We'll just see what those crooks at Sheffield Petroleum have to say when a congressman gets involved."

His wife appeared over his shoulder as he found the representative's website, located the constituency feedback form, and began to type a message. Andrea watched him for a while, and about a minute in, Albert felt a hand on his shoulder.

"I didn't realize how computer savvy you are," she said. When he glanced at her, he saw the same look on her face he'd seen the other day when he'd forgotten all about poor Ben Robinski.

"Not now, woman," he said. "I've built up a proper righteous indignation and I don't want to waste it."

He turned back to typing and felt Andrea's other hand come down on his other shoulder.

"Political activism too," she said. "I barely know who you are anymore, love."

He couldn't help but chuckle, especially as her fingers touched that ticklish spot on the back of his neck. He shook her off, though he didn't put much into it.

"Hold your horses," he said. "Or would you rather I not find a way to get those checks you've been on me about?"

That got her attention, but it only stopped her advances for a short time. Fortunately it was just long enough for Albert.

————

The thing that struck Brent the most as he sat in Colonel Richards's office was that this second experience was a good deal different than his first, when the colonel had, in his own subdued fashion, wowed the visiting professor. After all, during what other job interview could the man doing the interviewing ignore a fire in order to fully vet a qualified candidate?

The thing that made this visit a bit unusual was the colonel's body language. As Brent watched him, the way he sat, the way he put his hands on the desk and then immediately withdrew them, he seemed committed to discussing something that he didn't want to discuss. Brent, who had taken a psychology class or two on his way to earning his degree, theorized that the colonel was caught between a sense of duty and one of profound discomfort, yet he felt convicted enough about the topic to press on anyway.

The colonel shifted in his seat again, leaning forward and placing both hands around a cup of tea with the tea bag still in evidence.

"Dr. Michaels, we've been so busy since you returned from Afghanistan that I haven't thanked you for what you did for Captain Madigan," Richards said.

The statement caught Brent off guard. Judging from the colonel's discomfort, something like a simple thanks seemed to lack the punch necessary for the moment.

"I'm not sure thanks are warranted," Brent said. "Without Maddy slamming my head into a table, I probably wouldn't be here."

That drew a hint of a smile from Richards, with Brent coming to realize that a minimal curl of the lip from this man was the equivalent of a full-blown laugh from most others. Despite that, Richards shook his head.

"According to the report—and Amy—you took out at least two of them. And a firefight on foreign soil is far beyond the terms of your consult."

"Self-preservation will make a guy do crazy things," Brent answered with a grin, one that failed to penetrate the colonel's demeanor, as evidenced by the now-vanished smile.

"Dr. Michaels, I may be overstepping my bounds, but you have to realize that each and every one of these people is, for lack of a better word, family. What happens to one happens to all of us."

The colonel stopped and surveyed Brent, as if to see if the professor was tracking with him. A nod from Brent signified he was.

"It hasn't escaped my attention that you and Captain Madigan have become close during your time with us," Richards said, and in a flash Brent understood the real reason for the meeting, as well as for the colonel's discomfort. In fact, now that he knew what this was about, he felt a bit uncomfortable himself.

"I suppose that can happen when you spend a significant amount of time with someone," Brent said.

But the expression on Richards's face said he was not satisfied with the response.

"Amy has been my liaison for a good many outside consultants," Richards said. "And I can assure you that this one is a bit different."

The colonel let that hang there as he watched Brent, with the professor growing increasingly more uncomfortable under the scrutiny. For some odd reason he felt the need to apologize. And since he didn't like that feeling, he chose to get some kind of foothold in the conversation.

"Colonel, if you have something to say, then just come out and say it."

"Without trying to sound like Amy's father, I'm curious as to your intentions."

"I'm not sure I follow you."

The colonel held his stony gaze for another few seconds before allowing it to dissolve into a sigh. "You have to understand—Maddy has been a member of my team for many years, and consequently I've assumed what I can only describe as a parental concern, however inappropriate that might be."

Brent only nodded.

"What complicates things is that Maddy and I attend the same church." The colonel paused and fixed Brent with a hard look. "I'm sure that by now you're aware of the importance the captain places on her faith?"

Again a nod from Brent, although with wider eyes.

"My guess, Dr. Michaels, is that you're one of the few men Maddy has met who can keep up with her intellectually. Did you know that she received an invitation to fill a senior researcher position with NASA? That alone should tell you how bright she is."

Then the colonel allowed silence to fill the room, perhaps weighing what he would say next. After a while he continued, "Usually the consultants we hire come here, do what we ask, and then take their paycheck and leave. Most of them we never see again. And the defining characteristic of most of these people is a lack of personality, which seems common among those with doctoral degrees."

Brent had to chuckle at that.

"But for some reason Maddy has attached herself to you, and my concern is that you don't understand the significance of that."

Brent understood the backhanded compliment implied by the colonel's words.

"With all due respect, Colonel, I'm well aware of the captain's religious beliefs. And I've been nothing but honest with her about my own."

The colonel didn't ask him to expound on the nature of those beliefs, but Brent suspected he already knew. Instead, Richards broached another topic almost as sacrosanct as religion.

"Why aren't you married, Dr. Michaels?" Richards asked.

The question caught Brent more off guard than he would have thought possible. He knew that he didn't have to answer it—that it had nothing to do with the consult—and yet he felt as if he were somehow a knight of old defending a lady's honor.

"I guess I've just never met the right woman," he said.

"Which is likely the same reason Maddy would give if I posed the same question to her."

"Well, Maddy and I *are* both adults. Even in the military, I'm pretty sure she has the option of dating whomever she wants."

It took Brent several seconds, and the colonel's half smile, before he realized that he may have said something incriminating. And in reviewing his statement he suspected he'd found it.

"We're not dating, Colonel," he said. "Not even close."

In the colonel's eyes, Brent recognized triumph. But he also saw a weariness of sorts, as if constantly spreading his personal resources to cover both external and internal threats had exacted a toll on the man. The revelation made Brent reconsider anything he'd said that could have combated Richards's observations.

"I assure you that I have no ungentlemanlike intentions as far as Maddy's concerned," Brent said. "If my field has taught me anything, it's that personal beliefs are not easily trifled with. And if my relationship with Maddy continues beyond the consult, I promise I won't do anything that would put her in conflict with her faith."

Even as he said it, Brent understood that he was making a promise he might not be able to keep. Few things were more important to someone in his field than the truth. And were he to come to believe that Amy Madigan's faith lacked that essential element required of a belief system, he knew he would call her on it.

He suspected the colonel knew it too, which explained why, when the professor left the man's office, he felt the eyes on his back.

December 15, 2012, 12:10 P.M.

Brent's primary thought as he sat at the table that had become as familiar to him as his desk back at the university was an understanding that despite the vast resources of the federal government, and the new cooperative atmosphere touted among the various branches of the military and civilian organizations, pinpointing the source of a global threat was akin to finding a needle in a haystack.

From all the reports to which he'd been privy, there was nothing that anyone could point to that spoke of a global conspiracy tied to the Mayan 2012 phenomenon. Brent put little stock in that, because it would be difficult for anyone reviewing large swaths of data to avoid having their preconceptions compromised by a knowledge of what they were looking for. He was becoming convinced that the only way they would locate his polarizing event was to stumble upon it—to find something within a particular data set that at first they would find themselves unable to qualify—and only later would they realize it pointed to the thing they'd been looking for.

He was in his assigned office, and of course Maddy was there. It was the first time he'd seen her since his conversation with Richards that morning. If nothing else, he was gratified to learn that the dialogue between them had not found its way to Maddy, who reacted to him in the manner she always had, which was somewhere between a corporate professional and a schoolgirl crush. The troubling thing was that he felt the same way. But Richards had called him on any designs he might have, and that left Brent considering how to proceed.

The good thing was that Brent understood that the seriousness of their investigation superseded anything between them. Even so, that didn't make sitting in a room with her any easier.

Fortunately, Rawlings also occupied a place at the table, which forced Brent to concentrate on the business at hand. And with only six days in which to discover the polarizing event, the professor found that the distraction caused by Rawlings was for the benefit of them all.

Brent glanced over at Maddy, who with a laptop in front of her was studying a steady stream of news stories, working the keyboard with her good arm. Now that a tentative connection had been established between the incidents the team had investigated and the approaching 2012 phenomenon, Brent hoped that a thorough study of the data would reveal something they might have missed. A too hopeful stance perhaps, but one he had to take with the calendar mocking him.

He was settling back into his own work, reexamining the graphs he'd started to develop his first day on the job which had grown increasingly complex the more he worked on them, when Colonel Richards entered the room.

"There's been a coup in Cuba," Richards said.

All eyes went to the man standing in the doorway.

"The Fifth Battalion marched into Havana this morning,"

Richards continued. "In less than an hour they had control of every governmental agency, and if we're to believe the reports, they did so without firing a shot."

It took a minute, but Rawlings voiced the collective thought. "That doesn't make any sense. Every report we've seen over the last few years has told us that the political situation in Cuba was as normalized as it's ever been." He shook his head. "Did anyone see this coming?"

Richards turned to the captain, who replied, "There wasn't a hint of it until yesterday. And by then it was too late to do anything about it."

"So what does this mean?" Brent asked.

"I have no idea," Richards said. "The head of the Fifth Battalion is General Lopez, and nothing we've seen in his file indicates political ambition. In fact, he was close to retirement. Another few years and he could have turned in his stars and carved out a portion of the island for himself."

Perhaps it was because he was nonmilitary, but Brent could see that he was probably the only person there considering the weighty events of the morning with anything beyond a national defense interest.

"Colonel," he said. "Isn't this all a bit too convenient? From everything you're saying, Cuba has maintained a stable government for decades. And for it all to end now, when we're investigating instances of instability around the globe?"

"Which is why I stopped by to let you know, Dr. Michaels." The colonel fixed him with a look. "You'll find I'm not a big fan of coincidences."

Brent appreciated the validation, but his brain was already moving into clinical mode. "Okay, where is your information coming from?"

"We're getting reports out of Guantanamo and the embassy,"

Richards said. "So far neither of them has been touched. We're sending in additional troops to protect the base and to help evacuate the embassy." The colonel paused to address an internal issue and then added, "I doubt Lopez will go anywhere near Guantanamo. He knows that we won't do anything as long as he keeps it in the family."

"What about Castro and his brother?" Maddy asked.

"Raúl has already been dragged out into the street and shot," Richards said. "We have some nice footage of it courtesy of CNN. As far as Fidel, we don't have anything."

Then it hit Brent from out of nowhere. "Colonel, how are the stocks doing?"

Richards smiled. "We have someone on that right now. On the surface it looks like commodities are up and tech stocks down."

Brent absorbed that and said, "That makes sense."

"There's one other thing," Richards said. "Are you aware that stock prices for companies that manufacture weapons systems have risen dramatically?"

An innocuous question and yet Brent could see that everyone around the table understood the significance of it.

"Can you backtrack on some of those stocks and see how long they've been rising?" the professor asked.

"We're working on that too. With a little cooperation from the SEC, we should have an answer to that by the end of the day."

Which left them, in Brent's estimation, in roughly the same spot they were in before Richards arrived. What excited the researcher in him, though, was that by the end of the day they could have a good deal more data than they'd had when the day started. And with this team he was coming to understand that the data was everything.

———

One did not reach a position such as Canfield's without creating an enemy or two. The decisions required—the bridges burned—in order to clear the path ahead resulted in a list of people harboring varying degrees of animosity toward the aggressive executive. The flip side of that truth was that one seldom navigated that route without also building a network of friends.

One of those friends was a person in Human Resources who left a voice mail for Canfield telling him about inquiries into his personnel file. According to Nadine, these inquiries came from the highest of levels, which meant Van Camp's own administrative assistant. And while Nadine could not pinpoint anything concrete about the questions, she'd felt odd enough about them to return a favor Canfield had done for her long ago.

He'd received the message while driving to the office to put in a few hours, after which he would stop by the hospital to check on Phyllis, and the fact that Van Camp was working to create the necessary trail to lay blame on his underling if need be pulled a harsh laugh from his tired body. At least now he knew where his boss stood on the subject of Canfield's continued employment past December 21. In all likelihood Canfield would turn up dead in some seedy hotel room with a bullet wound to the temple. Even dead, he could still take the lion's share of the blame for Project: Night House. His only ace in the hole was that Van Camp had to keep him alive for at least another six days. If Canfield was killed prior to the completion of the Shackleton project, Van Camp would find it difficult to attribute that to his former employee.

He lowered the phone from his ear and, despite the fact that he'd been preparing for this, indeed putting into motion the means by which to circumvent it, it was still difficult news to absorb. So much so that he pulled the car to the side of the road and cut the engine. The resultant quiet that fell over the car's interior, a state broken only by the sound of tires over asphalt as other cars passed his, acted like a tonic.

He'd known what the events of recent weeks were building to, yet he'd viewed it almost as a distant thing, something whose eventuality might never materialize. He knew how foolish that sounded as soon as he thought it. The end of this—of the last few years of work—was as physical as the car in which he sat. All he could do now was manipulate what pieces he could to make certain that the man whose ambition this truly was would take the fall before Canfield, and to profit from it as much as he could. If Van Camp died and nothing of Night House was discovered, there were few people better positioned to step into the CEO chair. And if an investigation led back to the company, well, plausible deniability was a much maligned but very real course of action.

While sitting on the side of the road in his car, he felt a chuckle begin to form as he considered how the job he'd accepted, the one that now marked him for death, was managed with all the niceties such as workload management, flex time, and quality control. It was humorous to him how these things were categorized in the company records. The entire operation was either a gross misrepresentation of the free enterprise ethos or an evolution of a successful business model. Weren't multinational corporations the countries of the new millennium? He found it comforting, though, that he knew all the budget codes necessary to lay down bread crumbs for investigators.

Still, his seeing the humor of the situation did little to mitigate the sense of betrayal he felt. In the last three days he'd slept for perhaps six hours—fitful sleep from which he awoke wearier than when he'd closed his eyes. With the end of the project just days away, he suspected those six hours were a good deal more than he'd get—until his boss pushed the button that would separate the ice shelf from Antarctica. And to find out that he'd be taking the blame for it all was a hard thing for him to swallow.

Perhaps it was karma. While engaged in the project, he'd made decisions resulting in the deaths of more people than he cared to consider. Once December 21 came and went, would Van Camp be wrong for sending death after him?

He knew the answer to that.

The problem was that self-preservation, as a general rule, took precedence over a balancing of the karmic scale. Which meant he had to make another phone call.

The phone rang just once.

"There's been a little snag with the Antarctica project," Canfield said. "It appears that one of our drillers was injured and flown out early in the drilling."

He paused to listen to the response.

"No, the drill super didn't file a report on it. So now we have a loose end asking about workman's comp checks and threatening to call his congressman."

Canfield listened again and had to laugh at the colorful response coming from the other end of the line.

"Just take care of it," he said, reining in his mirth. "And do it quickly—before he can compromise us more than he already has."

After ending the call, Canfield started the BMW and pulled out into traffic, pointing the car toward the office.

———

"Hello, doll," Abby said. "Miss me yet?"

"More than anything," Brent replied. "Are you holding things together for me?"

"Sweetie, I am the glue that keeps you gainfully employed."

Brent couldn't help but laugh at the familiarity of the exchange. It was nice to know he could count on at least something to remain constant while his life was going in a hundred different directions.

"Speaking of which, when are you going to wrap things up and get back here? I can only keep your boss off your back for so long."

"I may need you to keep the heat off for a while longer. It looks like this job could go another week."

Abby's response was silence, which was something he seldom heard from his admin, but considering the circumstances it didn't feel like much of a victory.

"You do realize that part of teaching is actually being here to teach, right?" she asked.

"Funny how that works. Listen, Abby, I know how much extra this puts on you. When I finish up with this job I won't even consider another offer for a semester or two. I promise."

"Don't toy with me."

"I wouldn't dream of it," Brent said.

He knew Abby well enough to understand that she was only mildly put out by his extended absence. Were she truly upset, the conversation would have a whole different feel. He thought she was about to end the call, satisfied that she'd let him know who really occupied the driver's seat in the relationship, when he heard a quick intake of breath through the phone.

"Oh, I remember why I called now," Abby said.

"It wasn't just to harass me?"

"That was just a bonus. No, are you working on anything for the *AJS*? Because there was a guy in here yesterday talking to Dr. Hathaway and it sounded like he was getting some background on you for a journal article."

Brent had to think about that for a few seconds. It was conceivable that he had an article in the works for the *American Journal of Sociology*. Just because he couldn't remember it right now didn't necessarily mean anything. But he couldn't pull anything like it from the recesses of his brain.

"No, I'm pretty sure I'm not," he answered.

"Yeah, that's what I thought. Because I know pretty much everything you're working on, and that's not one of them."

"Okay, so if we both agree that I'm not writing an article, then who was this guy?"

"Excellent question, my dear Mr. Watson, which is why I offered him a glass of water."

Brent understood the sentence but failed to grasp the significance, or the smugness in Abby's voice.

"I don't follow."

"For fingerprints."

"You took fingerprints?"

"I thought he was creepy. And sometimes you just have to follow your gut."

"Even if you got his prints on a glass, how are you . . . ? Wait a minute, you're dating that cop, aren't you?"

"Ick, no," she said. "Where have you been? That's been over for weeks."

"But I'm assuming you at least ended things nicely?"

"Sure. In fact, I'm watching his dog next week when he goes out of town."

"And?"

"And it's a mixed breed. Mostly chow, I think."

"The fingerprints, Abby?"

"Oh. Well, they seem to belong to a guy named Gregory Hickett. One domestic violence charge, which was why he was in the database, but nothing other than that."

Brent's thoughts were going in a dozen places, the most important of which was why some guy masquerading as an employee for the *AJS* would be trying to dig up information about him. He was a boring old college professor. It took a few steps down that line of reasoning before he even thought to connect this mysterious visit to his present job. And when he made that connection a line of cold worked its way up his spine.

"Are you there, doll?"

"I'm here, Abby. Look, I need you to do me a favor. Can your cop find out everything he can about this guy and send it on to me?"

When his admin answered, her voice held concern. "Done. Is there something I should know about?"

Brent tried to infuse his response with his customary nonchalance.

"It's probably nothing. For all I know, it really was a footwork guy for the *AJS*."

"Who can't find out what he needs over the phone instead of coming all the way here to spend thirty minutes with your colleagues and to glance at a few of your papers?"

"You never know with the academic sorts," Brent said.

When a minute later he ended the call, he found that the chill was still there.

———

While the last few years were not without their anxious moments, Arthur Van Camp could not remember a time when he felt as if the entire project were teetering on the edge of a cliff. He suspected that was normal—that any large scale endeavor hurtling toward its culmination brought out the dormant fears of colossal failure. He also understood that he wouldn't feel that way if he knew what Alan was thinking.

One mistake his rogue vice-president continued to make was to believe that just because the cleanup team was his to command for the duration of Night House, they reported only to him. Van Camp knew that Alan was on task, that Shackleton was prepared, that more than a dozen additional global hot spots were being worked appropriately, and that the Russians were ready to announce a total freeze on wheat exports. With each domino that fell, Van Camp moved closer to achieving the objective he had laid out for himself in a Sunday school class so very long ago.

All of it told him that Alan had been the right man for the job.

It also told him that the man's endgame did not involve cutting and running. He was intent on finishing the project. After that, Van Camp could only guess.

It was a rare afternoon in that he wasn't in the office. Instead, he sat near Alan's wife in her private room, watching the monitor mirror the steady beat of the woman's heart. It was interesting to him how the line on the monitor seemed so strong. He suspected Phyllis's heartbeat had the steady regularity of a healthy woman. However, whatever was happening in her mind was keeping her from engaging with the rest of the world.

The seat he occupied, and the hospital room in which it sat, struck a chord in him whose origins were no mystery. When his own wife lay dying, he lost track of the hours he spent at her bedside, holding her hand as she readied to pass. According to the nurses, Alan had done much the same, although his presence did not seem to be as frequent as had Van Camp's just a couple of years before. It was further proof that Alan was still invested in the project.

Van Camp had already resolved to pay for the woman's hospital bills, even if her condition warranted an extended stay somewhere. It was the least he could do—a last gesture for a man who had given so much to the company. It was a pity Alan would not be around to reap the rewards of such meritorious service.

December 15, 2012, 3:48 P.M.

"No one would fault you for calling it," Maddy said. "Like the colonel said, you've more than fulfilled your obligation."

"I can," Brent said. "I can quit and go back to the classroom and worry until December twenty-first comes and goes, or I can stay here and do what you folks brought me here to do."

They were in the Pentagon mess. Brent was finishing up an exceptional Philly cheesesteak, after telling Maddy about the call from Abby.

"If I go home now, I'll just spend the next six days looking over my shoulder. And I'll probably just keep working on this on my own anyway. If you let me keep my computer."

Maddy didn't answer right away. She'd pushed the rest of her lunch away and let her eyes play over the other tables and the men and women, civilian or uniformed, who occupied them.

"I keep forgetting that you haven't been here very long," she said. "You slipped right in and it's almost like you're a real member of the team. I have to keep reminding myself that you're a sociology professor. You're not an anti-terrorism expert, or a spy. So when you get shot at in Afghanistan, and have some guy snooping around your workplace, it's probably not quite what you were expecting."

"You're right. It's not. But I'm having fun."

That drew a smile from the concerned army captain, which was what Brent wanted, but he also thought he owed her an honest answer.

"I know you're not expecting anything from me," he said. "This is just something I have to do. If I walk away now and someone else dies and I could have done something to help you prevent it, I'm not sure I'd be able to live with that."

That was the kind of answer he thought Maddy would appreciate, and from the look on her face it appeared to have hit home.

"Besides, you never know when you're going to need me to save you again."

She aimed a glare at him in response, and Brent accepted it with a grin.

"And there's something else," he said. "Say we don't find out who's behind this and the polarizing event happens and they reap whatever profit they expected to gain from it. Do you think that'll be the end of it? That they won't start trying to clean up some loose ends?"

He saw her take that in and roll it around, saw the look that came to her eyes as she did so.

"If nothing else, we have to get some security for you," Maddy said. "If they're bold enough to show up at your office, they won't be shy about showing up at your hotel."

"You mean if the man Abby saw even has anything to do with this."

"I guess we'll know more about that when you get the report you asked for."

"Until then I say we just keep plowing ahead."

"Fair enough," she said.

Brent rolled up his napkin and set it on his empty plate. He pushed his seat back, expecting Maddy to follow suit, when he realized that she hadn't moved.

"What's wrong?" he asked.

"What did the colonel drag you into his office for?"

While Brent could hear the casual tone of the question, he also picked up on the nervousness behind it. He wasn't sure how she'd picked up on the topic of the conversation, but she obviously knew something. It left him with a decision to make, and he decided to choose the path that someone with her ethical standards would appreciate: honesty.

"He asked me what my intentions were as far as you're concerned," he said, unable to keep the gleam from his eye.

The candid admission set Maddy back in her chair, eyes wide. "He didn't."

"Oh, but he did," Brent said. "The colonel thinks you're taking a shine to me, and I think he's worried that I'm not as good a catch as you deserve."

He enjoyed seeing how the news affected her. To her credit, she recovered quickly.

"He didn't actually say 'taking a shine,' did he?"

"No, I believe his exact words were that you and I 'have become close' during my time with you and the team," Brent said in his best imitation of the colonel.

Maddy couldn't help but chuckle, but she still appeared taken aback by the forwardness of her superior officer. Brent, always willing to add fuel to a good fire, decided to make her squirm a bit longer.

"So have we?"

"Have we what?" Maddy asked.

"Have we become close during my stay here?"

The question served a dual purpose. The first was to have some fun at her expense. The second, though, was to use the banter to see if the colonel might have been right. Brent was well aware that he'd thought a lot about Maddy over the last week and a half. It would be nice to know where she fell on the subject.

What he didn't expect was for the light atmosphere that had settled around the table to vanish. When she answered, after a pause long enough for Brent to have eaten another half of a cheesesteak, both her face and voice were without humor.

"Since you were honest with me, I'll return the favor. Am I attracted to you? Yes. You're smart, funny, and not too bad looking. In fact, you're probably just the kind of guy that I could see myself getting serious about." She stopped and allowed Brent time to process what she'd said. "But there's one big problem," she went on. "And I think you know what it is."

"You can't date someone who doesn't share your religious beliefs."

Maddy answered with a sad smile. "We're not talking a different denomination, or even a big point of theology that we can fight about. You don't believe in God at all, and for me that's a deal breaker."

Brent had no answer to that, because she was right. He'd considered and rejected the concept of a god a long time ago and he'd never found sufficient cause to revisit the topic. He was glad that Maddy's belief helped her, perhaps gave her life more meaning than it might have had, but he wouldn't cop to something he didn't believe in, even for someone he was interested in.

Maddy was the first to break the extended silence.

"The colonel's right about one thing, though," she said.

"What's that?" Brent asked.

"You're nowhere near as good a catch as I deserve."

And with that she picked up her tray, winked at the professor, and then left him there to think about it.

———

Dabir's mastery of English was a source of pride for him, but he had to admit to struggling with idioms. Some things did not translate well, lacking the proper context for a nonnative speaker. Tonight, though, he thought he was doing something called *stirring the pot*. What struck him as amusing was that in his country, a person stirred the pot to blend all of its elements, while what he was in the process of doing seemed more like taking a stick to a hornet's nest. That too might be an idiom, although he supposed such knowledge was not important for his current task.

The copy business, where he stood watching a stack of documents wind through a scanner, was six blocks away from his hotel. At least three such shops were closer, but he'd chosen this one because, as far as he could tell, there were no security cameras. Still, he kept his hat pulled down and avoided raising his head any more than was necessary to complete the transaction with the youth behind the counter.

He still was not sure what he hoped to gain from this act. Beyond the assignments he'd carried out for Alan Canfield, his knowledge of the man's other operations—if such existed—eluded him. Nor could he be certain that anything the man had ordered Dabir to do was connected to the company for which he worked. He thought it a reasonable assumption and yet he preferred dealing with facts.

If nothing else, the recipients of these pages would be able to make Dabir's former employer uncomfortable. But he would not make it easy—even for those who would face with him a common enemy. They had spilled the blood of his men at Afar and so he would give them no names. Only a picture. They would do the work themselves, or Dabir would move forward without them.

When the scanner finished its job, Dabir accepted his disk and walked out into the street.

December 16, 2012, 5:47 A.M.

Richards seldom arrived at the office before Maddy or Rawlings. The others, the ones more reluctant to greet the morning, would stagger in an hour or so after those two. The problem was that Maddy and Rawlings also stayed later than most. He suspected he would have to talk to them before too long, and remind them of the importance of a work/life balance.

He'd lived the life of the workaholic for too long and had only been preserved against its deleterious effects on his marriage by the saintly qualities possessed by his wife. Neither Maddy nor Rawlings was married, but the colonel understood that life existed beyond these walls. The worst part was that extended workdays were not requirements for a promotion. Richards would sign the papers recommending rank and transfer to just about anywhere either of them would want to go—and both of them knew that. Yet they kept coming in early and staying late.

The difference today was that both of them had an excuse. As did Dr. Michaels, who sat at the table with them, sifting through the data once again. Confining a search for a potentially catastrophic event into a period of a few days necessitated a temporary forgiveness of the admirable qualities of hard work and commitment. He himself had stayed until after midnight, only to return long before the dawn began to lighten the Washington sky.

"Good morning," Richards said, and by their reactions it seemed all of them were weary enough for his presence to have remained unnoticed.

After a chorus of acknowledgments, the colonel asked for a briefing from Brent.

"It's hard to tell, Colonel," Brent said. "Rawlings found . . ." He fielded a yawn that interrupted the thought. When finished he gave the colonel an apologetic wave and continued. "Rawlings had an interesting idea this morning that I think bears some investigation."

The professor looked at Rawlings, inviting him to elaborate, but the man had his coffee cup positioned beneath his nose, as if inhaling its rousing properties.

"Before Morpheus claimed the captain, he remarked on the percentage of news stories that seemed to coincide with the events you've investigated," Brent said. "He said it almost seems like the media itself is responsible for the uptick in violent events, if only to give themselves something to cover."

Before Richards could say anything, Rawlings roused from his coffee worship. "Hypnus," he said, eyes half closed.

"Pardon?" Brent said.

"Hypnus is the god of sleep. Morpheus is the god of dreams."

Brent raised an eyebrow, then exchanged a look with the colonel.

"Anyway," Brent said, "if you think about it, there are some news conglomerates that dwarf just about anything else out there."

Brent let that statement hang there for the colonel to mull over. Richards could see where Brent was headed, and he liked the fact that they were investigating every possibility, yet he found it an odd idea to advance. While Richards didn't know much about the news business, he thought of the industry as a reactive one—a corporate segment whose bread and butter involved how it responded to events, not how it manipulated them. But years leading a team with the charge of investigating the strange kept him from dismissing the idea out of hand.

"If you think there's any merit to it, then keep at it," he said. "If you haven't already done so, let the SEC know what you're thinking. They can start looking at stocks held by news corporations."

"They're already on it, sir," Maddy said. "They're looking at both domestic and foreign-owned organizations—all the networks, Reuters, the AP, the works."

The colonel took that in and found himself nodding. It seemed his people—and Dr. Michaels—had it all covered.

"I imagine the rest of the team will be here shortly," he said. "When they show up, tell them I've suspended anything that's not associated with this research."

"Yes, sir," Rawlings said.

After a last glance around the room, and a long look at Michaels to see if anything the two of them had discussed yesterday might have sunk in—of which he found no evidence—Richards proceeded to his office.

Sitting down at his desk, he logged on to his computer and went straight to email. Without fail, between the time he finished up one workday and started another, the email gremlins filled his box with no less than fifty messages. A number of them were sales-related, as the Pentagon's spam blockers seemed content to stand down and wave as malicious emails zoomed past. A handful were from facilities, with information about anything that might impact entrance to and exit from the building, as well as navigation through it, plus access to any of its services. Most of the rest were work-related—messages from people above and below him in the chain of command. These would be the first read and responded to.

There was, however, a last category that came through on occasion—something from outside that bore neither the defining marks of official business nor the impersonal subject lines that denoted junk. Most of these came from family or from church, schedules for elders' meetings or children's Sunday school. Despite the severe demeanor he displayed around work, he enjoyed finding out which Sundays he would get to spend with the second and third graders, supervising a craft or working his way through a Bible lesson. When Maddy had started attending his church, he'd sworn her to secrecy about this softer side of his character. And to his knowledge, she had yet to break that trust.

As he finished scanning his email, he saw something that reminded him of the last category of messages he received. Every once in a while the colonel was surprised by a message from the outside but that addressed some mission the NIIU might have undertaken. Nine times out of ten such a message came from a legitimate researcher—someone attached to a university or recognized scientific institution. The tenth one, though, was often the highlight of his day: an inquiry from a conspiracy theorist. As little as Richards smiled, few things could make him do so as easily as a late-night diatribe from a nut case.

It never ceased to amaze him the way a person's mind could work, creating government goblins around every corner, or sounding the alarm that the government was engaged in a campaign to keep the people of America from finding out the truth about Bigfoot, aliens, Atlantis, or any of a host of other things. The existence of his unit gave these people all the proof they needed of a government cover-up. The messages themselves were fascinating in their variety, from simple accusations featuring poor grammar and punctuation to well-reasoned, articulate letters that had at times made even the colonel think. Regardless, when he saw what looked like an email questioning NIIU activities, it got his attention, even before official business.

This morning he had one such message. Its subject line said: *I believe you may have killed some of my associates.* He opened it and began reading, a deepening frown spreading across his face. When the text ended, the file continued for another page, revealing a black-and-white photo. It appeared to have been taken in an airport. The man targeted by the camera lens wore a hat and sunglasses, and beyond the fact that he was one of the few fair-skinned people in the picture, he looked like any other businessman dressed for casual travel. Richards studied the picture for a few more seconds before reading through the first few pages again. Before he made it halfway he was sending it to the printer.

After snatching the page up, he took it to the professor's temporary office, sliding it in front of Brent.

"What's this?" Brent asked.

"It came in during the night," the colonel said. "It's an interesting read."

Puzzled, the professor pulled the paper closer and scanned it. Richards followed the man's eyes, and when Brent got to the end, the colonel watched him pause before jumping to the top and starting again. He gave the professor the time he needed to give it a second perusal. When Brent looked up, his eyes were filled with an odd combination of puzzlement and energy.

"This is a recounting of your Ethiopian mission," he said.

Richards nodded.

"I thought no one knew about this."

"Beyond the general, and whoever else he had to tell, no one should," the colonel answered.

Brent looked again at the paper, then back up at Richards. "So how does this guy know about it?"

Richards offered the professor his half smile that wasn't quite a smile. "Good question. I suggest we start by finding out who that is in the picture."

———

The colonel hovered behind Snyder as the man pulled up the report provided by the IT staff, and by the time Snyder finished reading it, the colonel had also reached the end so he didn't need to relay the information to him. However, for the benefit of the others, Richards motioned for him to share.

"They tracked the IP address back to a Kinko's in Atlanta," Snyder said.

"Why doesn't anyone email cryptic messages from home anymore?" Brent asked, but the colonel ignored him.

"One of the guys from IT put in a call to the place and they don't have any security cameras."

"Of course not," Rawlings grumbled.

Richards took the news in stride, and despite the irritability of his team, he knew they would too.

"If you find something you can't control . . ." the colonel reminded them.

"Then move on to something you can," returned Maddy. She took the picture and held it up for inspection. "At first glance there's nothing here that would give us a clue about who this guy is or where he is in the photo."

Richards knew that when Maddy began an explanation with the words *At first glance*, that meant that a more constructive second glance had already been performed.

"Do you see the dark blur on the wall here?" Maddy asked, pointing at what to Richards looked like a rectangular shadow.

"Not really," Brent said for all of them.

"We haven't done a layer lift yet, but with a microscope you can see that it's a poster," she said. She looked around the room, perhaps waiting for any one of the men to ask the obvious question. When none of them did, she released an exasperated sigh. "It's a poster advertising a theater production in Addis."

"So this is a terminal at Bole?" the colonel asked.

"And there's something else. The show on the poster had run dates of December sixth through the ninth."

That took a little longer for the colonel to process, and Michaels beat him to it.

"That puts this guy in Addis within a week of your Afar mission," the professor said. "Ten days at the outside."

"If the poster didn't stay up for a while after the show was over," Snyder said.

Richards considered both Maddy's discovery and Snyder's pessimism and came down closer to the former's side while reserving the right to change his mind at any time.

"If we can allow a week prior to the first performance for the poster to go up, and if we can accept the possibility that they still haven't taken it down yet, that leaves us with going on four weeks' worth of manifests to look through."

"Looking for what, Colonel?" Brent asked, and when he did, Richards saw that the professor was only speaking up because it appeared no one else was going to. "The only way to match this guy to someone in the airport's database would be to compare passport photos against a picture that's so grainy I can't tell this guy apart from Rawlings."

"Unfortunately, Dr. Michaels, it's all we have to go on at the moment."

The professor looked distressed at that and the colonel

couldn't blame him. Still, they'd solved a mystery or two with less evidence—although not much less.

"One of the things you learn in this job," the colonel said, "is that you don't marry yourself to a theory right out of the gate. We'll investigate this one concurrent with the others."

With that, the colonel turned on his heel and left, stopping by the kitchenette to get some coffee before proceeding to his office. Once at his desk he returned to the task of checking his email, suspecting he was behind in answering a few from his superiors. That was what made him so irritated when he saw that he'd received a new email message, this one from Congressman Bob Cooper.

Immediately, Richards had two distinct thoughts: that notes from congresspersons were always trouble, without exception; and that the subject line marked this email as one that might better fit with those from the conspiracy theorists. Anything with a subject line "I want my workman's comp checks from the thieves at Sheffield Petroleum, and by the way, no one seems to know where Ben Robinski is" had to be worth the read. But as Congressman Cooper had never sent him an email for anything beyond business, Richards knew there had to be a legitimate reason for forwarding it.

When he opened it, the congressman's addendum provided a bit of an explanation.

> Colonel Richards, I know you and your boys were out at Hickson Petroleum last week. This one mentions another oil company so I'm passing it along in case it's related. Besides that, I don't have a clue what to do with it. Bob.

Thus prepared, Richards dug into the body of the email.

It didn't disappoint, even if he did have a problem following everything. He had to admit it was one of the more entertaining ones he'd received. The part about a covert months-long drilling venture in Antarctica was a nice touch.

With a rare chuckle he closed the message and checked his watch. He had a meeting with General Smithson in an hour and nothing until then but to exhort his team to action, yet he knew they functioned better without him hovering. It left him with an unexpected—and unusual—block of free time that he wasn't sure what to do with. He gave a passing thought to starting work on the Bible lesson for Sunday but decided against it. His wife liked to help him with those.

He'd started drafting a letter the previous day and opened the file to see how it sounded after sitting for a while. But as he read through the letter, his mind kept returning to the email he'd just read, and he wasn't sure when it happened, but at some point the humor he'd pulled from it transitioned to something else.

The email was colorful, that was certain. But there'd also been something businesslike about it, despite the few expletives at the expense of Sheffield Petroleum. On a whim he pulled up a search engine and typed in the name Albert Griffiths and, for good measure, Pendleton Drilling Company, which was where Mr. Griffiths said he'd worked for twenty years. To his surprise he found a link to an employee page on the PDC website. On the page was a picture of Mr. Griffiths. According to the short bio that accompanied the photo, he'd been a supervisor.

The revelation that his email writer was not a complete nut case gave the colonel pause. After considering the matter for a moment, he followed his instincts, picking up the phone and dialing Madigan's office.

Captain Madigan stepped in soon after, and without preamble the colonel gave up his seat so that she could read the email. When finished she aimed a puzzled look at her superior officer.

"I don't follow, Colonel."

"I don't either," he admitted. "But I've already discovered that

Mr. Griffiths is alive and well and formerly a supervisor for an oil company."

Maddy absorbed that, although the result was another head-shake. But before she could voice her disagreement with this line of inquiry, Richards raised a hand.

"Maddy, just dig around for an hour or so. If nothing comes up by then, we'll drop it."

Maddy answered with a nod and set to work at the colonel's desk, which he allowed for the sake of expediency. Meanwhile, Richards picked up his coffee cup from the desk, stopped by the kitchenette for a refill, and headed down to the lab. When thirty minutes later he stepped back into his office, Maddy glanced up.

"I found him," she said.

"You found who?" Richards asked.

"Ben Robinski."

"From the email?"

Maddy nodded.

The colonel processed the news, but the meaning of the captain's statement took some time to arrive. "Wait. What do you mean you found him?"

"It turns out there *is* a Ben Robinski," Maddy said. "He lives in Des Moines, and his wife reported him missing this morning."

"He's missing?"

"According to the police report, which by the way is going to cost you a favor for the Des Moines chief of police, Ben Robinski signed on to a drilling team for a few months and his wife hasn't heard from him since."

"You mean . . ."

"I mean the guy who sent this to you," Maddy said, holding up a printout of the email, "is not out of his mind. This is legit."

———

"Albert, telephone."

As he crawled out from beneath the Charger, Albert grumbled about his wife's inability to tell whoever was calling that he was busy with something of the gravest importance. That would be the brake lines. What could be more important than that?

"Is it Pendleton?" he called back. "Or those thieves at Sheffield?"

"Neither, love," she said.

Had it been Pendleton, they would have asked him to come back to work, citing a lack of skilled drilling supervisors. He would have said no, at least not until the Charger was running. And with all he knew about the Charger's condition, they could avoid calling him for a few years. If the call had come from Sheffield, he would have been out from under the car fast enough to hurt himself. Now that the phone call from Ben Robinski's wife had got him thinking about the money again, he found it hard to get it out of his mind.

"Who is it?" he asked as he strode toward the house.

"I don't know," Andrea said. "He mentioned something about the military. It sounded important."

Albert took that in as he walked up the front steps and into the kitchen. What would the military want with him?

"I haven't missed some kind of compulsory service for immigrants, have I?" he asked Andrea, his hand cupped over the phone.

"Not that I know of," she said with a headshake.

"Hello," he said.

"Mr. Griffiths, my name is Colonel Jameson Richards. I'm with the NIIU out of the Pentagon."

"Are you now?" replied Albert. "Well done, then. I imagine that's a tough job to get."

The man who'd identified himself as Colonel Richards paused as if gathering his thoughts.

"Mr. Griffiths, I'm calling about the email you sent to Congressman Cooper yesterday."

That bit of news surprised Albert into silence. By his reckoning, there were only two reasons the military would be calling: to help him with his workman's comp issue, or to accuse him of threatening a congressman, which if his memory of the email was accurate, he hadn't done. Still, he didn't think a simple workman's comp claim, however serious to the one waiting for the money, was ever escalated to the military.

"So are you calling to help me out of this workman's comp jam?" he asked.

"Not exactly," Colonel Richards said. "I'm calling about the other part of the letter—the one that described the drilling activities in Antarctica."

"Oh, that," Albert said. "That's where I hurt my leg. You're right, we should probably start there."

"Can you tell me everything you can about what you were doing in Antarctica, Mr. Griffiths?"

Happy for a chance to talk about the injustice done to him via the holding of his workman's comp checks, Albert did just that, from the first call he'd received asking him to join the team to his time in the hospital in South Africa getting his leg seen to.

"So you see, friend," he said, "I left a bit of skin on that rock and so I want to be properly compensated for it."

Through the telling, this Colonel Richards hadn't said a word, and now that he'd finished, Albert was beginning to wonder if he'd lost the connection.

"You still with me, Colonel Richards?"

"Mr. Griffiths, can you tell me exactly *where* you were drilling?"

Albert thought for a moment. He failed to see what that had to do with his workman's comp checks. Unless this fellow was also wondering about Ben. "You don't think they up and left poor old Ben there, do you?" he asked.

Albert waited while the military man entertained another long pause. Finally, he said, "It's important we find out where you were drilling. If there's any way you can point us in the right direction, it would be very helpful."

Albert didn't quite know how to respond to that. This all seemed like a lot to go through to secure his comp checks, and to see to the health and well-being of Ben.

"Well, they never actually told us where we were in Antarctica," Albert said. "But a few of us had compasses, so I know we were on the eastern coast."

"That's a bit helpful," the colonel said. "Can you be more specific?"

"Sorry, but like I said, I wasn't there but a week or so, what with my leg injury."

The colonel asked a few more questions, which Albert answered to the best of his ability, and when it appeared the conversation was near completion with no mention of his missing money, Albert said, "So when can I expect my checks to start coming?"

"Thank you for your time, Mr. Griffiths," the colonel said. "We may be back in touch if we need more information."

Then the line went dead, leaving Albert holding the phone to his ear and feeling as if he'd just had an interesting conversation that ultimately had accomplished nothing. When he hung up he found Andrea waiting with an expectant look.

"From the Pentagon," Albert explained. "He called about the message I sent to our congressman."

"Really? I had no idea you were so well connected, love."

Given the look on his wife's face, Albert suspected he would not be crawling back beneath the Charger anytime soon.

———

With Maddy gone almost an hour, Brent had taken over her research as well as his own. The one thing he envied her—all of them, in fact—was the depth of the resources at their disposal. The report Maddy had been using a red pen to go through was compiled in less than twenty-four hours by one of the in-house research units. Within the almost seven hundred smartly bound and crisp pages were a large number of possible candidates for the role of polarizing event.

There was, however, one problem. Seven hundred pages' worth of results suggested that Maddy's search criteria was wrong. He had to believe that, because the other possibility was more frightening: that there really were this many potential events of volatile variables to meet Brent's needs. Brent couldn't imagine how Maddy could hope to go through all of it. Even to narrow the monstrous list to one half its size would take more time than they had. He had given up after a few pages in Maddy's book and had just started into his own work again, adding elements to his Poincaré map, when Richards and Maddy came back. And from the expression on Maddy's face, it looked like something was about to drop into his lap.

Or onto the table. Maddy slipped a page in front of him and waited while the professor read. When he looked up he raised an eyebrow. "I don't get it."

"Maddy said the same thing," Richards said. "What it comes down to, Professor, is that as a general rule I don't believe in coincidence. We have issues with two different oil companies, along with a missing worker and a story about some mysterious drilling project in Antarctica."

"Yet not a bit of it is probably related to what we're doing," Brent said, surprised that a man as levelheaded as the colonel was considering allowing this email to coax them down a rabbit hole.

"Dr. Michaels," Richards said, "I just got off the phone with Mr. Griffiths, and he had enough interesting things to say to pique my curiosity. And while I've said that I don't believe in coincidence, every once in a while I can be led by my gut. This is one of those times."

228

Not having a long association with the man, Brent didn't know how unusual it was for the colonel to make this leap of faith. However, Rawlings, who did have the experience and association Brent lacked, looked up from his work and regarded Richards with surprise.

That was when Maddy jumped in. "If nothing else," she said, "it may be worth asking Mr. Griffiths a few more questions. From what you told me, Colonel, we may get more if we do it in person."

She didn't say anything else, and neither did the colonel, leaving Brent to wonder if they were about to lose a critical day to a wild goose chase. His eyes then fell to the large stack of papers in front of Maddy, the loose charts and diagrams spread next to Rawlings, and his own work, all numbers and lines. All of a sudden the thought of sitting in this office for another minute didn't sit well with him.

"Maybe it would be nice to get out of here for a while," he said. And judging by the smile that appeared on Rawlings's face, Brent guessed he wasn't the only one in need of a break.

December 16, 2012, 3:41 P.M.

Unlike Brent's last field trip, where he and Maddy had resorted to commercial coach to reach their destination, this time they took the Learjet. The passengers were him, Maddy, and Rawlings. The colonel remained behind to manage the growing number of inquiries from Homeland Security, the other branches of the armed forces, and Washington. The simple consult for which the professor had signed on had grown into something much larger, and Brent did not envy the colonel the task of explaining it all. Snyder had remained behind as well, wading through the research, using Brent's notes as a guide. Brent didn't envy him either. What Brent still couldn't understand, though, was where or how he fit into this trip. While he was grateful for the time away from his office at the university, his skills were in research as opposed to fieldwork. He felt like something of a fifth wheel.

The black SUV cut through the Tucson traffic, the sun just beginning to pull in front of the vehicle as the driver aimed the vehicle west on E. 22nd Street, skirting the air force base to the south. Within twenty minutes they'd entered a suburb of modest homes, with the telltale signs of new business evident just about everywhere Brent looked.

The driver made a few turns, winding into a neighborhood that looked a bit slower in adapting to the new face of the suburb. Brent watched out the window until the truck pulled up in front of a house that, if Brent was to be charitable, looked lived in.

For one thing, three cars rested on blocks in the front yard, and as Brent surveyed the rest of the street with its well-kept lawns, he suspected the Griffiths might not be invited to many neighborhood functions. The front door hung open, with the screen door the only thing keeping bugs and people alike from walking inside.

Brent, Maddy, and Rawlings exited the truck and started for the front door, Brent being cognizant of the distance Maddy kept between them. Since their unexpectedly personal talk in the Pentagon cafeteria, she'd closed up a bit, although Brent suspected that had more to do with her than it did with him. He hadn't pressed things, mostly because he still didn't know which way to press them. He couldn't figure out if this was a passing thing or if the chemistry they shared deserved attention beyond the length of the consult.

He could almost say the same thing about the entire team. Looking back on all of his consults, he could not remember a time when he'd felt so in sync with another group of people. That was why he'd agreed to things so far outside the scope of this contract, including gunfights in Afghanistan and home visits in Tucson.

Rawlings had called ahead to make sure the trip wouldn't be wasted. Now the man mounted the three front steps and knocked on the screen door. No answer came from within the house. Brent stepped up next to Rawlings and peered through the screen door into the dimly lit living room. It was hard to see anything with the sun behind the house, and he couldn't hear any activity inside.

"You did call ahead, right?" Brent asked.

"I'm assuming you're the fellas from Washington?" came a voice from behind them.

When Brent turned he saw a man's head sticking out from underneath one of the cars on the lawn. The professor, a car guy in his younger years, recognized a Charger when he saw one.

"Are you Albert Griffiths?" Maddy asked, leaving the steps and crossing the lawn to meet the man, who had crawled out from under the car and was wiping his hands on his pants.

"The same," the man answered with an accent that Brent could have placed from either Australia or South Africa. He offered a grease-covered hand to Maddy, who without hesitating, shook it. "You folks want to talk about the work I did for Sheffield, is that right?" Griffiths asked. He bent down to retrieve a rag from the ground and, while using it to wipe his hands more thoroughly, started for the front door.

"That's right," Maddy called after him.

As Griffiths passed Rawlings and Brent, he gave them both a gap-toothed smile, ascended the stairs, and disappeared into the house, leaving the NIIU team members standing out on the lawn.

"I have to tell you" came the man's voice through the screen door. "I never thought complaining to a congressman would get this kind of a response."

Brent looked back at Maddy, who had joined the two men by the steps. She gave Brent a shrug, looking ready to call through the door, when Griffiths suddenly pushed open the door and came out onto the porch. In his hands was a six-pack of Guinness, one already pulled from the packaging.

"Wet your whistle?" he said, holding the beer toward his guests.

Brent started to reach for one when he heard Maddy clear her throat and he withdrew his hand.

"Suit yourself." Griffiths set the rest of the beer down on the porch and gave the team a once-over. "Almost makes me happy to pay taxes. I mean, a simple man like me makes a call and the army shows up." He took a long draw from his drink and then settled his eyes on Maddy, for reasons Brent couldn't argue with.

"Mr. Griffiths—" Maddy began before he cut her off.

"Call me Albert," he said.

"Okay, Albert. Can you tell me more about this drilling job you said you did?"

"Right. Well, we weren't a week into it before I got hurt. Tore my leg up pretty good." With his free hand he took hold of his pants just above the left knee and raised the material, revealing a long scar that wrapped around the calf. "So me and the missus came here when I got back Stateside, after the doctor gave me a 'good to go' on my leg, and all I can say is that it's been a regular odyssey trying to get my workman's comp checks."

"We understand that part," Maddy said, "but we'd like to know more about the project you were working on. What exactly were you doing in Antarctica?"

The question seemed to catch the man off guard. He stared blankly at Maddy, then shifted his gaze to both Rawlings and Brent before landing again on Maddy.

"Why am I getting the feeling that you're not here about my workman's comp checks?"

Maddy offered the man a tired yet warm smile. "Albert, it would be very helpful to us if you could tell us everything you remember about the project."

Albert responded with a shrug of his shoulders. "Well, the whole thing seemed a bit off," he said.

"What do you mean by 'off'?" she asked.

Albert raised his eyes to look past the group, toward the Charger, as if trying to put himself back on the southernmost continent. "I wasn't there for long, remember. I think we'd only started drilling the day before I got hurt. Which I thought was just fine once I found out I wasn't going to lose the leg. Thought I'd collect checks for a while on account of my injury and not have to deal with the cold." He paused to take another drink and then shivered, whether from the coldness of the Guinness or the memory of the work site, Brent didn't know.

"Do you have any idea how cold it is there? It's the biggest, flattest piece of ice you can imagine. The wind cuts through your clothes like you're not wearing anything."

Brent shook his head, while Maddy and Rawlings nodded.

"Then you know what I'm talking about," Albert said. "So I thought I'd just enjoy working on the Charger for a bit, while I healed up." His eyes moved to the car, and Brent found his going there too.

"Is that a 400 CID V8 in there?" Brent asked.

Albert fixed Brent with a grin. "What else?"

Brent's eyes lingered on the muscle car, long enough for him to see a truck that looked remarkably like their own SUV cruise past Albert's house. He watched until the vehicle reached the next street, then made a right and disappeared from view.

"If we can get back to Antarctica," Maddy prodded.

"Sure. Like I was saying, I think we'd only drilled a hole or two before I left. But Sheffield had a big crew there. Whatever they were up to, they weren't joking around."

"Holes?" Rawlings asked. "What kind of holes?"

"The round kind," Albert replied. Then, seeing that he was the only one amused, he added, "The one I saw was maybe nine inches wide and they were drilling down pretty deep. I'd say fifty feet at least."

Maddy and Rawlings shared a glance.

"What do you do with a hole that size?" Rawlings asked Albert.

The drill-rig operator finished his beer and bent to retrieve another one. Only after he'd opened it and sampled the contents did he answer. "In my experience there are only two reasons you dig a hole like that, and only one that makes sense considering where we were. Ice cores."

"Ice cores?" Brent said.

"Like you see on them shows on the Discovery Channel," Albert said. "When I was working up in Alaska, we'd sometimes drill out a core for some scientists before we got down to real business."

Brent saw Maddy processing the information. To Brent, what Albert Griffiths was saying sounded plausible. But then he remembered that ice cores were only one of Albert's reasons.

"What's the other reason someone would dig a hole like that?" he asked.

"See, that's where it gets strange," Albert said. "Because the only other place I've seen holes like that is when a crew is trying to cut through rock."

"And how does that work?" Rawlings asked.

"Well, you dig a nice hole, not too wide, slide a charge in there, set her off and, voilà, you have yourself a small pile of rocks where there used to be one great big one."

Brent tossed that possibility around in his mind, deciding the ice core idea made more sense. He was about to share that with Maddy when in his peripheral vision he caught movement around the corner of the house. Perhaps it was his recent experience with guns that caused his senses to be more attuned to the sight of one, but in the instant he had to consider things before the shadow resolved into a person, he knew the man was carrying one.

"Maddy!" Brent shouted, and the captain followed Brent's line of vision even as he rushed forward and took a surprised Albert Griffiths to the ground.

The man weighed a great deal more than Brent, which meant it was like running into a brick wall, but the tackle did the job and the two civilians were facedown on the porch before the bullets began to fly.

Brent rolled to his side to look for Maddy and Rawlings and spotted the latter down on one knee at the foot of the stairs, his handgun drawn. As Brent watched, he saw Rawlings squeeze off two shots and then glance over at him.

"Get him inside," Rawlings shouted.

After hesitating for only a moment, Brent grabbed a dazed Albert Griffiths by the arm and began urging him toward the door. It didn't take long for Albert to reclaim his wits and assist in the effort. Once inside, Brent tried to ignore the sounds of gunfire as he and his charge retreated deeper into the house.

"Is there anyone else in here?"

"No," Albert wheezed. "The missus went shopping."

Brent nodded, casting his eyes around the house, eventually bringing them back to Albert. "Do you have any guns?" he asked.

Albert gestured for Brent to follow him to a back bedroom. Once there, Albert retrieved two shotguns from a well-stocked gun cabinet. He loaded both and handed one to Brent.

"Stay here," Brent said once the gun was in his hands.

The look Albert returned was one of incredulity.

"Not on your life," the man answered. He moved to push past Brent when the professor put a hand on his shoulder.

"Either stay here or I'll have you arrested," Brent said.

Albert hesitated. "You can do that?"

"I can send you to Guantanamo if I want," Brent lied. Then he turned on his heel and walked away, leaving Albert there to consider things.

When he reached the door, he knew better than to rush out. Almost pressing his face against the screen, he looked around as much as his field of vision would allow, and the realization was slow in coming that he no longer heard any weapons fire. He pushed his way through the door, leading with the gun, which felt a lot better in his hands than had the handgun in Afghanistan. His heart racing, he edged forward on the porch until he reached the steps, keeping his eyes moving as he advanced. It wasn't until he reached the steps that he saw a pair of legs sticking out from behind a hydrangea. With quick but careful steps he descended the stairs and went around the bush, dreading what he would find, and almost dropped his gun when he saw one pointed up at him. Rawlings lowered the weapon and grimaced as he tried to shift positions.

From what Brent could see, Rawlings had taken a round in the thigh—a painful, but not critical, injury. Which allowed him to leave the man there and head in the direction from which the attack came, despite the harsh whispers from the wounded soldier behind him.

Maddy had been closest to the gunman when the shooting started, and while he fought with the sick feeling that threatened to make him vomit on Albert's lawn, Brent took comfort that he didn't see her body, or any blood indicating she'd been hit.

He used the same caution at the corner that he used at the front door, poking his head around slowly. He almost missed them, their movements on the street running behind the house nearly blocked by the thick bushes in the back yard. He knew it was a dumb thing to do, but he didn't have any choice. Ignoring the rapid beating of his heart, he slipped around the corner and advanced along the side of the house. He walked until he had a clear view of the street—at the men who were struggling under the weight of the woman they were carrying to their truck. The feeling of nausea that had followed Brent since he'd stepped out of the house increased tenfold, and he froze as one of the men slid open the door and, between the two of them, they tossed Maddy none too gently inside.

Then, as if forced into action by something outside of himself, Brent began to run toward the SUV. He brought up the shotgun as he ran and came a hairsbreadth away from pulling the trigger when it occurred to him that he might hit Maddy—a realization that left Brent defenseless as one of the men, masked and wearing jeans and a plain white shirt, spotted him. Whoever he was, he could fire a gun a lot faster than Brent. The only way the professor survived was by throwing himself to the ground. He forced himself into a roll, and didn't stop rolling until he reached the cover of a large pine tree.

As he tried to catch his breath he heard doors slamming, followed by the squeal of tires. By the time he reached the street, the truck was too far away for him to read the plate.

Brent suspected that Albert Griffiths had never considered that his house would be turned into a command center for several very agitated military personnel. For the most part, the man kept to himself, watching the activity around him with a bemused expression while nursing a Guinness. Albert's wife had come home not long after the shooting stopped, and she too seemed oddly amenable to the situation.

The rest of the team, with the exception of Addison and Bradford, whom Richards had left to continue their research, had arrived an hour ago. But the colonel's superiors had hedged at sending anyone else. It was always a tricky area for the military to operate domestically, and the call was made to let the FBI manage things. Brent looked at the colonel and could see that the decision did not sit well with him. There was something else as well, and Brent knew what it was without Richards having to speak it.

The truth was that they had next to nothing to go on. Neither

Rawlings nor Brent had gotten a close look at their attackers. And Brent hadn't caught the license number of the truck. Without those, there were few places for the investigation to begin. He caught it too from the expressions of the FBI agents, who had interviewed him and Rawlings—the latter while he was having a bullet extracted from his leg.

"How did they know we'd be here, Colonel?" Snyder asked. He'd been outside helping the feds pick up shell casings, and Brent suspected he was now starting to feel like the rest of them. "You only decided to send them here this afternoon. That shouldn't have been time enough to set up something like this."

The colonel shook his head and indulged a deep sigh.

"I don't know," he said. "The timeline suggests these people have someone on the inside."

"Not necessarily, Colonel," Brent said from his spot on Albert's couch. When Richards refocused his attention on the professor, Brent said, "Who's to say they came for us?" He gestured with his head toward Albert.

It seemed obvious to Brent, and he guessed the only reason the colonel hadn't thought of it was because of whatever walls he had to put up in order to keep functioning under the circumstances. Military training or not, losing two team members in the span of a few days was a bit much to handle. Brent understood, because underneath the calm that he was working hard to maintain, he felt as if his insides had been ripped out. And he knew that part of what he felt was guilt—the realization that he hadn't been able to keep Maddy safe. On some level he knew that was backward. She'd been responsible for protecting him. He understood that, but it still didn't make it easier to deal with. The only thing he kept telling himself was that a very real chance existed that Maddy was still alive.

"Colonel, we came here because Mr. Griffiths put a bug in a congressman's ear. Now, if there's really something going on in

Antarctica, and whoever is behind it learned that a former employee was bending ears in Washington, don't you think they might want to pay him a visit?"

At that suggestion, every eye in the room turned toward Albert, who after raising his Guinness in salute, suddenly realized what Brent had said. "Wait a minute. What's all this about a visit?"

"So you believe that Mr. Griffiths was the primary target," Richards said. "And the fact that the three of you were here was—"

"Coincidence," Brent said, finishing for him.

Richards's jaw set in irritation. "As you know, Dr. Michaels, I'm not very fond of coincidences."

"And yet sometimes they happen, Colonel."

Richards looked as if he might say more, but instead he turned and crossed to the screen door, letting himself out onto the porch.

———

When Catherine came running into his office, Arthur Van Camp immediately regretted allowing his emotions to get the best of him.

"Everything's fine, Catherine," he said, forcing a smile he did not feel.

Despite his assurances, she looked unconvinced, eyeing the broken vase on the floor against the office's interior wall.

"Believe me, it's fine. You can go back to your desk. And please close the door behind you."

Even with this second admonition, his admin seemed reluctant to leave. Yet she knew better than to ignore a request from her boss, however kindly delivered. Still, she stole one last glance at the broken vase as she walked out. Once the door closed behind her, Van Camp lowered himself back into his chair.

He'd reached the end. It no longer mattered that the project still lacked days. His return on the investment in Alan had ended;

the man was now a liability. His only wish was that Brunner had called him before he left for Tucson. Van Camp would have stayed his hand. Now his corporate security officers were holding an army captain at the safe house in Lubbock.

He felt the anger growing again, but then checked it before it could overtake him. He understood Alan's intent, to clean up the one loose end from Shackleton. He didn't fault the man for that. He could not have known that the same army unit that continued to poke their heads into portions of the project would be standing on the target's front door. In truth, much of the blame rested on Brunner, who should have called the attack with the added complications. Ultimately, though, everything went back to Alan.

Van Camp rose from his chair and walked over to where the expensive vase lay in pieces on the carpet. He bent down and, reaching a hand under the table, retrieved the Akbal. He studied the carving, noting the chipped corner. He ran a finger over the irregularity, then turned and walked back to his desk, returning the carving to its spot.

———

The woman hadn't made a sound since Canfield arrived at the safe house in Lubbock. Her hands were bound behind her, the rope threaded through the chair slats, and Brunner had pulled a hood down over her face. He could hear her shallow breathing and knew she was awake.

He looked past her, catching Brunner's eye, and gestured to Van Camp's security chief to follow him as he left the room.

"Did she see either of you?" he asked once Brunner had shut the door behind him.

"No. She was bound and blindfolded before we took off the masks," Brunner said.

An agitated Canfield ran a hand through his hair. He took a

few steps away from the door and then stopped as if unsure how to proceed.

"What are we supposed to do with her?" he asked.

Brunner didn't hesitate in his response. "There are at least three places within six blocks of here where we can dump her. She wouldn't be found for days."

Alan Canfield, a man responsible for more deaths over the last few years than he could recollect, almost shuddered at the dispassionate suggestion. Even so, it seemed the most logical choice; it was certainly the most convenient. However, if he'd learned anything under Arthur Van Camp's tutelage, it was that hasty decisions, when not necessary, were best avoided.

"Keep her here for the time being," he ordered. "I'll call you when I decide what to do with her."

As he turned to leave, he had no delusions that this situation had not already been reported to his boss. While the security team was at his beck and call for the duration of the project, Canfield knew the way the lines would fall on any org chart. Brunner reported to Van Camp; it was as simple as that.

It was a truth that meant there would come a point when Canfield would no longer be able to use the team, when whatever target he gave them would be superseded by one designated by Van Camp. Canfield's only ace in the hole was that he still had the detonator. Without that in his hand, Van Camp would hesitate before striking his subordinate down. Still, it was with profound relief that he made it out into a Texas evening without a bullet in the back of his head.

December 17, 2012, 7:17 A.M.

As much as it went against every feeling in his gut, Brent could not fault the colonel for bringing the remnants of the team back to Washington. After spending most of the night at the home of Albert Griffiths, doubtless setting the neighborhood ablaze with speculation, the colonel had come to the conclusion that they could provide no real assistance to the FBI. He suspected they could do more to help Maddy by continuing the work than by standing idle in a private residence in Tucson. Brent agreed, although it didn't make him feel any better about what seemed tantamount to abandoning Maddy to her fate.

"I'm not even sure how to go about investigating this, Colonel," Rawlings said. "Especially not in the time we have."

"That's why I'm giving this to you," the colonel told Rawlings. "I think satellites are our only chance, and there's no one better at finding a needle in a haystack than you."

Rawlings returned a slow nod.

"We're not set up to do that here, sir," he said.

"That's why I've got the plane ready to take you to NORAD. They're already pulling data so it will be ready for you when you get there."

"Yes, sir," Rawlings said.

After Rawlings left, Richards turned his attention to Brent, who gestured toward the door through which Rawlings had just passed.

"Is it reasonable to think that he can find something over a surface area as big as Antarctica?"

"Eastern Antarctica," Richards corrected. "And whether it's reasonable or not, we're running out of avenues to explore."

Brent conceded that point with a nod.

"How's your research progressing, Doctor?" Richards redirected.

"I'm not entirely sure. I knew Maddy was waiting for a report from the SEC, so I used her computer to access her email." As soon as the words left his lips he realized the security implications of tapping into a military officer's computer, and he hesitated, waiting for Richards to react. But when the colonel did not so much as raise an eyebrow, Brent pressed on. "To be honest, the report is a lot less helpful than I'd hoped. While there are a number of companies that have seen better than average gains over the last year, none of them jump off the page. And most of these companies are so big that it's difficult to link stocks across their various lines of business." He shook his head in frustration. "Maybe if they had more time, but I think this is just a second haystack."

As the colonel absorbed that, Brent switched gears.

"But I've been thinking," he said. "Colonel, I don't know about you, but I've never met a captain of industry who wasn't a complete narcissist."

"I haven't met many captains of industry" was the colonel's dry response.

"Most people who end up controlling huge corporations have a certain personality type. They're completely ego driven, which can cause them to take risks most people wouldn't take. Because the more the deck is stacked against him, the greater the ego validation if he wins."

"And if he loses?"

"Then it's because of things he couldn't control. No CEO worth his pay would admit a personal failing in the face of a loss."

Richards was thoughtful for a moment before saying, "I'm with you so far. Now tell me what you're getting at."

"What I'm getting at is that a significant part of the ego validation comes from other people being aware of the accomplishment," Brent said. "If no one knows, is it really a win?"

He saw the colonel frown.

"I'm not following," the man admitted.

"What I'm saying is that if this guy is your typical CEO, he won't be happy unless people know what he was able to pull off."

"I like the psychology," the colonel said, "but I'm not sure it fits here. With something as large a scale as this, my thought is that someone with the resources and intelligence to pull it off would also exercise sufficient self-control to ensure he isn't caught."

"I agree," Brent said. "But he's been working on this for a long time. My guess is as far back as Y2K. That's a lot of time to drop a hint or two. And more than likely he wouldn't be aware he'd done so. Braggadocio is just part of his DNA."

He watched as the colonel considered his argument and then asked the next logical question. "Even if you're right, how do you expect to follow it up?"

"I'm not sure. But everyone else has a haystack."

That pulled a slight smile from the colonel, but it vanished an instant later.

"While you're pursuing your theory, you may want to see what you can find out about the name Miles Standish."

The professor gave a thoughtful nod. "That's the guy that Griffiths said recruited him for the drilling operation, right?"

"I have Bradford talking to Sheffield Petroleum. He hasn't given a full report yet, but at first blush it appears they haven't had a crew in Antarctica for at least three years."

Out of all the pieces of news he'd received during this consult—if it was even appropriate to call it that anymore—the one just delivered by Richards stole any response he might have made, and it took him a while to determine the reason. Until now, he had only appreciated the magnitude of the plot they were uncovering on a clinical level. It was one thing to read about a series of small events occurring at points around the globe. It was quite another to understand that whoever was behind this had the wherewithal to construct a shell corporation atop a real one, recruit a few dozen men for a job in a remote part of the world, and provide them with all the resources they needed to engage in what was shaping up to be a mammoth drilling operation. For some reason, the weight of the thing was now settling on Brent's shoulders.

The colonel, as good a reader of people as Brent had met, tried to take a portion of that weight from him.

"One thing at a time, Dr. Michaels. We'll get it all sorted out."

It wasn't much of a pep talk, but Brent appreciated it nonetheless. And as the colonel left to check on Bradford's progress, Brent dug into his new line of inquiry.

———

Alan Canfield was accustomed to dealing with a sense of loss. In his understanding, loss went hand in hand with accomplishment.

One did not succeed without giving up much. In his estimation, he'd sacrificed a great deal to achieve what he had—both on a personal level and for the company. His marriage had been in tatters long before Phyllis took the pills; his health had certainly suffered; he couldn't remember the last time he'd pursued a leisure activity of any kind. In fact, his efforts toward advancement had stripped him to the point that he had no idea who the man was who looked back at him from the mirror.

And so to accept the prospect of yet another loss—his life this time—lacked most of the raw emotion it might have otherwise had.

When he'd arrived back in Atlanta after leaving the safe house in Lubbock, he drove home with the intention of catching a few hours of sleep before making what might well be his last appearance in the office. He could feel the noose tightening, knew that all the pieces were in place and it was time now to find a hole from which to watch things unfold. Pulling into his driveway, he saw it right away.

On his leaving the house for a business trip, Phyllis always left the light on in the front room. He would see it through the window when he pulled in. It was, he supposed, a greeting of sorts if he arrived home after she went to bed. When he left the day before, he'd flipped the light on in some small sentimental gesture that his wife would doubtless have appreciated. But when he returned, the light was off.

Canfield had cut the engine and sat in the driveway, watching the darkened house. Nothing was moving as far as he could tell, but he understood how little that meant. After ten minutes, half expecting the sound of a gun tapping on his window, he exited the car and walked to the front door, key in hand. In the dim lighting provided by the streetlamp, he could see nothing to indicate a forced entry. He opened the door and went inside, deciding not to switch on the hallway light.

A thorough canvassing of the house yielded no sign of an intruder and he relaxed. He was ready to laugh it off, assuming he simply had not turned the light on as he thought, when he stepped into his office and found his eyes moving to the bookshelf. Only a man who had built the shelf with his own hands and who had stocked it with great care would have recognized that some of the books were out of place.

He crossed to his desk and opened the bottom drawer, from which he pulled the gun that Phyllis hated keeping in the house. Then he ascended the stairs, grabbed a suitcase from the closet, and tossed in as many articles of clothing as he could fit. Once he'd lugged the suitcase down the stairs, he paused in the hallway, his mind racing to think of anything else he should take with him. It took only seconds for the realization to hit that there was little there he couldn't do without. Less than a minute later he had pulled out of the driveway.

Now his car idled outside of the hospital. He'd thought about going in and seeing Phyllis but knew that if Van Camp had marked him for termination, someone on the team would be watching the hospital entrance. He'd already taken too much of a chance in going to his office to collect a few things. He'd taken the loading dock entrance and then used the service elevator to get to the lobby, after which he'd chanced the second elevator bay, where an elevator took him to the twentieth floor. The remaining twenty flights of stairs had provided more exercise than he was accustomed to but had enabled him to collect a number of important files, check and send email, and satisfy himself that some of the open-ended portions of the project were falling into place.

He also retrieved the item his boss had been seeking when he sent men into Canfield's home. The ultimate success of Project: Night House relied on what happened at their southernmost battlefront. After the millions of dollars spent readying the ice shelf for separation, he couldn't consider it not happening. If nothing else, it would make the loss of life an incalculable waste. While Canfield wasn't the religious sort, he suspected that abandoning the project now would mean a monumental misuse of assets—a true disservice to the dead. Before he left the office, he pulled the detonator from behind *The Art of War*, a book that held a prominent place in his office library.

He slipped the detonator into his briefcase, took one last look around his office, and walked out the door, turning the light off behind him.

————

Dabir truly enjoyed purchasing expensive things, especially when he could procure them with the money of others. Such was the case with the CheyTac M100. He held the high-end sniper rifle across his lap, his fingers running over its surface. He'd only held its like one other time, on a training exercise in Saudi Arabia. His teacher had been impressed by Dabir's steady hands, the accuracy of his shots. And Dabir had been impressed with the optional surface-to-surface missiles that one could send on its course with deadly accuracy. He had not opted for such with this purchase. For this mission, stealth and finesse were all that were required.

He stood and placed the gun on the hotel bed. He considered disassembling it now, knowing he would have to do so before carrying it from the room, but decided against it. There was something almost spiritual about seeing such a fine instrument of death ready to be picked up and used.

The Eritrean padded across the dingy carpet to the sink, where he poured himself a glass of water. As he drank he inventoried himself in the mirror, an introspection that served to help him focus, to banish everything that was not the mission. Satisfied with what he saw, he checked his watch and then lifted his suitcase onto the bed, the lid opening over the M100. From the suitcase he pulled his prayer rug.

He spread it on the floor and then knelt upon it, finding east before starting to pray.

26

December 17, 2012, 10:11 P.M.

Brent thought that what he saw as he looked out the window of the cargo transport was how the world would look minutes before it breathed its last: a maelstrom of ice chips riding winds that obeyed no meter, spires of ice towering over frozen deserts, glimpses of monstrous cracks in the fabric of the earth that looked dormant but seemed to hold the promise of fire and magma issuing from the earth's molten belly.

Added to that was the very real possibility that he would make use of the airsickness bag before the plane alighted on terra firma.

He realized, as he watched the plane split the elements in two, that it was insane for him to be there. The stakes in this thing exceeded what he'd signed on for. There was no set of axioms that should have resulted in his sitting in a seat in the cold cargo hold of a plane that vibrated as if it would shake itself apart, knowing that if it did there wasn't another living soul around for a thousand miles save for the foolhardy adventurers who had chosen to brave the elements with him.

However, as he looked around him, taking in the faces of the men he'd come to know over the last two weeks, he saw nothing but an equanimity that bespoke another day at the office. Taking his cues from them, he decided not to cry.

Rawlings had made quick work of the satellite imagery. The first thing he'd noticed was the rerouting of several commercial satellites that seldom were rerouted. At first, Rawlings and the technicians, whom NORAD had loaned him, approached the problem linearly. The technicians, accustomed to altering orbits to gain a better view of a target, attacked this problem with the same mind-set. It was Rawlings, more used to approaching things with a unique perspective, who suggested that the satellite moves might not have been meant to bring something into focus but to blur something else. From that point it was a simple matter of finding the manufactured blind spot, which lined up precisely with what Albert Griffiths had recalled about eastern Antarctica.

However, as Rawlings had explained to Colonel Richards, the effectiveness of creating a blind spot rested on making sure *everyone* turned their heads. And while whoever had organized the altered orbits had demonstrated a frightening array of resources, the type of task they'd assigned themselves was impossible to pull off. Someone was always watching.

Rawlings suspected whoever had orchestrated the satellite moves would have known that. They would have acted accordingly.

It took Rawlings and the technicians—with the captain allowing the techs to do what they did best—to find faint yet regular energy signatures where none had ever been recorded. Now with a place to look, the team had gone for a visual, but the one old satellite that could provide a picture had a lens that wouldn't grant the pictures enough detail to make out anything beyond the emptiness of a forbidding continent.

Thus, another field trip.

The plane dropped as the air pockets shifted around it and Brent grabbed hold of the armrests. But in a second it was over—the plane resettled at its new, if not entirely chosen, altitude. Brent wondered if that said something about the concept of free will, but he chose to relegate that thought to a time more appropriate for trolling the depths of it.

All of a sudden the plane began what Brent assumed was a controlled drop, a rapid descent he hoped was dictated by radar and pilot expertise, and through a break in the opaque clouds he saw a flat surface. Less than fifteen seconds later the wheels of the plane touched something solid and Brent's lunch fought against making a reappearance. He was thrown forward as the pilot hit the brakes, as the transport locked down on the ice of a world the professor had known existed but had never considered in empirical fashion.

It took the plane almost a quarter mile to stop, although Brent just registered it as a long time. He forced thoughts from his mind of the plane either running into a mountain or running out of road and falling into the sea, and waited for someone to tell him what to do. As it turned out, he had to wait a while.

As the plane powered down and the team—their numbers supplemented by Army Rangers on loan from General Smithson—jumped into motion, he found that not one of them paid him the slightest bit of attention. Each one had a series of prescribed duties to execute before acknowledging anything outside of that list. Rawlings, who had assumed responsibility for Brent in Maddy's absence, was the first to include him among those duties.

"Stick with me," he said. "Don't go anywhere and don't touch anything."

"Got it," Brent said.

They told him the clothes they'd outfitted him with were good for forty below zero, but when the bay door opened and the team spilled out onto the ice, it was difficult to convince his face of that. As the team assembled, Brent saw a number of pieces of equipment that he hadn't witnessed the team using up to that point, and he suspected the weather necessitated use of the big guns.

The team moved as one across the frozen surface, led by Rawlings, who consulted his handheld device. When enough distance separated them from the plane so that Brent lost sight of it, he felt the beginnings of panic set in. What kept that panic from becoming debilitating were the attitudes of the rest of the team, all of whom acted as if the loss of a visual on the plane meant nothing.

How long they progressed over the ice, Brent didn't know. It seemed to him that they traveled far past the time he'd heard the colonel say a person could survive in this place without the proper equipment, and it was at some point during this journey that he realized he trusted these people. And with that realization came the knowledge that he had no idea why he trusted them. On the sociological chart that mapped the progression of relationships, he understood that his camaraderie with them was the result of a compressed relational period defined by stress and a shared agenda, and for one of the few occasions in his professional life, he was ready to toss all his theories out the window. He liked and trusted these folks, for no other reason than they were good people. Despite the career sociologist in him, he decided that was enough.

Rawlings, walking a step ahead of Brent, stopped and Brent did the same. Rawlings consulted his scanner, turning his body first to the left and then to the right.

"I've got something, Colonel," Rawlings yelled over the wailing of the wind. He used his gloved hand to wipe particulate matter from the scanner and set his body in the direction of whatever the machine had revealed to him. "About fifty yards that way."

Rawlings started off and the rest of the team followed. Brent hung somewhere at Rawlings's elbow. The fifty yards unfolded below them, and by some inward count that only someone used to measuring distance without the proper instruments could utilize, Rawlings slowed and the team spread out. Brent, who had no idea what to look for, remained at the man's side. It was with a growing feeling of uselessness, then, that he suddenly fell down a hole.

It wasn't a deep hole, perhaps sixteen inches, yet the ground beneath his feet felt soft. It was enough, however, to turn his ankle and to require help from Rawlings to find solid ground again. After the officer pulled him up, Brent spent a few seconds looking into the hole.

"It felt like it might go down farther if someone pulled the loose snow and ice out of it," he said.

At that, Rawlings knelt down, bringing his monitor closer to the hole. Then he set the instrument down and cleared some of the snow away until he'd revealed a hole rounder than nature could have produced in that environment.

"Score one for Albert Griffiths," he said, looking up at Brent. "This was drilled."

He touched a button and a rectangular piece of what looked like metal slid from the front of the scanning unit. Rawlings lowered the monitor into the hole and held it there for at least thirty seconds before withdrawing it. When he pulled it from the hole he touched another button with his gloved finger and sent the rectangular sensor back into the machine. Within fifteen seconds he was flagging down the colonel.

"Traces of octanitrocubane," he shouted to him.

While the layers of protective gear kept Brent from seeing the true effect of this pronouncement on the colonel, he saw the man's body go taut. Seconds later he was calling the rest of the team, and the loaned Army Rangers, around.

"Rawlings found traces of octanitrocubane," he yelled, point-ing at the hole. "We're looking for shallow depressions, about eight inches in diameter."

With that as their charge, the team set off. Brent stayed with Rawlings, but he didn't move from his spot, giving the rest of the team a point from which to spread. Fifteen minutes later, Brent saw Snyder begin to wave from about twenty-five yards away. Ten minutes after that, one of the Rangers made another hit. Even to Brent's unpracticed eye, he saw that the three holes formed a straight line.

The colonel sent Bradford and Addison in opposite directions, overshooting Snyder and the Ranger by the same distance that sepa-rated those two from Rawlings. When, after a bit of searching, each man returned a wave, the colonel made a hammering motion in the air, followed by a circle. As Brent watched, each person positioned at a hole pulled a stake-mounted flag from his pack and drove it into the ground, after which they started back to Richards, who motioned them into a tight circle.

"Dr. Michaels was kind enough to take one for the team and find a hole for us," Richards said. "And it looks like we have some others in a straight line. Now, what does that mean?"

The thing about working with a group of smart people was that it seldom took long for someone to venture an opinion. In this case it was Addison.

"We're at the grounding line, Colonel," the man said. "It can't be coincidence that we have holes filled with the most powerful non-nuclear explosive known to man, spaced about twenty-five yards apart along the line. My guess is that the line of explosives covers the entire length of the grounding line."

"So you think someone's going to blow the ice shelf," Richards said.

"Yes, sir."

The colonel nodded. "That's what I think too."

Richards looked past Addison, following the line marked by the flags, imagining flags heading into the distance as far as he might see on a clear day.

"Too many to dig out," he said. "And probably too dangerous."

Snyder shook his head.

"It's a pretty safe explosive, sir. Safer than just about anything out there. Your problem is time."

The colonel grunted and studied the flags for a while longer as if they might offer up a suggestion. Finally he turned to Brent.

"Dr. Michaels, it looks like we've found your polarizing event."

———

"So what does this mean?" Brent asked Richards as the team finished boarding the plane.

Before the colonel could respond, Addison cut in.

"Colonel, there's going to be a simple triggering mechanism, probably no bigger than a remote control."

"Where?"

"It could be anywhere, sir. It would feed a signal to a satellite, which would set off each of the explosive caches simultaneously."

"And I'm guessing there's no way to keep that from happening?" the colonel asked.

"Technically, whoever has the detonator could blow the whole thing right now, from anywhere in the world," Addison said.

The fact that Addison was the most cerebral member of the team and, as such, often delivered information with the passion of someone reading the newspaper, added a peculiar weight to his statement—enough to make everyone within earshot stop for a second, including the colonel.

"I doubt we're in any danger now, Colonel," Brent said. "Whoever planted these charges—whoever's responsible for everything we've seen to this point—will wait until the twenty-first. They won't do it any sooner."

The colonel nodded, turning his attention to the rest of the team.

"Can they do it?" he asked. "Can they really separate the ice shelf from the continent?"

While he waited for an answer, the plane rumbled to life.

"It depends on how deep they drilled," Addison said. "And how much octanitrocubane they're using." He paused and seemed to do some calculations in his head. When he looked back up at the colonel, his face was grim. "It's possible, sir."

On the heels of that, the plane began to move and Brent almost lost his footing. The colonel motioned for everyone to take their seats. Once everyone was seated and buckled in, Richards swiveled his seat around so that he faced the team. The Rangers, who had fulfilled their obligation, clustered in the back, talking amongst themselves.

"What happens if the ice shelf goes?" Richards asked, but then immediately held up a hand. "And I know we don't have enough data. I'm looking for conjecture, folks."

"I think the first worry is a tsunami." This came from Addison, again, who was in his element with a puzzle like this one. "A slab of ice this size basically falling into the ocean could create a wave that would reach who knows how many miles inland if it were to hit a landmass."

"Okay," Richards said. "What else?"

"Rising sea levels," Bradford said. "The shelf will break up over time and parts of it will float into warmer water. And with the size of this thing . . ."

The colonel nodded. "Anything else?" Richards looked around at the faces of his team, but no one seemed ready to make another guess.

"What it will do is make otherwise sane people panic," Brent said. When everyone turned to look at him, he ran a hand through his hair and leaned back against the seat. "In less than twenty-four hours after the event, the stock market will crash. You'll see people all over the world making runs on stores, stockpiling food and gas. At first, most governments will tell everyone to be calm. They'll try to present a good public face. But then they'll start issuing orders about what people can buy and when they can buy it. And there will almost certainly be pockets of unrest that spring up during the first week that will require the National Guard. At least in the U.S. In the rest of the world they'll do whatever it is they do to secure the peace."

"All so that someone can profit," Richards said.

"And profit they will," Brent said. "Gas companies, food manufacturers, weapons and survival gear dealers. There are people who stand to get rich from something like this."

The silence that settled over the plane was tomblike and was only broken when Colonel Richards, not willing to let the mood of his team sink to a place from which he wouldn't be able to bring it back, forced them to reengage.

"So our job is to make sure that doesn't happen," he said. "Addison, is Sheffield still insisting they haven't had a team here in three years?"

"Yes, sir."

"Do you believe them?"

"I'm inclined to, sir. Bradford helped me speed through their financials. I don't think they're a big enough company to have pulled off something like this."

"And Albert Griffiths?"

"They claim the first time they ever heard of him was when he started calling and asking for his workman's comp checks," Addison said. "They say he was never on the payroll. Neither was anyone named Ben Robinski."

Richards grunted and turned to the window to watch the clouds roll by.

"If we're going to assume they're telling the truth," he said, "then we're left with someone who co-opted their name, assembled a large, well-provisioned drill team, shipped them all off to Antarctica, and then drilled thousands of holes in a straight line across hundreds of miles, filling each one with an explosive so new that there should be records of every ounce of it that's been produced."

"In a nutshell, sir," Addison said.

Listening to the back and forth, Brent couldn't help but laugh. And as he did so, he realized that it wasn't just for the nature of the conversation but the nature of the whole thing. The fact that he was in an airplane over Antarctica, discussing how they were going to keep the largest nonnuclear explosion in the history of the world from happening, was something he would never have imagined.

"Something amusing, Dr. Michaels?" Richards asked.

At the question, the laughter threatened to overtake Brent, but he did his best to keep it in check.

"No, sir," he said with a small wave. Except that then his eyes began to fill with tears and the laughter came even harder. And once the laughter started, he found that all the trying in the world couldn't make it stop. At one point he glanced over at the colonel, apology in his eyes, and was gratified to see that he didn't seem to mind. In fact, there was a twinkle in his eye that suggested he understood. When he could catch his breath, he said, "I mean, yes, sir. This whole crazy thing, it's hilarious."

When the colonel arched an eyebrow, Brent said, "Colonel, if you can't understand what it is about this situation that makes me feel like I've hopped down into the rabbit hole, then I've been reading you all wrong."

The moment he said it he realized the colonel could take that as an insult, but as he suspected the man would, Richards let the corners of his mouth curve upward.

"Dr. Michaels, welcome to my world," Richards said. "More than half of what we do is so absurd it almost reduces me to tears."

The whole team shared a few seconds of genuine warmth in the chill of the airplane's cabin, although it was short-lived as the immensity of the task before them reasserted itself.

"Colonel, there are only a few facilities producing octanitro-cubane," Addison said. "I suggest we get the feds to subpoena their records—find out if any of them have increased production enough to do something like this."

Even as Richards nodded his agreement, Brent suspected it was wasted energy.

"Whoever did this wouldn't have gone through any registered facility," Brent said. When everyone looked at him, he offered the same half smile the colonel had volunteered moments ago. "They would have figured out how to do it themselves."

The coldness of that fact silenced them all. Brent waited for a few seconds and then he turned to look out the window, and he kept his eyes there until he fell asleep.

Alan Canfield understood he had set foot in his office for the last time. Yesterday's visit to the Van Camp building had stretched the limits of good sense, with his knowledge of what the company leadership considered acceptable in the name of expedience.

His decision to spend the night somewhere other than his home proved the right one. Instead, he rented a car—one with dark-tinted windows—and drove through his quiet neighborhood. When he did so, he came up with one of those ideas that, were he still gainfully employed by the world's largest media company, he would have committed to a memo and sent to the Fleet Services Department. He would have told them to rotate the vehicles assigned to the security team monthly. That way, a potential target would stand less of a chance recognizing the same vehicle parked in the same spot over consecutive months.

Canfield picked out the Altima with the scratch on the side panel right away. The GMC Jimmy was a bit harder to spot, but that was only because whoever was behind the wheel had parked it in the strip mall lot adjacent to his neighborhood. Canfield had driven right by his home, confident that whoever was conducting surveillance wouldn't see through the dark glass of his rental car.

With his suspicions confirmed, Canfield drove on to the bank.

Collecting sufficient cash to remain safe for an indeterminate period of time held greater risk than just pointing the car away from Atlanta and driving until the gas tank gave its last. Yet he understood the logistics involved in trying to conduct a proper flight without adequate resources.

He pulled into the parking lot and chose a spot with a view of the front entrance, as well as most of the other cars in the lot. From what he could see, all of them were empty and there was no obvious Van Camp security presence around the bank. But then why would there have been? He wasn't supposed to know about the impending change in his work situation. He suspected that had he been caught unawares by the assassination team, they would have made it look like a suicide. With his termination paper work making its way through the HR Department, and with his wife not expected to recover, most crime-scene investigators would accept the suicide theory as the most likely. And since Van Camp had initiated termination proceedings, the company had plausible deniability in the face of any investigation. After all, who would murder an employee who was in the process of being fired?

After five minutes, Canfield cut the engine and exited the car. There was no line and so he picked one of the two available tellers.

"I'd like to close my account, please." He slid his driver's license and, for good measure, his passport toward her.

"Certainly, Mr. Canfield," she said. "Do you mind if I ask why you've decided to take your business elsewhere?"

Canfield offered the woman his most winning smile. "I've taken a position as regional manager for one of your competitors," he explained. "It's probably best if I show I can trust my own company with my money."

It was the sort of explanation that left slim room for argument, and in less than twenty minutes Canfield left the bank with more than fifty-two thousand dollars.

The next stop at a second bank, the one with which his company did business, proved trickier. But part of succeeding as a senior executive was imagining any number of doomsday scenarios. A month into his current role, he'd taken the liberty of producing a fair number of helpful documents, which enabled him to make his exit with considerably more than the meager sum he'd pulled from his own bank account. In this case it was a check, a very large one.

It took a bit longer this time, requiring a phone call to the director of the Finance Department at Van Camp Enterprises, who Canfield suspected, was as much in the dark regarding his pending unemployment as he was supposed to be. There was no reason for them to deny the request, especially since the instructions to disburse funds at Canfield's discretion had come from Van Camp himself.

By the time he left, almost an hour after walking through the bank's front door, he carried a briefcase holding almost two million dollars. It wasn't the sort of sum that would set him up for life in some far-off country with feeble extradition laws, but it was sufficient to let him burrow into hiding somewhere while he watched the whole thing play out.

As he got into the car and set the briefcase on the passenger seat, he again considered the possibility of going to the authorities. He had enough information to implicate more than a dozen people, and while he knew nothing he could offer prosecutors would absolve him of the blood on his own hands, it might buy him his life.

As with the other times he'd considered it, though, he dismissed the idea. Even considering his present circumstances, it was difficult to discount the possibility that he could emerge from this unscathed. With the detonator in his hands he had complete control over the ultimate success or failure of the project. And if he stayed the course, two potential paths opened before him. The first of them was flight, a permanent disassociation from everything he knew. While not ideal, it had the benefit of allowing him to live. The second was the elimination of the man who wanted him dead. He thought it could be done, but it was all about timing. It had to happen after Shackleton; there was no way around it.

Soon after leaving the bank, he reached the hospital and then spotted the Altima within seconds. As he kept his rental car in motion, his hands tightened on the wheel. With them watching the entrance, he wouldn't get in undetected. It meant that he would not get to see Phyllis for a while—perhaps never again. He pulled the car back onto the street and, after taking and releasing a long breath, pointed the car toward the airport.

———

For years, Colonel Richards's team had operated under the radar, and he liked it that way. On rare occasions he found himself in front of someone higher up the chain of command, answering questions about something unusual discovered by the NIIU, but those instances were exceptions to the rule, which saw him and his team left alone to play with eyeballs or explore things that most people discounted out of hand.

Had he any career ambitions beyond his present role, that might have bothered him, but he'd long accepted the fact that he was where he belonged. That made appearances like the one he'd had that morning uncomfortable. After reporting the Antarctic findings to Smithson, the general had solicited a meeting of the Joint

Chiefs of Staff. In Smithson's opinion, it was time to get this thing out into the open.

Richards did not begrudge these men and women their need to know about a threat to national security. What did irritate him, though, were the number of instances in which he had to respond to a question with the words *I don't know.* Consequently, he entered a room filled with clueless bureaucrats and left that room having armed these same men and women with enough information to convince them there was a significant issue but not enough to get them to understand the full extent of the danger. What he had accomplished was a commitment of whatever resources he deemed necessary to counteract the threat, and for that he was grateful. The problem was that he wasn't sure what resources he needed.

It didn't matter how fast they got a crew working to remove the explosives from the holes dotting the grounding line. According to Addison, they would never remove enough of them in time to change the outcome. And so Richards was left staying the course, trying to determine the mastermind behind the entire affair. In three days.

That was why he didn't feel as bad as he might have about missing his Sunday school commitment. It was a rare occasion that he missed his turn teaching the kids. To the best of his recollection it had been almost five years since the last such forfeiture of his duty. He was considering the lesson he wouldn't be able to teach when Addison entered his office.

"I've finished my analysis of what we can expect if the ice shelf is separated," he said without preamble. Without waiting for an invitation he took the seat across the desk from the colonel. "It's actually not without precedent. In April 2010 the Larsen B ice shelf collapsed and the entire thing was captured via satellite imagery. And of course you have Wilson. The reason that one was such a big deal was because of how quickly it happened."

"That's right," Richards agreed, although he had no idea what Addison was talking about.

"Now, neither of those caused serious problems because, first of all, they're both a lot smaller than Shackleton. But the main reason is that both of those ice shelves, for lack of a better word, disintegrated."

The colonel didn't respond, aware that Addison would take his silence as a prompt to continue.

"A closer scenario would be Lituya Bay," Addison said. "In 1958, a piece of ice broke away from the North Crillon Glacier, producing a tsunami more than fifteen hundred feet high. And what we're talking about with Shackleton is one and a half million square miles of ice dropping off the coast and displacing more water at one time than has probably ever been displaced before."

By the time the man finished, he was breathing harder, the prospects of such an event obviously touching his hot button.

"Put it in layman's terms for me, Captain," Richards said. "If the ice shelf breaks away, what exactly can we expect?"

"Near the point of entry, next to nothing," Addison said. "Oh, it will look pretty impressive, because the entire ice shelf will drop and disappear below the surface for a few seconds, but then it will bob right back up. Over time, as it floats away from the grounding line, it will start to break up and we'll wind up with colossal icebergs that will cause havoc in shipping lanes as they move north. But the real problem happens where you can't see it."

Addison took a breath before going on.

"You can't displace that much water without it going somewhere, and if my figures are accurate it's going to trigger a subsurface wave traveling primarily northeast."

"Meaning?" Richards prodded when Addison's pause extended longer than normal.

"Meaning that a tsunami bigger than any in recorded history

is probably going to hit mainland China about thirty-six hours afterwards."

Richards thought it was amazing how a simple series of words strung together in a particular order could cause most of the air to escape from his lungs.

"How far inland?" he managed to ask.

Despite the scientist in him that enjoyed measuring the facts and figures of something like the largest tsunami in the world, even Addison seemed to channel a portion of his human side, because it was in a subdued voice that he said, "Maybe a hundred miles, Colonel."

Richards didn't have to be as smart as Addison to understand the incredible loss of life such an event would entail.

"How sure are you?"

Addison offered a slight shrug. "Eighty-five percent." When the colonel didn't respond, Addison said, "But that's not the worst part, Colonel."

At that, Richards's face hardened. "We're talking about millions of lives lost," he snapped. "And that's not the worst part?"

"Sir," Addison said, his voice quiet, "when it's all over, and when China has the chance to send researchers to the area to study how it happened, they're going to know that it wasn't a natural event. They'll look at the even split from the grounding line and they'll see all the evidence of a series of explosions and they'll know that someone planned it."

It didn't take long before the colonel understood what the other man was implying, and the thought was almost crippling.

"They'll assume we did it," he said.

"In their eyes we'll be the only ones capable of pulling off something like that, sir," Addison agreed.

Richards had the phone in his hand a few seconds later.

———

Those who insisted that Allah did not answer prayers simply did not understand the subtle nature of divine direction. The thought had hit Dabir as he prayed, seeking guidance as he developed a plan for dealing with Alan Canfield, the coward who had used a fake name to obscure his objectives. And when it came to him, he thanked Allah for the simple things missed by wise men.

Canfield worked for Van Camp Enterprises, and Dabir knew enough about the workings of multinational corporations to know that someone with Canfield's power did not rise to his position without the blessing of his superiors.

And so he had begun his investigation into Arthur Van Camp, the man who had developed a media empire out of a single cable television station, and who now commanded more wealth than most men in the world. A worthy adversary—one who seldom left the protective sphere of his office or his security team. A target like Van Camp made Canfield seem like a man barely worthy of interest, even if that interest was more personal than the clinical one that encompassed his interest in Van Camp.

What aided Dabir in seeking retribution from Van Camp was his knowledge that Canfield would not go anywhere without the knowledge of the Eritrean. That was another thing he liked about America—the preponderance of businesses that offered a foreigner the means to track a person. Alan Canfield was still in Atlanta, and when Dabir was ready, he would find him.

For now, he had things to consider. If one was able, one did not kill a man without coming to know what that death would cost those around him.

———

It took Brent longer to flag the colonel down than was normally the case, and when Richards broke away from Addison and approached the professor, Brent saw that regardless of the news he had to present to him, he did not have Richards's full attention.

"How are you at haystack analysis?" Brent asked.

At Richards's puzzled look, Brent said, "Miles Standish was a member of Plymouth Colony. He was a brutal military commander who slaughtered Indians any chance he got." Seeing that the colonel had brought his attention to bear, Brent continued, "Granted, most of what I've read about Standish doesn't have much bearing on our situation. He was responsible for the protection of the colony and used any means necessary to get that done."

Brent paused to consult his notes.

"But what's interesting is that in 1625, he was sent to London to negotiate with a group called the Merchant Adventurers. According to one written report, Standish gave a speech in front of the Merchant Adventurers in Newcastle. In fact, it was such a powerful speech that a number of them voted to cancel the colony's debt immediately."

"That's all very interesting, Dr. Michaels," Richards said, "but I hope you're coming to the payoff soon."

"I am, Colonel," Brent assured him. "In his speech, Standish makes repeated references to the wealth of Solomon. He mentions it so often that it sounds like a buzzword for him."

"The wealth of Solomon?" Richards repeated.

"So that got me to thinking and I plugged that into a search engine. And after going through about fifty pages of results, I found something interesting."

"I'm listening."

"I'm not sure how up you are on biblical history," Brent said, "but according to legend, King Solomon was the richest man who ever lived. And according to some theologians, no one would ever have the wealth he amassed by the time of his death." He could see he was losing Richards, so he cut to the heart of it. "So I searched for any speeches or addresses that used the phrase *the wealth of Solomon*. And while it took a while, I finally found a reference."

"I admire the follow-through, Doctor, but I really need you to cut to the chase."

"In 1998, a businessman by the name of Arthur Van Camp gave a commencement address at Stanford. The gist of it was how anyone who worked hard enough, who sacrificed, and who was smarter than their competitors had a chance to achieve incredible wealth. I read the whole thing; it's a pretty good speech. But do you know what's so interesting?"

The colonel didn't respond to the rhetorical question, but Brent saw a glimmer of interest in his eyes.

"Arthur Van Camp is the same guy who runs Van Camp Enterprises," Brent said.

The colonel frowned. "The TV guy?"

"The TV guy. But that's not all. According to the SEC, Van Camp holds stock in almost a hundred different businesses, including a few weapons development firms."

He stopped and aimed a mischievous smile at Richards.

"And I'll give you one guess which way almost every single one of his stocks has gone over the last two years."

Richards was silent for some time, and Brent saw the man working through the information he'd presented him. It was only a theory, so the professor couldn't do anything beyond make his case and let the other man run with it.

"Does he have the resources?"

"More than enough," Brent avowed. "In fact, I'd bet he has more money than two-thirds of the countries in the world."

Brent knew his case was shaky, but he also understood that time was running out, and to this point, they had nothing on anyone else. Still, he had to allow the colonel to come to his own conclusions.

After what seemed a very long time, Richards nodded and said,

"Run with it. But it would be helpful if we could get something more concrete than a fourteen-year-old commencement address."

"Understood."

The colonel started to walk away and then, as if having an afterthought, he half turned and called back to Brent, "And if you can do something to verify the picture we got via email, that would be helpful too."

Then he was gone, leaving Brent with both a feeling of triumph and one of regret for the work ahead.

December 18, 2012, 5:43 P.M.

Van Camp could not recall a single occasion over the last twenty years when something outside of his influence was playing out on the world stage. Few situations were immune to the pull of money and a forceful guiding hand. Today, though, he found no shame in admitting that this thing he'd started a few years ago—this grand plan that stood to increase his personal wealth by a factor unparalleled in human history—had spiraled out of control. Perhaps it was his own hubris that had allowed it to happen. Regardless, all he could do now was plan for what the future might hold.

He'd begun consolidating some of his financial holdings, pulling what money he could into shelters that would withstand whatever the fateful day might unleash. He thought he had all of his ducks in a row, suspected that nothing could happen beyond the enrichment of his own accounts, but so much had happened beyond the scope of the plan that, at this point, there was simply no way to know for sure.

If only he could locate Alan.

By his accounting Van Camp had already amassed a fortune surpassing that of anyone else alive, although it would be months before his calculations were verified by those entities that corroborated such things. So in that sense Project: Night House had already succeeded. But only Van Camp, who understood the importance of fulfilling a childhood dream, knew that without the final push that would send governments flocking to purchase weapons and to lay hedges against the rising prices of agriculture, he would be remembered as but one rich man among many.

Alan had the detonator; there was no way to escape that. And after consulting with his tech staff, it had been determined that there was no way—at least in the time they had available—for Van Camp to find some other means to detonate the charges that occupied the shelf. Without the calving of the ice shelf—a project that was, ironically, Alan's idea—the events of the last several years might as well have been for naught.

Every resource at his disposal was occupied with looking for the man, and if they found him, no amount of meritorious service would protect him from Van Camp's anger.

For now, though, Van Camp had to leave Atlanta, at least until this business was concluded. There was no sense remaining there and allowing the army unit Alan had agitated to put the pieces together in time enough to pick him up—not before he had the chance to finish what he'd started.

———

They had gathered for a briefing from Brent, but the colonel exercised his authority to co-opt the first part of the meeting.

"I'm sure you've heard by now that Addison has projected the damage that calving Shackleton will cause," Colonel Richards said, and a look around the table told him that was true. "I spoke with the Joint Chiefs . . ." He hesitated and then took a deep breath before continuing. "At this time, they're not going to issue a warning."

Brent's eyes went as wide as those of everyone else.

"What are they thinking?" he asked.

"They're thinking that it would be foolish to tell several million Chinese to make a run for the interior of the country," Richards said. "Besides the logistics involved in organizing an evacuation of that size, they'd never get it done in time. And then there are the number of people who will lose their lives trying to get away from the coast."

"But that's nowhere near as many who will die if the tsunami hits and we don't warn them."

The colonel gave the professor a grim nod. "The problem is that there seems to be some doubt as to whether the artificial calving of an ice shelf is even possible. A few of their scientists-advisors, to be blunt, think we're wrong."

Brent looked across the table at Addison, watched the man's face cloud at the suggestion that his figures were inaccurate. But the man didn't argue his case. He knew the data was right, as did the others seated around the table.

Brent thought to continue the discussion, but Richards cut him off before he could start.

"Dr. Michaels, I let my superiors know that some madman was about to blow a million tons of ice to smithereens and that it would plunge the world into a panic the likes of which they've never seen. And do you know what their reaction was?" He paused to see if the professor might hazard a guess. When it was clear Brent would not, Richards said, "They all nodded and thanked me for my report. Then they said they'd study it."

Anything Brent might have said after that would have been fruitless. He wouldn't just be arguing with the colonel but with a group of nameless and faceless men and women with advisors who would most likely contradict any claim he might make.

"Our best hope of stopping this, gentlemen, is to find the person responsible."

That was Brent's cue. He stood and pressed a button on the projector remote.

"His name is Alan Canfield," Brent began. "Arthur Van Camp promoted him to VP of Business Development three years ago."

The man's picture was projected on the wall next to the black-and-white photo that their unknown assistant had sent them.

The rest of the team—with the exception of Snyder, who was still verifying the stock records they'd received from the SEC—studied both photos, and Brent saw the doubt on their faces.

"I admit it's hard to tell with how grainy the first picture is," Brent said. "But I'm sure this is our Miles Standish."

"What can you tell us about him?" the colonel asked.

Brent had enlisted Bradford to help him dig up information about Alan Canfield, so the professor turned the floor over to him.

"He's the youngest vice-president in the history of Van Camp Enterprises. Married. No kids. His wife's in the hospital."

"What for?" Snyder asked.

"Attempted suicide," Brent answered. "Apparently she almost got the job done, because the prognosis is severe brain damage—if she ever wakes up."

Richards nodded. "What else?"

"His record's clean as far as our federal friends are concerned," Bradford continued. "But they did find something interesting. Not only is he the youngest VP in company history, he's also the most traveled. He's logged ninety-five business trips this year, and he has access to a lot more Van Camp cash than any other company employee in a similar position."

"Do you have any itineraries?" Richards asked. "I'd be curious what that would look like plugged into your charts, Dr. Michaels."

"I have a partial," Bradford said. "Working on the rest. It can get more difficult to do that when the subject uses local carriers."

"And we have a number of flights booked under the name Standish," Brent added. "The passport photo, while similar to Canfield, isn't him. But that's not surprising. If you're working with a fake passport, all you need is someone who looks enough like you so that if anyone questions it, you can just tell them you either lost or gained some weight."

"Alright then," Richards said. "We have a possible. Now, what do you have on Van Camp?"

"Well, for one thing his personal stock has spiked over the last eighteen months," Bradford said. "The SEC pointed out a number of shell corporations that they're pretty sure funnel directly back to him."

"What kinds of companies would those be?"

"I'm glad you asked, Colonel," Brent said with a smile. "It's a pretty varied bunch, but some of the notables are weapons systems, handguns, canned goods, and wilderness supplies. The big one is weapons systems, most of them developed for and sold to the U.S. government." He paused and fixed them all with a grin. "I guess that's you guys."

The implications of that hit everyone at about the same time.

"It almost seems as if a war with China would really help his bottom line," Rawlings remarked.

Richards weighed that against the rest of the data and then looked at Brent and Bradford. "Anything else?"

"He lost his wife five years ago," Brent said. "Cancer."

"So could that have been his stressor?"

"No. I don't think so, Colonel," Brent said. "Something like this would have been in the planning stages for a long time. Long before his wife died."

The rest of the team listened to the data that Brent and Bradford had compiled, and when they had finished, the professor saw Richards frown.

"The problem I'm having," Richards said, "is that Van Camp is one of the wealthiest men alive. And if your stock projections are accurate, he might well be at the top of that list. For a billionaire to manipulate the world markets, and to threaten an untold number of people with death, solely to fatten his bank account seems like the province of a James Bond villain."

Brent shrugged. "Well, maybe the world is filled with a lot more of those kinds of villains than we know. Most of them, though, don't have this guy's ability to pull off a grand scheme like this."

Richards appeared to ponder that answer, tossing it around in his head. Then he met Brent's eyes and said, "You don't really believe that, do you?"

"Not entirely," Brent agreed. "But right now it's all we have to go on."

After spending so much time with Richards's team, Brent was beginning to understand its special dynamics and he saw the colonel's appreciation for his position.

"So if you're right," Richards said, "Canfield is a footman for Van Camp."

"I believe so. After all, Van Camp is the one who stands to gain here—not Canfield."

"Besides," Bradford added, "Canfield seems to have gone underground. From what we can tell, he cleaned out his bank account this morning and he hasn't been to the office. No flights either. Not yet anyway."

The colonel looked ready to ask a follow-up question when Snyder hurried into the room.

"Colonel, it looks like Van Camp is on the move," he said. "His pilot just filed a flight plan to Eduardo Gomes."

At Brent's questioning look, Richards explained, "That's the major airport in the state of Amazonas in Brazil."

Bradford glanced down at his notes. "Van Camp has a home there."

"When are they leaving?" the colonel asked Snyder.

"In a few hours. There's no return flight scheduled."

To Brent, the fact that their subjects had flown the coop—or were in the process of flying the coop—was more than coincidence. He was the first to break the silence that had settled over the room.

"He's going there to wait things out," he said.

"Right," Richards said. "He doesn't know what we've figured out." The colonel paused, and in that space, Rawlings, after glancing around the room, jumped in.

"If we're right about what they're planning in Antarctica—and I'm pretty sure we are—then how come we can't send someone to pick up Van Camp? Or at least go in and grab all his files and see what we can uncover?"

If Brent was any judge of facial expression or body language, he could see that his suggestion sat well with each member of the NIIU, although it seemed to run into a roadblock when it reached the colonel.

"It just doesn't work that way," Richards said. "Even with the drilling in Antarctica, all we have is a theory, and that's not enough to go charging into the offices of a Fortune 500 company and grabbing anything we want. For one thing, we're not even allowed to operate domestically."

The colonel looked around the room as if gauging the effect of his words. Apparently what he saw was not what he'd hoped.

"And I can't just turn this thing over to Homeland Security; they'll laugh me out of their office."

"So what do we do?" Brent asked, feeling the exasperation growing.

The colonel sat there for perhaps a full minute, his eyes unfocused, as if working through a plan in his mind. Everyone else in the room let him do it.

Finally, Richards said, "Snyder, I need everything you can give me about his home in Brazil. And see if you can get us clearance for a border crossing."

He turned to Rawlings. "Get the plane ready for a trip south. Heavy armament."

At the surprised looks aimed his way, Richards explained, "Since we can't operate within our own borders, how about we remove that border from the equation?"

———

Brent was in the office he'd come to think of as his own, flipping through papers that he no longer needed to flip through, except that it gave him something to do. When the meeting ended, with all the team members going off to prepare for the trip to South America, the feeling of being a fifth wheel began to set in. Regardless of the fact that the threats he'd suffered granted him a stake in the outcome of this investigation, he had to face the fact that he'd done what he'd been hired to do. His presence from this point on was likely to be more of a hindrance than a help. In fact, he expected Colonel Richards to step into the office at any time, thank him for his help, and send him on his way.

It was as he was nursing that last thought that the colonel came in. Brent acknowledged the man with a half smile, and Richards took a seat, watching the professor sort papers that would likely wind up in the shredder once the NIIU closed the case file.

"Something on your mind?" Richards asked.

"A few things," Brent said. "But the big one is my wondering when you folks are going to let me go."

"Very astute of you, because that's why I'm here."

Brent frowned, dropping the papers and leaning back in his chair.

"Dr. Michaels, we're not about to cut you loose just yet. We owe it to you to keep you on until we see how everything plays out."

That news had an immediate effect on Brent, easing a tension he hadn't realized had taken hold in him.

"Does that mean I get to tag along to Brazil?"

"I wouldn't have it any other way."

It struck Brent how much a couple weeks could change a man. Before meeting this team, the thought of crossing the border to try and apprehend a criminal mastermind had never crossed his mind.

He thanked the colonel, then sat up straight in his chair and met the man's eyes. "About Maddy . . ." he began and then trailed off. Since coming back from Arizona, he hadn't heard anyone on the team mention her. It was as if she'd ceased to exist.

"That's another reason I'm keeping you on," Richards said.

Brent answered with a raised eyebrow.

"I stand by what I said before, Dr. Michaels. At some point during your time with us, you made her care. And because of that . . . well, I can't send you home yet."

"How altruistic of you," Brent said with a weak smile, one that quickly disappeared as he thought of the missing captain. "Honestly, Colonel, what do you think—?"

"I don't know and I'm not going to speculate," Richards said. "All we can do is hope for the best and, if you're so inclined, pray."

"And if one is not inclined in that direction?"

Before answering, Richards released a heavy sigh. "Then I'll pray for the both of us."

December 19, 2012, 4:52 P.M.

While Dabir thought it justified to hold American airport and border security in contempt, he was nonetheless careful crossing through to South America. In Africa, one could cross borders with impunity, and on those occasions in which poor timing or the will of Allah dictated border detainment, an exchange of money or other valuables ensured continued passage. In this hemisphere, one could often traverse borders with equal ease, but the penalties for being caught were often more unfortunate.

Although, now that he was there, he found much about this country to like. In many ways, the rain forest rivaled the jungles with which he was more familiar, both in expansiveness and the undercurrent of ferocity pervading them. He did not, however, force a kinship between the two, as that would have lulled him into a sense of dangerous familiarity when he did not know the landscape's deadly creatures, large or small.

After debarking from the single-engine plane that had brought him from Miami, he had rented a motorbike to take him over the nearly impassable roads that wound through and around the forest.

It seemed to him that Allah smiled on his mission: otherwise how to explain the ease with which he found the information he needed, as well as the timing of such. After observing Arthur Van Camp's movements, Dabir knew when the man's apartment would be empty, and breaking into the place, even if protected by an alarm, was a simple matter—another skill he'd learned in Saudi Arabia.

It was in Van Camp's study where the Eritrean found the man's notes: scribblings really. But there was enough there for Dabir to piece some things together. What he was coming to realize was that his part in this play was a minor one, and whatever it was building toward was fast approaching. A firm hand had written a date just two days from the one Allah's eternal provision now granted Dabir to enjoy.

His wish was that neither man live to see whatever their sins had fashioned.

To that end, he had followed Van Camp to the airport, where getting the man's flight plan became another simple matter. He would punish this man first, this one he had never met. He would save for last the one with whom he had shared tej. Alan Canfield/Miles Standish was Dabir's personal devil, and for that he would be Dabir's final act.

The Eritrean slipped his backpack off and, setting it down and unzipping it, withdrew the pieces of the M100. He sat on the forest floor, crossed his legs, and began to assemble the weapon, surrounded by sights and sounds so very much like his own world and yet very different.

———

As a child, Brent had understood that his life would include a variety of experiences. He knew it in the way some people knew they were destined to surpass the physical or ideological confines of their upbringings. His life, then, had been an effort toward solidifying the dreams of youth. With his advanced degree, occasional research work, and no attachments to speak of, he had thought he'd achieved his youthful vision.

How different could the passage of a month render the perception of one's personal landscape.

"I still don't know what I'm doing here," he whispered to Richards.

Here was a forest in Brazil—a wild land whose inhabitants barely grasped the existence of a world unfolding beyond their tribal fires. They'd come in from Colombia, someone in their military owing the colonel a favor, and twenty miles over the border they were in position to either prevent a global catastrophe or start a war.

The way Brent understood it, the Brazilian government had no idea an American team was operating on their soil, which was another indication that things down here unfolded in a different way than they did up north. Brent couldn't imagine a foreign military unit wedging its way into California without being detected in minutes.

"You're here because we wouldn't be here without you," Richards explained. "But when things get hairy you'll stick with Rawlings. You won't see any action."

Brent glanced at Rawlings, who had a look on his face that suggested irritation at being told he would have to remain with the civilian while the rest of the team risked their lives.

Before anyone could argue about the arrangement, Snyder emerged from the forest and crossed to the colonel's side.

"They have a moderate presence around the perimeter," he said. "All light armament from what I could see."

"Any way to breach without being spotted?" Richards asked.

Snyder shook his head. "They have motion detectors and

cameras. It would take us a long time to circumvent their systems. I think we can take them all from the tree line; there's not a one of them that's hunkered down."

"But if they were hunkered down, you wouldn't see them now, would you?" Brent asked.

Richards smirked and returned to surveying the scene through binoculars. He remained that way for a few minutes before lowering them. He removed the radio from his belt. "Bradford, meet Snyder and me by the rise ten degrees off the front gate. Addison, set up on the southeast corner." He didn't wait for a response before gathering Snyder with his eyes and rising to disappear into the forest.

The thing Brent registered most was the unnatural quiet of the forest, as if the animals around them had paused to see what would happen.

"Sorry you have to baby-sit," he said to Rawlings, whose only response was a grumble the professor couldn't translate.

The two men passed the minutes in silence, both sets of eyes fixed on the compound below them. Their single target, along with the sounds of the forest, lulled Brent into a sense of complacency— which meant that he nearly jumped out of his skin when Rawlings spoke.

"Are you sure about this, Doc?"

Brent didn't have to ask what he meant.

"Because it's something to kill a man," Rawlings went on. "If you're going to do something like that, you better believe one hundred percent that it's the right thing to do."

The soldier might well have been reading Brent's mind. The entire flight Brent had tossed the question around in his head, and each time he did, he came down on the side that said Van Camp was the one they were looking for. Too many things lined up for it not to be true. And there was also Maddy. Brent suspected his judgment was clouded by the prospect of finding her, and he could only hope he wasn't passing judgment on a man based solely on his admiration for a woman.

"I'm as sure as I can be" was the professor's honest answer.

Rawlings studied him for a moment before nodding and turning away.

Then Brent heard the voice of Colonel Richards coming through on Rawlings's earpiece. Brent couldn't hear what he said, but when he finished, Rawlings handed Brent the binoculars.

"They're ready," he said.

Brent didn't want to, but he accepted them and used them to review the compound. Magnified, the shapes he'd watched moving around below now took on faces. He raised the binoculars to try to spot Richards and the others positioned near the front gate, but the dense forest swallowed everything up. He brought the binoculars back to the trio of men guarding the gate, and the moment his hand stilled he saw a man's head explode in a mist of blood. It happened so fast that he almost dropped the binoculars. Just seconds later the two remaining men met similar fates.

When all movement stopped, Brent found that he couldn't pull the binoculars from the scene. It wasn't until Rawlings put a hand on his forearm and gave a soft tug that Brent lowered them. He turned a somber face to Rawlings, who nodded and then motioned for Brent to follow. Without a word, the soldier rose and started off down the slope.

————

Van Camp stood on a second-floor balcony overlooking the rain forest, which stretched as far as he could see, crossing the border into Peru, Colombia, and Venezuela in one direction and spreading into the country's wild interior in the other. From this spot he could nurture the belief that he was there alone, as he could not see the security team in evidence, nor did the existence of the city less than ten miles away intrude upon his solitude. Manacapuru was one of the larger cities in Amazonas, which meant it could supply anything Van Camp might need yet was small enough to allow the forest to block it from his consideration. While his wife still lived, they would sometimes take a motorbike the ten miles to the outskirts of the city, where they would browse among the fruit stands and small shops, sampling coffee and pastries.

He took a deep breath, tasting the scents he hadn't sampled in a long while. It was his first time back to this place since his wife's death and he was disquieted by the circumstances behind it. Had everything gone according to plan, he would have watched the culmination of the project from Atlanta, sitting in his office atop the company he'd worked to build.

However, with Alan's disappearance, and the detonator with him, he'd come to the conclusion that remaining in the United States was imprudent. There were too many trails and he worried at least one of them would lead past his vice-president of Business Development.

Even so, he doubted anyone would be able to put the pieces together to form a clear enough picture to implicate him. His team of lawyers would see to it that any case presented against him remained tied up for so long in the courts that he could well be dead before anyone discovered the true extent of the operation.

Van Camp harbored little ill will toward Alan, even considering the position in which the man's actions had put his boss. In hindsight, Van Camp saw that putting that much responsibility on the shoulders of one man was a mistake. Perhaps he thought he'd noticed something of himself in Alan, something to be developed, refined in fire. He couldn't even fault Alan for cleaning out the expense account. Had Van Camp been in a similar position, he would have done the same.

Van Camp sipped at the Mouton. When he'd selected it from the wine cellar, he'd meant it for the final tick of the clock. But he yielded to the urge to uncork it early, understanding the truth that the only ceremony granted a moment was that which a man gave to it.

His only hope was that wherever Alan went, he would do the one deed now denied the one whose plan this was. He suspected he would. Shackleton had been Alan's idea after all—a grand one. And after it was concluded, and after the stocks susceptible to such things either rose or fell according to their types, he expected that Alan would try to come for him. In the same fashion in which he sought to put the entirety of the blame on Alan, so would the man seek for him.

Arthur Van Camp stood on the balcony for a long while as the warm wind pushed through, carrying with it the smells he remembered from years ago. He could have gone to any number of houses around the world, all of them similarly stocked and secured. He'd chosen this one because it had been his wife's favorite, which was the reason he had not visited since her death. Before now, it had seemed wrong to be in the house without her.

He emptied the wineglass and went back inside.

His office, normally as orderly as the ones he kept all over the world, was cluttered with the things the impromptu flight had forced him to bring. His aide had left three boxes against the wall opposite the desk, upon which were spread several file folders and a loose stack of papers—all the items he needed to keep the business running. A member of his IT team had installed a new computer, as the passage of five years had left the system there inadequate for his needs, which included the ability to web-conference with his leadership team.

Aside from these, the only other addition to the office was the one thing Van Camp considered most important. His wife's painting now hung on the wall to the right of his desk.

He retrieved the Mouton and poured himself another glass and then sank into the guest chair.

The one thing he most had to consider was the one thing he seemed least inclined to entertain, and he imagined the reason for that rested in the sheer number of ways this whole operation might play out. And even acknowledging that bothered him. As a younger man, he would have charted every possibility and developed plans for dealing with them all. Not a detail would have escaped his notice; no contingency would have remained unaccounted for. Now, he just felt tired. Once Alan pressed the button—if he pressed it—Van Camp's personal portfolio would increase by a factor of five; of that he had no doubt. But would he, after finally achieving the dream he'd sought for so long—which at times seemed childish and at others an all-consuming fever—be a man without a country? For despite all the resources at his disposal, there still was no way of knowing.

Finishing the second glass of Mouton, he emptied the rest of the bottle into it.

———

When Rawlings, with Brent trailing, reached the bottom of the slope and joined the others, with Addison only now rounding the tree line to meet them, the colonel and Brent shared a look. The professor's drawn lips apparently told the man what he needed to see. Richards offered a grim nod and then turned to his work.

"There's a sensor on the gate, Colonel," Addison said. "If you open it from the outside, it triggers an alarm."

Richards nodded.

"If you look right there," Addison went on, directing the colonel's attention past the gate bars, "you can see the panel Van Camp's security team uses."

Richards held his response as he considered their next move. Brent knew the man was weighing the need to do this correctly against the danger posed by allowing the dead bodies to remain as testament to the presence of the Americans.

"How does security get back in if they have to leave the compound?" Richards asked. "They can't just hope someone's going to be around to open the gate for them."

Without waiting for a response, Richards walked toward the gate, and after a slight hesitation, the others moved with him. When they reached it, Brent saw that one of the security guards had collapsed nearby—perhaps close enough.

The professor knelt in front of the bars and reached an arm between two of them. Try as he might, he couldn't reach the dead man from that position, so he dropped onto his stomach and, with his face pressed up against the cold metal, pushed his arm through up to the shoulder. Even straining he was barely able to insert three fingers around the man's belt, and once he'd done so he discovered he had no leverage to drag the man forward.

"Hang on to him," he heard Rawlings say, and then the professor felt hands around both of his ankles. The soldiers pulled him backward as Brent held on to the dead man, who was a good deal heavier than he looked.

Addison took over, kneeling and fishing around in the man's pockets. He found it in the second pocket and handed it to the colonel, who gave it a once-over before holding it out and pressing its only button. In the top left corner of the gate a light that had been red turned to green. Snyder quickly pulled the gate open, then closed it again once they were all within the perimeter.

Seen from within the walls, the house was massive. And in the middle of the forest it looked like something that had grown up independent of the hands of men. Brent was struck by the beauty of the structure, understanding the inappropriateness of that when three dead men lay on the ground behind him. He avoided looking at them. He had watched them die and felt no need to relive any part of the experience.

The team spread out over the compound while Rawlings and

Brent remained by the front gate. Brent watched as Snyder and Richards disappeared around one side of the house, with Bradford and Addison taking the other side. In less than a minute they were coming back and gesturing for Brent and Rawlings to advance.

"The perimeter's clear," Richards said once the others were within earshot. He looked toward the front door. "We have no idea what's inside, so Rawlings and the doctor will stay out here until we clear the interior."

Brent offered yet another apologetic look to Rawlings. The soldier gestured with his head, indicating Brent should follow him away from the door. It was as Brent moved to comply that he heard a single shot. As when Rawlings had spoken to him in the trees, the loudness of the sound caused the professor to nearly jump out of his skin. Eyes wide, he whirled to see if he could find the shooter and instead found confusion setting in when he saw Snyder with a pistol in his hand, smoke rising from the barrel. Brent followed the line of the man's gun. It was pointed somewhere past Brent's right shoulder, and as the professor turned he again saw the three men the team had executed from afar. Except Brent was certain that one of them was not in his previous position.

"We didn't put him down the first time, Colonel," Snyder explained.

Richards took a second to assess the situation and then began barking orders, the element of surprise now gone.

Instantly Rawlings pulled Brent away while the rest of the team converged on the entrance, Snyder leading and Addison taking a position halfway up the steps, his weapon trained on the door.

Bradford pushed the door open, and after an eerie moment during which no shots rang out, he slipped past the doorframe and disappeared inside. Snyder and the colonel were right on his heels.

December 19, 2012, 7:19 P.M.

Van Camp understood the meaning of the sound before the blast dissipated. Yet he did not end his review of the documents spread out on the desk. With a red pen he made a note in the margin, and after scanning the rest of the page he capped the pen and returned it to its place.

No other shots rang out after the first one, but now he could hear voices in the courtyard below. He turned to the computer and checked his email. A quick perusal revealed nothing earth-shattering, nothing that couldn't wait. However, considering his present circumstances, he thought it prudent to send a few updates to his executive leadership team. It took less than two minutes to compose his thoughts regarding the Stratford Industries takeover, and his thoughts about network programming for the coming season, and his decision to try for a share of Major League Baseball broadcast rights.

After the email was on its way, he pushed his chair from the desk and closed his eyes. Without looking outside he had no way of determining what was happening. It was possible a member of his security team had accidentally discharged his weapon. It was also possible that one of them thought they'd seen something beyond the wall and overreacted. There were other possibilities too, but he chose not to consider them. He wondered if the small military unit that had so vexed Alan would have followed him to Brazil.

With a sigh, Van Camp stood and looked over at his wife's painting. "Great deeds are usually wrought at great risks," he whispered, quoting Herodotus. He studied the painting for several seconds before turning and stepping out onto the balcony. Looking down into the courtyard, he saw two uniformed men. Despite what their presence signified, he could not help the smile that came to his lips. One of the men below looked up and saw him.

———

"Rawlings," Brent said, gesturing upward.

The soldier glanced up and released a curse.

"Colonel, Van Camp is on the second-floor balcony," he said.

Brent heard a muffled reply coming from Rawlings's headset, but he couldn't decipher it, which didn't matter because all of his attention was on the man standing above them, a man they had traveled a very long way to find.

"Good evening, Mr. Van Camp," Brent called, and it seemed an appropriate thing to say, because unless he was seeing things, the ruthless corporate CEO and potential murderer of several million people was smiling at him.

Meanwhile, Rawlings had raised his gun, aiming it at Van Camp. "Sir, I want you to put your hands above your head and wait for my team to get there!"

Brent had no doubt that Van Camp had heard Rawlings, and yet the man didn't move.

"Mr. Van Camp, I don't want to shoot you, but I will if I have to."

Still no response from the billionaire. Rawlings exchanged an exasperated look with Brent and then refocused his attention on Arthur Van Camp.

Brent saw the shot strike before he heard it, which was the only way he knew that it had not come from Rawlings's gun, nor from the weapon of anyone inside the house. One moment Van Camp was standing and looking down on them with his strange smile, and in the next instant he was carried back by something that seemed to lift him from the ground before sending him back through the balcony doorway. Only then did Brent hear what sounded like thunder, except that the sky was the purest blue.

Before Brent could make sense of what was happening, Rawlings had his arm in a viselike grip, dragging him toward the open front door.

The first thing that struck Brent was the coolness of the air inside the house—something he registered despite the fear that a second bullet would take him even as it had taken Van Camp. When they were through the doorway and around the corner, Rawlings released his arm and Brent nearly collapsed, keeping himself upright by leaning against the cold tile of the wall.

"Colonel!" Rawlings shouted into his headset. "A sniper took out our target!"

Through the headset Brent heard Richards curse, and he wasn't sure what surprised him more—that the colonel had uttered the word or that Brent could understand it through the headset speaker.

———

What struck Van Camp most strongly was how quiet it was—like a tomb.

He'd landed against his desk, more surprised than anything,

at least at first. It wasn't until he tried to move that he realized what had happened. And even with that realization he couldn't stop smiling.

Out of the corner of his eye he could see his wife's painting and it seemed fitting. With great effort he turned his head until he could see its entirety. He stared at it for what seemed a long while, the thought that what he had purposed to do would have abhorred her not lost on him. She would not have seen the great deed in it, and he wouldn't have wanted her to.

It was something he had a hard time explaining to himself; that he would do something like this as a monument of sorts for a person who wanted nothing more than to walk through beach sand with bare feet and watch the sunset. He supposed it was one of those grandiose ideas that, once started, could not be halted. At this point far too much water had passed under the bridge for any sort of penitent act. And even had that not been true, he was now out of time.

He wished he could have a last sip of the Mouton.

Then there was movement around him, hands pulling him away from the desk and then lowering him to the floor. He could hear them, but as garbled things. They leaned over him, and through all of it Van Camp smiled.

———

When Brent and Rawlings entered the room, Addison and Snyder were bent over Van Camp, who wasn't moving. Richards walked past them, reaching to close the balcony doors. Brent understood the necessity of the act, yet he suspected the sniper had hit his only target and had since disappeared.

Moving closer to the huddle of people surrounding Van Camp, Brent found himself marveling at the fact that the man looked so normal, not like some Machiavellian monster. And despite the large bloodstain spreading across Van Camp's chest, he was still smiling.

For some reason, Van Camp's eyes picked Brent out of the group. His lips moved, but Brent couldn't make out a word. He leaned in closer.

"It's not here," Van Camp whispered.

"What's not here?" Brent asked, although he already knew.

"Alan," Van Camp managed before a cough took his next words. When the fit subsided he found Brent again. "Alan has it."

"Where?"

"Safe . . ." Again more coughing. "Safe house." His eyes moved to the desk.

"Will I find information about the safe house in there?" Brent asked him.

Van Camp nodded. The rest of the team had pulled back, understanding there was nothing they could do for the dying man. Brent, though, had to ask the one question that needed an answer.

"Why?" he asked the man.

Van Camp's smile grew wider, and Brent saw blood on his teeth. But when he answered, his voice was as clear as Brent had yet heard it.

" 'To sin is a human business, to justify sins is a devilish business,' " Van Camp said.

"Tolstoy," Brent breathed.

And then the man was gone.

December 20, 2012, 3:47 A.M.

From the outside it looked dead—not a single light or movement to indicate anyone was in there. But this was the address for the safe house, right where Arthur Van Camp had said it would be.

Sitting in the SUV, Brent watched the members of the NIIU donning the rest of their gear and checking their weapons. He was under strict orders to remain in the vehicle, and as tired as he was, Brent hadn't argued. After flying directly from Brazil to Lubbock, Texas, without even sparing the time to clean up the mess they'd made, the team was on the verge of exhaustion. But they were also infused with an energy the professor could feel.

They were nearing the end of their pursuit, and all of them could only hope that the prize they sought was inside.

Without a word the doors of the SUV opened and all but Brent slipped out, and so well did the men blend with the shadows that Brent lost them after only a few steps. At some point he must have nodded off, because he was awakened by the sounds of muffled gunfire, which served to propel him to alertness. He snapped upright in his seat and watched the front door, where he saw no movement. After a time the sounds of weapons fire faded and Brent suspected that was a win for the team. He thought about stepping out of the SUV, but then he remembered the colonel's strongly worded admonition and resolved to wait until they came and got him.

A moment later he almost missed the shadows that passed by around the building, heading toward the blackness of the street, yet their clothes weren't as dark as the team's. As Brent watched, the forms—three of them he could see now—started off down the street. They moved oddly, almost as if the outer two were supporting the one in the middle.

Brent had the SUV door open before the thought could finish forming, and as he stepped out onto the street, he reached back inside and retrieved the pistol that Richards had left him for protection. On tired legs he started after them.

Brent had no experience with this sort of thing, so he did the only thing he could think to do: he shouted. The effect on the three people in front of him was instantaneous. Two heads turned as if on swivels, and seeing their pursuer, one pushed his baggage off on the other and reached for his belt.

The professor nearly froze as the man's hand closed on his weapon and swiftly brought it up. Brent was late in reacting; the man got his shot off first and it struck true. Brent found the pavement rushing up to meet him, a searing pain in his stomach. But he had the presence of mind to try to break his fall with his free hand, and before he could no longer focus, he steadied his hand enough to squeeze off what he hoped was a straight shot.

Whether the bullet hit its mark or not he couldn't tell, because his arm suddenly went out from under him and he came down hard on his shoulder. He forced himself to roll over onto his back until he was staring up at the sky, wincing in pain.

Then it occurred to him—as the sounds around him fled so that everything became quiet—that this was how Van Camp had died. He thought there was something poetic about that. But then as his eyes began to feel heavy, Maddy's face entered his mind, which caused him to smile. He wondered absently if this was why Van Camp had smiled—if he was thinking about someone too.

And then Maddy was gone, and Brent felt an immense sadness take her place. It took several precious seconds for him to understand what it was, and when he figured it out, that too made him smile. His last conscious thought was to lament that he wouldn't be able to tell Maddy that he'd come down closer on his mother's side after all.

———

From the motel it was hardly more than a hop to the border. The single-level building sitting just off the 55—its dirty white stucco falling off to reveal the gray surface beneath—had eighteen rooms. Seventy-five miles in one direction lay Los Angeles; in the other direction an inconstant line that marked the division between two countries, a line from which a commingled culture emerged that did not pay homage wholly to either.

The going rate for someone heading north, who looked like they might not have a car, and who may have just survived a trip through the desert, was ten bucks. For anyone with white skin, the rooms went for forty-five. Canfield had one of the more expensive rooms that looked, he imagined, just like one of the less expensive rooms. He also had one, according to the desk clerk, with a working air-conditioner, although when he went to turn it on, the thing shook to life only to discharge air perhaps half a degree cooler than room temperature.

Canfield was in the closetlike bathroom, sitting on the edge of a tub that appeared to have remained unwashed from the day the motel opened. He took a long drag on a cigarette. When he'd stopped for gas a hundred miles out, he bought a pack, his first in more than eight years, and had since worked his way through four cigarettes.

The faucet dripped into a sink holding the remnants of the hair dye that had taken him from brown to blond, the box left on the sink in the absence of a wastebasket. Looking at himself in the mirror, he'd decided he didn't look good as a blonde. The light from the single bulb flickered as he finished the last of the cigarette. He tossed the butt into the sink, where it hissed as it landed against the wet porcelain.

For the last several hours he'd clicked through all the news outlets, searching for any hint of what was happening with his former company. He knew Van Camp had left for Brazil; he still had friends to tell him things.

He planned to catch a few hours' sleep and then try for an early morning border crossing, perhaps at six o'clock, when the business travelers began to hit the checkpoint hard. At that time he stood a better chance of being waved through. He wanted to be somewhere remote, someplace where no one knew him, when he pressed the button.

His only worry about the border crossing was that one of the guards would pull him out of line for a vehicle inspection. Explaining a half-million dollars in small bills in a suitcase underneath the spare tire in the trunk might be tricky.

He thought about pulling another cigarette from the pack, but instead decided he needed food more than anything. He couldn't remember the last time he'd eaten; he didn't think it had been in the last forty-eight hours. Grabbing the room key and his wallet, he stepped outside into a mugginess that belied the month of December. He stopped for a few moments to peer out over a land rendered in tans and browns that stretched out past the 55, as far as his eyes could follow. If he stared long enough, he thought he could see a hint of higher land—maybe a mountain—far off in the distance, but a sun disappearing below the horizon made that just a guess. In a way, the indiscernible presence of a mountain offered a hint of what lay before him. Abandoned behind was the sum total of all by which he had defined himself; ahead lay a murkiness that frightened him. Feelings of liberation and loss formed something completely different, something as indefinable as the muddied cultural waters around him.

He released the deep breath he hadn't realized he'd been holding and started off toward the lobby, his path taking him past a number of other doors, most marked with graffiti in two languages. As he passed one, he thought he could hear crying coming from the other side and yet it didn't move him. Entering the lobby, a blast of cold air greeted him. He met the desk clerk's eyes, and if the man noticed the change in hair color, nothing on his face suggested such.

A trio of vending machines lined the wall opposite the front door: candy, chips, tiny doughnuts, beef jerky, and trail mix. Nothing that nutritious, but he thought he might find enough to keep him satisfied until he crossed into Mexico tomorrow. Two minutes later, with something from each vending machine food group, he made his way along the walkway back to his room, skirting a Colt 45 can that hadn't been there a few minutes ago.

Inside his room, he deposited his wares on the dresser. Before starting into his meal, he walked to the window and pushed aside the shade. As had been the case when he'd arrived, there were three other vehicles in the parking lot in addition to his own. It wasn't that he was worried; there was no way anyone could have known he'd run, not this soon anyway. And even had they known, they wouldn't have tracked him to some seedy motel in the middle of nowhere. He let the shade fall back in place.

Opening a bag of trail mix, he settled into a wooden chair near the air-conditioner and pondered what would come tomorrow.

On the nightstand, next to the mangled cord that might once have belonged to a telephone, he'd placed the handgun he'd pulled from Van Camp's desk drawer—a trophy of sorts, along with the other thing he'd taken, the detonator. His eyes lingered on the gun, as if it were a concept for meditation rather than a physical thing. And it was, in a fashion, a totem of betrayal. A seemingly innocuous thing. And then his gaze shifted a few inches. Even though he knew what the other object was, it was difficult to distinguish from a television remote. He wondered, for perhaps the hundredth time, how the knowledge of his treachery had settled over his former employer, how the fact that Canfield had fled with the detonator had affected the man. It had to have been in a way none of his other traitorous acts could have.

Minutes passed in that fashion, with the absent munching of the trail mix, the unconscious staring at the dark gray metal. He wasn't sure when he first felt it, when the thing that seemed just a bit off first took some kind of shape in his mind. It might have been the moment he'd stepped back into the room, when he dropped his purchases onto the dresser. It might have been with him the entire time as he gazed out the window, watching for a threat beyond his door. All he knew was that he felt it now—the corner shadows that seemed to creep further into the room, the single light bulb that seemed to dim even as his eyes remained on the gun. So it did not startle him when a voice came from somewhere he couldn't see.

"Why do you run, Mr. Standish?" the voice asked.

Canfield emptied the last of the trail mix into his palm, tipping his head back and pouring the handful into his mouth. After he'd finished, after he'd dropped the empty bag to the floor, he released a sigh. "Hello, Dabir."

It seemed as if the African materialized from out of nowhere, although Canfield knew he must have come from the bathroom, where he'd been waiting and listening all this time. Like the ghosts of Canfield's past, who waited and listened and would have continued to do so regardless of how far he ran. Dabir stood for them all—all those he had betrayed, who had gone to their deaths on his order. Somehow it made it easier.

He knew there was no point in attempting to lunge for the gun. He wouldn't make it, and even if he did, Dabir would have emptied the cartridge. Dabir had always been careful.

"What now?" Canfield asked, knowing full well what was next.

Dabir chose to spare him the indignity of a monologue, or of an unnecessary wait for the inevitable. In that way, Dabir was merciful. He fired a single shot, and Canfield's eyes snapped open as if surprised by the speed with which death came. After his body had crumpled to the floor, Dabir offered a brief prayer, as he did for all the dead, and then he walked over to the door. He did not take Canfield's wallet, or the handgun on the table next to the remote control, or even the interesting carving he'd found while rummaging through the man's bags.

Instead, he left everything in the room just as it was, disappearing into the night like the ghost he'd always been.

December 22, 2012, 10:10 A.M.

Brent had already received more than his share of visitors, but he wouldn't have turned any of them away, especially the one who came in on crutches. Maddy was covered in bruises but mostly intact. She had been the human baggage between two of Van Camp's security personnel, and all it had taken was Brent's one shot, which hit nothing, to cause both of them to drop her and run. Brent wished he'd been awake when the team found her on the street; he would have liked to have been there for her.

He would have liked to have seen a lot of things, including the team's recovery of the detonator from a motel room near the Mexican border. But a chemically induced sleep stretching into two days had robbed him of the opportunity to witness some of the loose threads drawn up.

According to Richards, Alan Canfield's body had been found in the same room. In fact, that was the only reason the team had been able to locate the detonator. When local police had sent Canfield's name through the national database, they'd found the link to the NIIU investigation. The team had torn the room apart looking for the detonator, and Rawlings offered Brent a crooked smile when he recounted how close he'd come to using the thing to turn on the television. Had Snyder not snatched it away from him . . .

"We've got a dozen drill teams pulling up the octanitrocubane," Snyder said. "But it'll be at least a month before they're finished."

Brent simply nodded, too spent to comment. He had a passing thought about the possibility of someone somewhere on the planet—maybe someone with a malfunctioning garage door opener—accidentally detonating the explosives, but he had sufficient trust that the team of exceptional men and women had that covered.

A few minutes later found all of the others gone except for Maddy, who lingered, and Brent was glad she had. Despite the fact that his stomach hurt, and that he felt woozy from the medicine they were pumping into him, he wanted nothing more than to spend time with this woman. And at some point, if he hadn't already burned that bridge, he wanted to share his dying epiphany with her.

ACKNOWLEDGMENTS

As always, there are many people to thank for helping to get this book into print. The staff at Bethany House—Luke Hinrichs, Dave Long, Debra Larsen, Noelle Buss, Jim Hart, and a whole host of others—have once again guided me through the process, and I am grateful for their dedication and patience.

Thanks to Eric Humphrey for sharing his knowledge of all things military.

My ongoing appreciation for all that Les Stobbe does on my behalf.

And, of course, thanks to you for buying this book.

ABOUT THE AUTHOR

DON HOESEL, the acclaimed author of *Elisha's Bones* and *Hunter's Moon*, lives in Spring Hill, Tennessee, with his wife and two children. Don holds a bachelor's degree in mass communication from Taylor University. When not writing novels, he spends his days working in the communications department of a large company.

More Exciting Suspense from Bethany House

A Scorching Read of Arson, Murder and Second Chances

Firefighter Aidan O'Neil is reeling from a horrible accident as a dangerous arsonist descends on Reno. As the flames burn ever closer, he must confront his fears before it's too late.

Through the Fire by Shawn Grady

Chase the Angel of Death and You Might Catch Him

When paramedic Jonathan Trestle revives a man found sprawled on a downtown sidewalk, the man's mysterious last wish plunges Jonathan into a maze of mystery, murder, and danger.

Tomorrow We Die by Shawn Grady

The Nightmare is Coming...

Maia Peters is not impressed by the new amusement park, Ghost Town. But when its haunted house proves to be more than illusions, she finds herself in a dangerous struggle for the truth on the edge of the spirit realm.

Nightmare by Robin Parrish

⬧ BETHANYHOUSE

Find Us on Facebook.

Free, exclusive resources for your book group!
bethanyhouse.com/AnOpenBook

Stay up-to-date on your favorite books and authors with our *free* e-newsletters. Sign up today at *bethanyhouse.com*.

an open book